PRAISE FOR THE CRAFT OF KINGS SERIES

'Derek Birks has taken his usual high standard of storytelling .... level. **Scars From the Past** is impossible .... this book and not want to .... ted.'

The R...

'As wi.. .... he reader learns fascinating period detail, w... ... ... .tertained by an experienced author who knows his trade.'

Historical Novels Review

'I have to say, Derek Birks has done it again! **The Blood of Princes** is a masterpiece of adventure and intrigue.' *Sharon Bennett Connolly*

Echoes of Treason: "First-class historical fiction and beautifully written. A gripping Wars of the Roses yarn with totally authentic and believable characters. Highly recommended for fans of the period!"

Angus Donald

PRAISE FOR THE REBELS AND BROTHERS SERIES

Kingdom of Rebels: 'It is well written, full of action and the picture of fifteenth century life is skilfully woven by the author. Thoroughly recommended.'

Historical Novel Society

'It is impossible not to feel invested in the characters - they are flawed and damaged, but trying their best to survive and you find yourself willing them on.'

The Review

Also by Derek Birks:

Rebels and Brothers Series

    Feud

    A Traitor's Fate

    Kingdom of Rebels

    The Last Shroud

The Craft of Kings Series

    Scars from the Past

    The Blood of Princes

    Echoes of Treason

THE

LAST OF

THE ROMANS

DEREK BIRKS

DEREK BIRKS

This is a work of fiction.
Names, characters, places and incidents
are either the product of the author's imagination
or are used fictitiously, and any resemblance to any
persons living or dead is entirely coincidental.
Derek Birks asserts the moral right to be
identified as the author of this book.

THE LAST OF THE ROMANS

Published by Derek Birks

Copyright © 2019 Derek Birks

Maps designed by Katie Birks, www.katiebirks.co.uk

Front cover courtesy of Sharpe Books

ISBN: 978-1-910944-43-1

For all those fellow writers who gave me support and encouragement when I started out on this fantastic journey of creating historical fiction. You are far too numerous to name, but I remain very grateful to you all.

DEREK BIRKS

Acknowledgements

I would like to acknowledge the debt owed to my creative team for their constructive suggestions and astute observations. I am especially fortunate to have an excellent graphic designer, Katie Birks, without whom the maps would have remained as jumbled ideas in my head.

Thanks are also due to Richard Foreman, of Sharpe Books, for helping me to dip my toe into an entirely different period of historical fiction.

Finally, as always, I must thank Janet, not only for her constant support, but for dragging me away from the writing desk once in a while!

DEREK BIRKS

CONTENTS

The Players in The Last of the Romans   11

Glossary   13

Map of the Roman Empire c.450 AD   15

Map of Caracotinum c.450 AD   16

Part One: Death of a Legend   17

Part Two: Friends and Enemies   65

Part Three: Caracotinum   151

Part Four: Ships and Harbours   234

Historical Notes   305

About the Author   311

DEREK BIRKS

The Players in The Last of the Romans

The Aurelius Honorius family:

Dux Ambrosius Aurelianus*, an elite bucellarii commander under Flavius Aetius

Aurelius Honorius Magnus, commander of the Roman fort at Caracotinum

Aurelius Honorius Petro, son of Magnus and half-brother of Ambrosius

Aurelius Honorius Gallo, son of Magnus and half-brother of Ambrosius

Honoria Florina, daughter of Magnus and half-sister of Ambrosius

Honoria Lucidia Clutoriga, daughter of Magnus and sister of Ambrosius

The Bucellarii:

Flavius Marcellus (Marco) Constans, a Roman friend and deputy of Ambrosius

Aurelius Varta, a Frank and also a long-time friend of Ambrosius

Aurelius Marianus Onnophris (Onno), an Egyptian engineer from Alexandria

Aurelius Maurus Rocca, a soldier from North Africa

Aurelius Xallas, a soldier from Baetica in southern Spain

Aurelius Molinus Caralla, a cataphract (heavy cavalryman) from Britannia

Flavius Silvius Germanus, a Burgundian soldier

Flavius Romanus Cappa, a former thief from the back streets of Rome

Flavius Rusticus Placido, a Vandal from North Africa

Uldar, a young Hun archer

The Freed Slaves:

Inga, a Saxon whore living in Verona

Calens, a Greek serving as a physician to the bucellarii

Canis, Ambrosius' personal servant and also the lover of Calens

Others:

Petronius Maximus*, a prominent Roman senator

Heraclius*, head of the emperor's household

Flavius Corvinius Puglio, tribune of the Imperial guard [Schola Scutariorum Prima]

Stavelus, commander of the Roman garrison in Verona

Prosperus, a soldier of the Roman garrison at Caracotinum

Clodoris, a Frank leader who raised Ambrosius from boyhood to manhood

Childeric*, a young Frank chieftain

Canaris, a young Frank

Lepidus, Cratus, Anticus, Fistulus, Ravidus & Crevicus, Imperial guards

Remigius, a sea-farer in Caracotinum

NB. Those characters marked with * are actual historical figures.

Glossary

apse: a semi-circular alcove seen in late Roman buildings and rooms such as triclinia

auxilia: support units in the late Roman army

bucellarii: a group of mounted soldiers personally loyal to an individual

cataphract: heavily armoured horsemen

caupona: a fairly basic inn or lodging house

coloni: tenant farmers in the late Roman empire

comes: a high-ranking official of the late Roman empire – either military or civilian

dux: a high military office in the late Roman empire, below the rank of **comes**.

foederati: other tribes who were bound by treaty to fight as allies of Rome

insulae: town blocks of tenement housing

liburnia: a common Roman ship with 2 banks of oars carrying 50-80 oarsmen

magister utriusque militiae: a supreme military commander of the late Roman Empire

navis lusoria: a small, shallow, military ship for use on rivers with oars and a sail

scutarii: members of the Schola Scutariorum Prima unit of the imperial guard

solidi: gold coins of the late Roman Empire

spatha: a long, straight, double-edged sword used widely in this period

tribune: a Roman officer

triclinium: a formal dining room

DEREK BIRKS

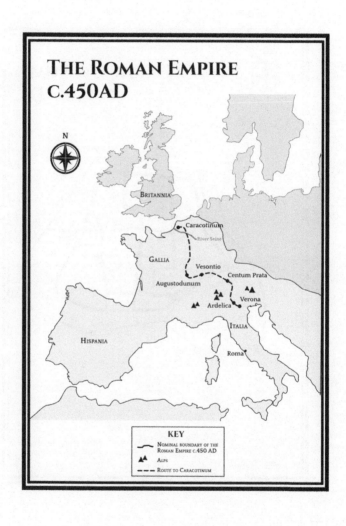

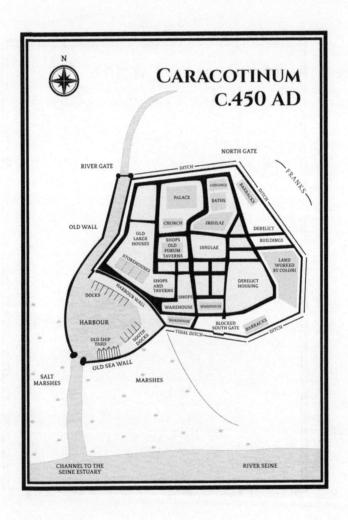

Part One: Death of a Legend

1

September 454, in a caupona at Ardelica on the shores of Lake Benacus in northern Italia

Brushing aside a handful of unruly red hair, Ambrosius squinted across at the other occupant of the bed. He always slept alone – yet he had allowed the girl to stay. Dear Christ, he was surely growing softer by the day! Sleeping alone made a lot of sense; it was safer. His work was bloody and covert – his mandate delivered where no-one ever saw or heard. If ever a man was born to dwell on his own in the shadows, it was Ambrosius Honorius Aurelianus.

For the past three years Rome's supreme military commander, the Magister Utriusque Militiae, Flavius Aetius, had sent Ambrosius wherever trouble erupted across the failing empire. Wherever an army was too many, or an assassin too few, he and his band of disparate bucellarii were despatched - and death went along for the ride. They slew every zealot, every ambitious politician, every fool and murderer, across the empire from the west coast of Galicia to eastern Thrace. In truth, Ambrosius and his comrades did little else but send men to an early grave.

Since he was recruited in Gallia, he reflected that his own fortunes had become inextricably harnessed to those of Magister Aetius. He could not resist a grim smile of admiration for the man who, against all the odds, still held the fate of the western empire in his firm grip. Without him, Ambrosius would still be a renegade bandit living among the Franks in north-western Gallia. Instead he was the commander of an elite band of mounted warmongers and carried the rank of dux. He was both feared and despised by his enemies - and very likely by some of the imperial guard as well.

Thus, Ambrosius slept alone; yet, there she lay... half-covered by the coarse blanket. So, yes, he was getting soft. But then, after the sudden demise of the Hun king, Attila, everything had changed. Peace had come to Rome – albeit a fragile peace brokered by exhausted combatants, but a peace all the same. And, in the wake of peace, it seemed that the wolf must be caged. So, Ambrosius found himself marooned in this shabby caupona on the shores of a lake far from the imperial court. While he preferred to remain at the inn, most of his bucellarii made frequent visits to nearby Verona where they were no doubt even now exhausting whatever coin they had left.

"Even you need to stop killing eventually," Aetius had told him. "Believe me, you need a rest from it; I know that better than anyone: killing eats into your soul..."

And somewhere, deep in his heart, Ambrosius feared his mentor might be right: there had to be an end to the carnage... sometime. Yet, removing the enemies of Rome and, where necessary, the enemies of Aetius, was what earned him his high status. If there did come a time when the dark skills he possessed were no longer required, what would he do? Fighting was all he knew... His rapid promotion had won him many enemies and some of those - both in Rome and Ravenna - would be only too pleased to see him taken down.

Until now, he ate the best food, drank the best wine – often too much of it – and had the most spacious quarters. Now all that was in the wind as he languished at this decrepit, lakeside caupona, awaiting orders; but for a long time now, no orders had come.

He glanced at the girl once again, his eyes following the smooth line of her exposed leg. She was pretty enough, but so were they all when first they were brought to the brothels of Verona where he had acquired her. It was not the first time he had bought a whore – indeed his good friend, Marcellus, had given him another telling off for doing so.

"It's become a habit, Dux," he complained, "and a pointless one! You find some good-looking, fair haired whore, buy her – usually at a grossly inflated price – and then you don't even keep her! You give her money and set her free! There's surely something seriously amiss with you!"

Marcellus, of course, was right: there was something wrong with him – badly wrong. Being abandoned in the north during these wretched months of peace was a slow-burning agony. He did not know why he freed the whores, but if it staved off the boredom of inactivity, he was going to continue doing it, at least until his ill-gotten income ran out… Sooner or later, if Aetius did not summon him, he would probably squander all his wealth on freeing the girls. What then? He must pray that mischief did not slumber too much longer in the empire of the west, for he could root out mischief better than anyone.

His eyes returned to the girl about whom he knew nothing, except what he could see - as Marcellus described: fair hair, light skin and blue eyes. Though she had barely said a word, he reckoned her accent hinted at an origin far north of the Rhine – Alemanni, perhaps, or even Saxon. Since her youthful beauty was still intact, she had clearly not been in the trade for very long - or so he hoped… but then he always hoped that. Though she was not the first whore he had bought, she was the only one he had suffered to remain for more than a few hours. Something about her must have drawn him in, though he could not say what.

Lying on her side, turned away from him, she was very close, yet not touching. Was that a barrier of her making, or his? He really should have asked her name, but very soon she would be gone – like all the others - so what was the point?

Sensing a subtle change in the light, he began to contemplate another dreary day. With a sudden shiver, the girl woke up and her anxious eyes scoured the chamber for a way out, before coming to rest upon him.

"Have you forgotten where you are?" he asked.

She stared at him, transfixed like a startled doe; then she gave another shiver, before lowering her eyes in submission. "No, master," she replied. "I was just… cold."

Behind her eyes, he saw wariness – but also perhaps a trace of contempt?

"You're safe here," he told her.

"Safe?" Nothing about her curt response was submissive.

"Safer than Verona, anyway," he murmured, intrigued by the little spark of defiance.

"You've not touched me all night, master," she said, "so, what is it you want with me?"

In her tone, he heard a tremor of fear– and yes, that lingering resentment too.

"Are you offended that you've been left untouched?" he enquired.

Again she lowered her eyes.

"How long have you been a whore?" he asked.

"I've been a slave for a year... master," she replied, emphasising the distinction.

Reaching for a small purse, he tossed it onto the bed in front of her. "So, now you're a freed slave," he told her, "and there's coin enough there to get you started."

With only the slightest hesitation, she pulled open the pouch of coins and peered inside. If he expected any gratitude in her expression, he found none.

"Get me started, master?" she asked.

"You don't need to call me master now," he said.

"What should I call you then?"

"What everyone else calls me: Dux."

"So, I'm free... Dux, just like that. And I can walk away with all this coin?"

He nodded. "You could give up whoring though."

"And what if I don't?" she said.

He gave a shrug. "You're free; I can't force you..."

"Hah!" With that brief retort, her disbelief slapped him in the face.

"I mean... I... won't force you," he said.

Why did she linger, he wondered? She should have left by now - raced out of the chamber, clutching her handful of coins, on a tide of elation.

"Where should I go then?" she asked, giving another shiver.

"Find my servant, Canis, on your way out; he'll tell you…"

Sitting perfectly still, he felt the draught of cool air against his cheek and sniffed the air; then he made a swift deduction that he should have made a good deal sooner.

"Christ's tomb!" he muttered.

By God, he was getting careless! The first time she shivered, he should have noticed that the door was ajar – not to mention the absolute, deathly silence outside! The caupona was never that quiet - even around dawn! That's what came of months of doing piss-all: you ended up with your head jammed firmly up your own festering arse!

Tossing the girl onto the floor, he had his knife out by the time the first man hurled himself up from the floor beside the bed. Slashing the eight-inch blade across the assassin's chest, Ambrosius paused - but only for an instant. Others were hurtling in: three more - no four – and all armed with knives.

As the nearest one came at him, he managed – just - to turn aside the thrust with his knife. Aiming a swift knee to the groin, he seized a flailing arm to swing the man around to block the attack of the next. Carving his blade across the throat of the third attacker in a spray of blood, he then despatched the man he still held in an iron grip. By the time Ambrosius took a breath, three victims lay unmoving on the timber floor.

With the element of surprise gone and three of their number dead, the two remaining assailants hesitated. They were right to think twice because, however skilled in their craft they might be, they would know now that the dread reputation of Ambrosius Aurelianus was well-deserved. Fleeing at once might have saved them, but instead they drew out their spathas – their second mistake. Moving to block their way to the door, Ambrosius snatched up his own sword belt and cast aside the leather-bound scabbard.

"Who's first then?" he enquired.

His weary tone should have given them a final warning, but of course they were contracted to kill - or be killed. After exchanging a swift glance, the pair came at him together. Why wouldn't they? But it would make no difference; he was too quick and too strong. The knife, hurled from his left hand, flew at the further of the two whose flapping arm could not prevent it from lodging in his windpipe. While the dying man choked on blood, his wretched accomplice backed away and reached down to pluck the cowering girl up from the floor. Hauling her up in front of him, he cast about with desperate eyes for another way out.

"I'll kill her!" he cried.

"So? She's not my wife, you fool!" declared Ambrosius. "She's just a slave..."

For a moment, doubt clouded the man's expression but, as the girl tried to pull away, he slid the edge of his spatha across her bare shoulder, drawing a thin line of blood. She stiffened but did not cry out.

Impressed by her mettle, Ambrosius took a step closer, meeting her eyes for the very first time.

23

"I mean it!" snarled the assassin.

"Oh, so do I," replied Ambrosius, still looking only at the girl. "I don't even know her name."

With a slow shake of the head, she glared at him – bitter, sapphire eyes flashing bright with anger.

"She means nothing to me," continued Ambrosius, raising the point of his spatha until its tip rested against her thinly-covered breast. "And this fine blade will run the pair of you through well enough."

Still holding her gaze, he drew the blade back a few inches and she gasped, eyes pleading with him now, as anger turned to alarm. Without warning, he kicked her hard on the outside of the left ankle and, as she dropped to the floor with a yelp, he thrust his blade into his opponent's chest – not far, but just enough. The man gulped a short breath, shuddering on the point of the spatha, as a trickle of blood dribbled down onto his belly and his weapon fell from trembling fingers.

"Who?" demanded Ambrosius, pressing the blade in an inch further. "For a swift death – which you don't deserve – tell me who sent you."

After a brief pause, the ashen-faced assassin whimpered only a single, grim word: "Heraclius…"

Ambrosius gave a weary sigh. "Of course," he said. "Who else but the sodding eunuch could have planned such a thing out here… so far from the imperial court, eh?"

Without pause, he drove the sword in hard, before swiftly wrenching it free again to allow the body to fall.

As he bent down to examine the stunned girl, the chamber door crashed back against the wall. Swivelling around to face the new threat, he found only Marcellus on the threshold, sword in hand.

His friend surveyed the carnage that littered the room with a wry smile. "I suppose you're alright then, Dux," he said.

"Morning Marco," said Ambrosius. "These fellows were a gift from Heraclius - or so I'm told…"

But Marcellus looked grave. "On their way to you, Dux, they were swift and… thorough. They spared no-one who got in their way: the owner, his wife, children, even a few of the slaves…"

"No witnesses," said Ambrosius, with a sigh. "What about Canis?"

"Sleeping in the stables… to calm the horses, he told me…"

Ambrosius raised an eyebrow, but made no comment.

"But what possessed Heraclius to attack us at all? The emperor's eunuch knows very well how Aetius will react. I may command a few bucellarii, but I can't believe I'm that much of a nuisance to the imperial chamberlain!"

"Well, whatever his reasons, at least you've dealt with it now," said Marcellus.

With a bitter shake of the head, Ambrosius murmured: "No, Marco, I don't think I have…"

"You think more will come?"

"Heraclius can't be acting alone - he must have the support of the emperor for this – he simply must!"

"But Aetius rules, Dux, not Valentinian III – everyone knows that…"

"But, I wonder, Marco, does Aetius still rule?"

Marcellus paled. "You don't think…"

Staring back at his friend, Ambrosius hardly dared contemplate the prospect. He sat down heavily on the bed, where the blood of one of the assassins had not yet congealed.

"Who did we leave with Aetius?" he asked.

"Boethius and Lippa."

"Then I suppose we must wait to see if they send word. You'd better go to Verona and gather the men."

"God's breath! They'll be scattered all over the damned town now," grumbled Marcellus.

"Then you'd best make haste, my friend!"

"What about this girl?" asked Marcellus.

"What about her? I've just freed her."

"By Christ! Not another one, Dux! Is she even still alive?"

"Yes, I'm alive!" cried the girl, massaging her ankle as she got gingerly to her feet. "But no thanks to him!"

"I thought it was every thanks to me!" said Ambrosius.

"You can't just abandon her here, Dux," said Marcellus.

"Just go," Ambrosius told him, with a final clasp of his arm, "and leave her to me - and hurry back!"

"I'll be a few hours at least. What if others come – I mean if they come at you hard…"

"I'll just have to manage, Marco," muttered Ambrosius. "Now, go and fetch the men - if you can find them all, let alone prise them from whatever shithole they've fallen into."

"I'll see you by noon at the latest-"

Ambrosius smiled. "-or in the afterlife…"

It was what they always said on parting, but Ambrosius wondered if today, it might just come true.

When his friend had gone, he turned back to the girl, who slapped him, hard across the face. Had he not caught her slim, but surprisingly strong arm, she would have struck him again.

"Inga!" she spat the word at him.

"What?" he said, aggrieved.

"My name… is… Inga!"

"Very well, Inga," he growled at her, "but you might think whether a badly-bruised ankle is better than a badly-severed head! Now, if you've finished hitting me, you can be on your way!"

"On my way… where?" she cried.

"Back to Verona, for all I care!"

"Ah yes, the town where I'm a whore!"

"Well, go north then – there are settlements along the lake…"

"What settlements? What do I know of them? Ever since I was brought to Verona, I've spent every hour in the town… in the brothel… on my back… pleasing men like you!"

"Well, you can't stay here…" said Ambrosius, unsettled by her vehement response.

"You said I was free, so why can't I stay here?"

"Not a chance!" said Ambrosius. "We may need to ride hard for the mountains. I've freed you and given you some coin – enough to keep you off your back for a while… now, for your own sake, go!"

For a moment he thought she might strike him again, but instead she favoured him with a look of undisguised contempt and snatched up her cloak and newly-acquired pouch of coins.

"Well, I may as well go back to being a whore," she cried, "because I was good at that!"

"Wait!"

"What?" she snapped, with a scowl.

"Be still!" His terse command stopped her.

While she stewed in grudging silence, he stood by the door, listening, and almost at once his head sank forward in dismay. Briefly, he considered flight, but it was fifty yards or more to where the horses were stabled at the rear of the caupona. The new arrivals would be upon them before they could even cross the courtyard.

"So, I'm going then!" said Inga, stalking towards the door.

Reaching out, he caught her by the arm. "Too late, Inga..."

"What?"

"Pity you didn't leave when you had the chance..." he said, pulling her away from the door.

Heraclius was known for his thoroughness, so he would not rely upon just one group of killers: he would send men after them - men upon whom he could rely absolutely. They would most likely be men Ambrosius already knew - but how many would there be, he wondered? A loyal handful perhaps, at the core of the emperor's personal bodyguard - but in his present circumstances, a handful of such men would be enough...

"Hide yourself in the inner chamber," he told Inga. "If they find you, tell them you don't know me. Tell them you're just a slave."

He didn't tell her that it would make no difference, that they would butcher her anyway.

At first, she seemed inclined to argue, until she heard the crunch of boots on stones. Even then, she just stood staring at him with those blue, bewildered eyes.

Easing her aside, Ambrosius walked to the half-open door and peered out. Barely thirty yards away, crossing the courtyard, were half a dozen of the imperial guard. When they saw him on the threshold, they exchanged a grim smile and drew out their weapons. They looked sore and exhausted; they must have ridden their mounts to death to get to him so quickly. It was not much, but it might help him a little.

Backing into the chamber, with spatha in his right hand and the knife once more in his left, Ambrosius was astonished to find that Inga had still not moved.

"What are you doing?" he hissed at her "You must convince them that you're not with me!"

But on Inga's face was a look of resignation and, reaching down to retrieve one of the assassin's bloody knives, she said: "It won't matter whether I stand or hide, will it?"

"If you carry on standing there, that's where you'll die!" he told her.

"Yes, but not as a slave," she breathed, "and not as a whore... If I die, I'll die a free woman, won't I?"

"You'll still be dead!"

"Who knows?" murmured Inga. "Perhaps I'll visit you... in the afterlife..."

"I doubt it," he murmured. "Not where I'm going..."

Before turning back to face the door, he surveyed the chamber as if it were a battlefield – which of course, any moment now, it would be. And there he was, wearing only a woollen tunic he had just pulled on - no mail shirt and no helmet. He felt like a tethered goat.

2

On the threshold, the snap of their boots faltered and died as they halted to contemplate the fallen bodies within.

"Oh, gods!" muttered Inga, in sudden fright, throwing herself down behind the bed.

Ignoring her, Ambrosius kept his eyes fixed upon the men at the door – men he knew very well indeed. Long jealous of his privileged position, they would be confident that together they were more than a match for Aetius's lone hunting dog.

"As you see, lads, I always have a warm welcome for visitors," he remarked cheerfully. "But today, it seems I grow ever more popular."

"Dux," acknowledged Ravidus, with a curt nod, managing to inject just enough disdain in his tone.

Being the fastest of them, Ravidus was sure to come through the door first. Lepidus, who was by far the most powerful swordsman, would follow; Crevicus and Fistulus, competent enough soldiers, would go wherever Lepidus led. For Ambrosius, the simple fact was that even he could not fight all four at once and survive; his oft-lauded speed and power would not be enough. Even if by some miracle of God, he overcame them all, then the massive Cratus would fall upon him, with the wily Anticus, lingering out of reach as he observed every flexed sinew and savoured every savage thrust.

Further conjecture was abandoned the moment Ravidus darted forward. But, though fleet of foot, the man was slow of wit. With a subtle sway of his body, Ambrosius easily wrong-footed his assailant, swept aside the ranging sword arm and plunged his knife deep into an exposed armpit. Even as Ravidus was falling, Lepidus hacked at Ambrosius with his spatha. While he defended with his sword, Ambrosius sought an opportunity to use his knife.

Lepidus would be gambling that his superior sword arm would overpower his opponent before Ambrosius could do any serious damage with the knife. When Crevicus joined the fight, with frequent short stabs at his torso, Ambrosius was obliged to employ his knife simply to fend off the attacks.

Trying to keep Lepidus between him and Crevicus, Ambrosius concentrated for a time only on defence. If he was patient, his moment would come for, strong though Lepidus was, he was far from battle-hardened. Sure enough, as his opponent began to tire, Ambrosius was able to risk the occasional lunge at him. Then, judging the moment had come, Ambrosius went on the offensive, battering his spatha against Lepidus until he saw that he was weakening further. Only then did he strike, hard and fast with his knife, low into his adversary's groin. With a grunt of pain, Lepidus jerked back a pace but, just as Ambrosius aimed to carve his sword across him, Crevicus darted forward and stabbed Ambrosius under the ribs. Cursing his sluggishness, Ambrosius knew that the wound, though not deep, would at the very least cause some loss of blood, which he could ill afford!

In a blur of rage, he spun around and went for both men. Ramming his knife down twice in quick succession into Crevicus' thigh, he then slashed his spatha down across Lepidus with every ounce of strength he could muster. The mighty Lepidus collapsed onto his knees, blood pouring from the savage wound. Crevicus cried out, clutching at his leg where blood was already pumping out between his fingers. Allowing him to slump forward against him, Ambrosius plunged his knife into Crevicus' throat and left it there until he felt warm blood run down his wrist.

Kicking the dying Lepidus aside, Ambrosius prepared to meet the fourth man, Fistulus. Knowing very well the effect it would have, he hurled the lifeless body of Crevicus at him. Distraught at the sight of his comrade and lover bleeding out onto the floor, Fistulus could only roar with anguish. Seizing his chance, Ambrosius carved his spatha down through shoulder and neck until it bit into the edge of the breastplate but, by then of course, Fistulus was already dying. Mortally wounded, he toppled over to fall upon his dead beloved.

Above the last moans of the dying men at his feet, Ambrosius could hear Anticus urging Cratus forward. After a glance down at his bloodied torso, Ambrosius gave a groan for, with two more men still to face, the wound would surely hamper him. But there was no respite as the giant Cratus, encouraged by Anticus, lumbered forward. Though Ambrosius drove his spatha into the great man's stomach, Cratus seemed oblivious to the sharp steel as he lifted his opponent clean off his feet.

Tossed against a wall, Ambrosius had the spatha torn from his grasp. Even as he slammed into the plaster and slid to the floor, he was certain he had inflicted a severe wound. Yet Cratus still lived, still breathed and still moved; and, all the while, Anticus stood waiting, sword drawn, ready to deliver the fatal blow.

Cratus, however, was far from finished and bending down, he seized Ambrosius' head in one of his great hands. Thick fingers probed and pressed against Ambrosius' scalp as Cratus hauled him up from the floor.

He's going to pull my head off, thought Ambrosius. The bastard's just going to rip it clean off… But instead Cratus propped him against the wall and, for the first time, examined his own wound.

What he saw clearly displeased him, for he growled: "I'm going to crush your skull, Dux."

Ambrosius nodded, for though he still gripped his bloodied knife in his left hand, he knew his resistance was almost at an end. Both men knew the gut wound would kill Cratus but, long before that happened, Ambrosius would have been smashed to a pulp.

Anticus, as ever, exhorted his comrade to greater things. "Finish him, Cratus – finish him and the glory will be yours!"

"You had me when I was on my arse, Cratus," said Ambrosius, with a grim smile. "You should have pounded me to death then."

When Cratus, with a dismissive grunt, pressed both hands against Ambrosius' head, he summoned up what little strength he still possessed and forced his knife blade through the giant's side in the vain hope that the tip might just burrow through all the muscle to reach the man's heart.

But it did not, and worse still, he could not free the blade for a second strike.

Cratus gave a rueful grimace of pain. "Good try, Dux," he conceded.

Wondering what it was going to feel like when his head exploded, Ambrosius shut his eyes, but a wild cascade of screams persuaded him to open them again. Clinging to Cratus' back was Inga, her hands scrabbling at the giant's face. At first Ambrosius thought she must be trying to claw out the man's eyes, until he saw the shaft of an assassin's blade protruding from Cratus' left eye. When Ambrosius felt the pressure ease upon his beleaguered skull, he knew that, this time, the man mountain truly was dying.

Next moment though, the sword hilt of Marcus Anticus cracked onto the back of Inga's head. Crying out, she fell to the floor and lay still. But her brave attack had won Ambrosius a brief respite. Dropping his shoulder, he pushed aside the weight of Cratus and, rolling onto the floor, retrieved his spatha in time to meet Anticus' first stroke at the crouch.

This adversary was different from all the others - relying upon stealth, not strength. Moving his feet fast, Anticus tried to turn his opponent but, desperate to gain a little more breathing space, Ambrosius lashed out with his spatha, sweeping it across the shocked face of his opponent. And, for once that day, Ambrosius had a little luck. Blood spurting from his splintered nose, Anticus staggered backwards and reached out for the door frame to stop himself falling.

"More will come, Dux…" he said, spitting out a mouthful of blood.

"But why?" snarled Ambrosius. "Why?"

"Because your man is dead, Dux; Aetius is dead - slain by the emperor's own hand - and very soon, you will be too…"

"No!" roared Ambrosius, striking with merciless fury and chopping first at Anticus' outstretched arm, then shoulder and neck until the imperial officer fell across the threshold in a quivering, blood-soaked heap.

Catching his breath, Ambrosius leant against the door frame.

"Aetius… dead…" he groaned, with a shake of the head. "No… that can't be! The death of Aetius would be… it would be… the end of Rome… the end of it all…"

He glanced along the passage and into the yard, but both were empty. No raised voices, no rap of boots on stone. No-one else would trouble him – at least for now.

He took several deep breaths causing more blood to seep from his wound.

"Careless fool!" he berated himself, for it would need binding up before he rode anywhere.

Stepping across the room he found Inga on her belly where she had fallen. Though there was a raw wound at the base of her skull, it would heal. When he touched her arm, she cried out, shrinking away from him.

"It's me," he said.

She lifted her head and looked up at him, eyes not truly focussed. "Are you still alive, or are we both… in the afterlife?"

He gave a shrug, which also turned out to be quite painful. "I can only speak for me."

She grasped his outstretched arm, fingers slipping on the blood there, and winced as she stood up. "My head feels sore..."

"It ought to feel sore," he told her, "but you'll live. You're lucky! He could have sliced his sword right through you..."

When it came, her reply was bitter. "I'm just so lucky today, aren't I?"

"Luckier than anyone else in this charnel house..."

Eyeing his still-bleeding wound, she muttered: "We should do something about that..."

Though reluctant to concede that he could no longer stand, he sank down onto the bed with a great sigh.

"Aetius... dead," he murmured. How many times before had he expected to hear those words? But not now – not now, when the struggle was all but won!

Tearing a strip of cloth from her linen shift, Inga bound it around the lower part of his chest, all the while avoiding his eyes.

"You were brave," he said, "and, I owe you a life. If you want me to, I'll take you out of here with me, but it's up to you where you go after that."

When she had dressed his wound, he did what he could for her scalp. "I have a man, a Greek called Calens – a man of salves and potions. When he returns from Verona, he'll see to it better than I can. Stay here."

Leaving her in the chamber, he ventured out to fetch the horses. If he was wrong and more trouble arrived, he wanted a means of escape. He would not survive another such fight today. Crossing the yard, he entered the caupona where several bodies littered the floor. The owner and his family, who had shown him so much kindness, had found themselves in the wrong place. He stared down at the bloodied body of the youngest boy who had somehow armed himself with a small blade – to no avail, of course. He recalled the initial looks of apprehension when he and his comrades rode in that first, balmy evening. Perhaps that night the innkeeper had somehow foreseen his fate… and now they were all dead, simply because Ambrosius Aurelianus chanced to stay under their roof.

∞ ∞ ∞ ∞

Several hours later, they waited in the yard, watching the dust cloud billowing up from the east.

"Is it more of them?" asked Inga.

"My eyes can't see through dust any better than yours," he said.

"But it could be, couldn't it?"

"It could be…"

"Should we run?"

"Not if it's my own men." He was unused to such questions – his comrades knew better.

"Well, how soon will we know?" she persisted.

"When it's too late to run," he replied.

Pausing only to glare at him, she turned to stalk across the yard.

"Where are you going?" he called after her.

"If it makes no difference, I might as well rest in your chamber to await my fate!"

With a sigh, he touched his fingers to his torn ribs. The binding had slowed the bleeding, but he needed Calens – and needed him badly.

Perhaps Inga had a point: if running would do no good then enjoying one's last few moments of peace was probably the more sensible option. He stiffened as it dawned upon him that there were far more horsemen approaching than there were in his small band of bucellarii.

"Oh, shit of a dog," he breathed.

He half-turned towards the caupona with her name upon his lips, but she had already made her choice. Of course it wasn't fair on her – for she had fought well and deserved to live. Following her to the chamber, he drew out his spatha. He would make a stand beside her; however futile the gesture, he owed her that much at least.

At his back, the thunder of hooves grew ever louder as he approached the room where the bodies of Anticus and the others still lay painting the floor with their blood.

"Inga?" he called.

She was lying on the bed, so he sat down beside her, though she would not look at him.

"I'm sorry," he said. "This is my doing."

"Of course it's your doing!" she replied, though there was little venom in her response. "You just thought one day that you'd poke your finger into my poor little life and make it better. Well, I suppose for a very, very short time there, you did..."

"There are many more this time," he said, "and they'll not be gentle with you. If you wish it, I can end it quickly for you now."

"So now you want to kill me too?" she said.

"Of course I don't want to kill you!"

"Then don't…"

"But-"

"Am I free, or not?" she said.

"Yes, of course, free…"

"Then at least let me choose how I die, since it's the last – and only - freedom I appear to have…"

"You want to fight?"

"I did before, didn't I?"

"But it's different this time; this time, Inga, there really are too many…"

"Then there's nothing to fear, is there?" she said, jumping off the bed.

Skidding on the slick of Cratus' blood, she was only saved from falling by the swift hand of Ambrosius holding her fast. When he released his hold on her arm, she took a step closer.

"Shall we meet them in the open," she asked, "with the sun on our faces?"

He handed her one of the discarded knives and she moved to the door.

"Coming?" she said, stepping carefully over the bloody remains of Anticus. She mouthed something more but her words were all but drowned out by the raucous shouting of the horsemen pulling up outside in the courtyard.

With a shake of the head, he gripped his spatha firmly in his right hand and followed her out.

When they emerged, weapons at the ready, the throng of soldiers slowly fell silent and then a great roar of laughter rolled around the courtyard as Marcellus dismounted to greet his friend.

"No!" cried Inga, punching Ambrosius hard in the stomach. "Why did you put me through all that?"

That brought another crescendo of laughter.

Ambrosius, bent double and clutching at his ribs where the blow had released a little more blood from his wound, grunted: "I didn't know…"

Inga sank down onto the cobbles, shaking uncontrollably.

"You two alright?" asked Marcellus, with a grin.

"No, Marco, we're not!" replied Ambrosius. "When I heard so many coming, I assumed the worst. How have you raised more men so quickly?"

Marcellus was no longer grinning. "A few of the local garrison joined us when news reached Verona that-"

"-Aetius is dead?" said Ambrosius.

"You know then…"

"Anticus was kind enough to explain - before he… passed away…"

"Anticus was here?"

"And Cratus, and Lepidus… need I go on?"

"How are you still alive, Dux?" cried Marcellus.

"I… had some good fortune." He glanced across at Inga, whose head wound was at last being tended to by his skilled Greek, Calens. "And a little help too."

"The girl fought with you?"

"Inga. Her name's Inga… not that it matters much. According to the recently deceased Anticus, more will be despatched."

"They have been and they're already in Verona," murmured Marcellus. "Tribune Puglio arrived, looking for you – for us."

Ambrosius raised an eyebrow. Flavius Corvinius Puglio was the strong right arm of Petronius Maximus who, as the long-time enemy of Aetius, had more to gain than anyone from the general's murder.

"And?" he prompted.

"That's where the local garrison chipped in. A bunch of them trapped Puglio and his men in the gatehouse."

"Why? Why did they do that? They must know that Puglio's the trusted man of Maximus."

"Puglio told them a little too cheerfully that Aetius was dead – and our master is well remembered around these parts, Dux – as are you. No-one's forgotten how we harried Attila to a standstill up here in these hills. That's enough to make men choose the right path."

"Even so, you know Puglio. Once he gets out, he'll show no mercy – and then he'll follow."

Marcellus grinned. "He'll need more men though – I fear some of those he brought with him protested a little too much."

"I can't see much humour in any of this, Marco," grumbled Ambrosius, still struggling to accept that the great survivor, Flavius Aetius, could actually be dead.

"So, what are we going to do then?" asked his friend.

"Get as far from Rome as possible!" said Ambrosius. "Corvinius Puglio is a tribune of the Schola Scutariorum Prima - by Christ, he has the whole imperial guard to call upon if he needs it!"

"Where to though, Dux? The Emperor's reach is very great..."

"We'll have to ride north into the mountains…"

"And after that?" asked Marcellus.

"After that, my friend, we contemplate life without Aetius…"

News of the murder of Aetius, apparently by the hand of the emperor himself, would soon throw everyone into disarray. Though he shared the rage of those among the Verona garrison who had chosen to throw in their lot with him, he knew this was not the time to grieve for their dead general. As Aetius himself once told him, 'only the living can fight back, Dux.'

When Ambrosius finally allowed Calens to tend to his rib wound, he noticed that Inga stood alone in the yard. Surrounded now by noisy, cursing soldiers, and jostling horses, she stared around her, eyes dulled by despair. Once his wound was dressed, he went to join her.

"Come," he said, offering her a hand, which Inga ignored.

"Canis!" he bellowed, scanning the yard for his other servant.

The older man appeared, bent low under the burden of his master's weapons and armour, and leading a great black horse.

"We'll need another horse," he told him, indicating Inga.

Viewing the girl with obvious disapproval, Canis conceded: "We've a few spares, I suppose."

"Find her one – a good and gentle one – or you'll be giving her yours!" ordered Ambrosius.

"I'm sure we can find more horses, Dux," said a voice nearby.

"Stavelus!" cried Ambrosius, with genuine pleasure, clapping his old comrade on the shoulder. "You commanded at Verona?"

"I did."

"So I have you to thank for Puglio's... inconvenience?"

"That," said Stavelus, with a smile, "was a sheer delight, Dux. But where will you go now?"

"Don't know, my friend – no time to think it through yet," he replied. "For now, we'll head into the hills towards Bergomum and Lake Larius.

With a glance at the sun, already past its zenith, he called the men to order. In the gateway of the crowded yard, he raised a hand in salute and waited for the soldiers to shuffle into silence.

"Our magister militum is dead," he announced, though they knew it already, "killed by the hand of a lesser man, perhaps even the emperor himself. I am resolved to serve such an emperor no longer. I make no secret of it: I am done with Rome. Aetius was Rome's last hope and now the dogs of chaos are let loose, nothing can save Rome."

Cries of outrage arose at once around the packed yard, but he shouted them down.

"I shall take the road north through the mountains!" he declared. "If any man wants to ride with me, he'll be most welcome!"

"Dux! Dux!" they yelled, clashing their spathas against their shields.

Above their tumult, he roared: "Come on then!" and rode away along the south shore of the lake, heading west towards Bergomum. If Puglio dared to follow him, so be it; he would be ready.

3

Early October 454 in the evening, in the hills above Leucerae

Ambrosius looked up as Marcellus sat down beside him.

"How many today, Marco?" he asked, tossing several more branches onto the fire.

"Only a score or so – thank God," replied his comrade. "But that still makes more than two hundred, Dux – thanks to your generous invitation! We can't even feed them all!"

Ambrosius nodded. "I know. I didn't expect word to travel so fast - nor so far…"

"By now, Petronius Maximus will know exactly where you are - and how many you have with you! He'll take that as insurrection and assume you mean to oust the emperor."

"But why would he think that?

"Sometimes you're just a fool, Dux," said Marcellus with a shake of his head. "He'll think it because you've just invited half the army to join you!"

"Bah! I only spoke to a few men!"

"Yes, but countless others have heard your words now – or a version of them! I don't know what possessed you!" grumbled Marcellus. "We've always been a small, tight unit."

"I don't know either," lamented Ambrosius. "The words just came into my head. When Stavelus and the others detained the tribune, Puglio, in Verona, they crossed a line. I suppose I wanted to offer them a way out…"

"A way out of what?"

"I'm not even sure of that… I don't know anymore – perhaps a way out of Rome?"

"Hah! Rome will endure, as it always has," his friend assured him.

"Will it though, Marco? I don't see how it can. Where are the men now to defend it? Petronius Maximus is not Aetius!"

"Perhaps not, but with Attila gone, the Huns are less of a threat, so who is there to defend against?"

Ambrosius smiled sadly. "Have the past few years putting out fires across the empire taught you nothing?" he asked. "We've been defending a graveyard, Marco, not an empire… not even a great city. In the east, Rome's legacy might live on, but the west is finished. And now that Aetius is gone, the wolves will tear the flesh off Rome's living corpse! Someone else will rule here soon enough."

"Yes, and Maximus fears it'll be you!"

"Well, it won't be!"

"I don't know," said Marcellus. "Perhaps after all, that's what you should do – overthrow Emperor Valentinian, kill Maximus and take over. You could avenge Aetius and save Rome - you could do it, Dux. The army would support you!"

"The thing is, Marco, I think I'm done with saving Rome," said Ambrosius, clutching his friend's arm. "I'm done with it. It's finished…"

"But we're all still Romans, Dux…"

"Are we though, Marco? You might call yourself Roman because you were born close to the city itself, but look around at our comrades. What are they? They come from Egypt, Thrace, Greece, North Africa, Gallia – even from far beyond the Rhine and Danube. They've fought for Aetius, but they have little in common with each other."

"But you, Dux, you're Roman."

"Me? I'm just like the others, Marco: Roman, yet not Roman – in truth, I'm more of a Frank than a Roman. I grew up among them - lived among them for years! And what is a Roman anyway? A thin skin of Roman culture doesn't change where you come from. My Gallic father counted himself as Roman - he ate the food and wore the clothes of a Roman. But my mother, she was not a daughter of Rome, she was a slave…"

Regretting where he had allowed their conversation to stray, he got to his feet to put an abrupt end to their discourse.

"Whatever you decide to do, Dux, we can't stay here much longer," advised Marcellus.

"I know," conceded Ambrosius.

"And we can't take all this lot with us," Marcellus insisted.

Waving aside his friend's concern, Ambrosius said: "I'll take a walk around the camp - take the measure of our new arrivals."

Stalking off into the shadows, he tried to banish the unwelcome reminder of his mother. She had a proud heritage, until her kin had sold her to the Romans as a slave. By chance, her beauty had attracted the attention of his father - at least for a while… Memories of her were few - far too few to share with anyone else – even Marcelllus. Indeed, there was little he cared to remember from his bitter childhood at all, but those last words with his mother… they were carved into his soul.

Making his way up the slope in the half-light, he gazed in despair at the numerous campfires which now illuminated patches of the hillside almost down to the shore of Lake Larius. Damn Marcellus, because, as usual, he was right. Though it was never his intention, Ambrosius had recruited an army. Now what was he going to do with it? For a time, as darkness gradually enveloped him, he remained brooding there alone, until a slight figure ghosted down to sit beside him.

He greeted her with a long sigh.

"I wondered where you were," said Inga.

"If I were you," he said, "being the only girl in this camp full of soldiers, I wouldn't go wandering about in the dark on your own."

"Well, I'm not on my own now, am I?"

"Why did you come with me?" he asked.

"You said I could – and where else would I go?"

"Anywhere else..."

"Anywhere usually means nowhere – and I was hardly going to be safe at that caupona, was I?"

"No, but you could have stayed at any of the villages we've passed through – or at Bergomum."

"Perhaps I wanted to stay with you."

"But why?"

She stared at him. "Well, at least I know you won't harm me – that's a start! And it's giving me time to think…"

"There's no future for you with me."

"But… that night… at the brothel, you must have… wanted me then? Why else would you have paid a fortune to take me with you? So I just assumed…"

"That I wanted my own personal whore?"

"No, not that; more than a whore; I've seen it happen with other girls - it's not uncommon for rich men to buy a whore… to marry."

"Marry? You think I want to marry you? When I told you, that first time, Inga, to leave, I really did mean it."

"Oh."

"I thought I was being very clear: I gave you a purse of gold coins and said you were free to go."

"Yes, but… a lot happened after that…"

"Nothing good happened after that!" he grumbled.

"Oh. I thought you at the end… that you wanted me to stay."

"Well, I didn't!" His denial sounded harsh – harsher than he intended.

"Oh."

"Stop saying 'Oh'!" he said, glaring at her. What else was he to say? He just wanted her gone, but she met his uncompromising stare with one of her own.

"When you didn't touch me that first night," she told him, "I feared the worst. But then, when you didn't abuse me either, I thought it was must be out of respect – that you thought more of me… Why do you think I helped you, against that ogre? I thought perhaps we might…" Her voice faltered.

"You should think a great deal less!" he said. "Because, there is no 'we'.

"Well, why buy me if you were just going to send me away?" she cried.

"I just did; and I'm already sorry I did! God's faith, girl, just accept it, as a gift!"

"I'll always have a scar on the back of my head because of you…"

"Yes, a scar and a bag of gold – so not such a bad outcome. Now please, take your scar and your gold and leave me alone."

"I could work for you…"

"You're no longer a slave; I've freed you!"

She put a hand upon his shoulder. "Then why do I feel like some babe abandoned on a barren mountain?"

Her touch unnerved him and he stood up. "I'll take you back to the camp; we're leaving tomorrow, but you should stay here in Leucerae. It's your last chance to stay behind before the mountains."

After he pulled her up, she released his hand but remained close, almost touching, though not quite.

"But… if I am truly free," she whispered to him, "then I can do as I please…"

4

Early October 454, Ambrosius' Camp in the hills above Leucerae

They did not leave the following day, because Ambrosius realised he must bring some sort of order to the chaotic jumble of men scattered in small bands across the hillsides above Leucerae. Used to managing a score of bucellarii at most, he was bewildered by the sheer numbers who had gathered to join him. Somehow he must reduce their number to a core of reliable men. During the day, he walked among them, appointing captains to represent all the different groups and then, when darkness fell again, he summoned those captains to his blazing camp fire.

"Friends," he began, "I am blessed to have such loyal comrades. That so many of you have come here has... humbled me. But it's also made me think hard about what I should do next. Some may have come here thinking that I will seek revenge against the emperor for the death of our beloved Aetius, but I will not."

At once a chorus of objections and questions arose, of which the most common was: "Why, Dux? Why let the murderers of Aetius go free?"

Feeling the raw power of their anger, he was tempted, there and then, to raise his sword and declare war upon Emperor Valentinian III. Even the prudent Marcellus seemed minded to encourage him on such a treasonous path when he declared: "The army of Rome is at your back, Dux!"

"Perhaps it is Marco," murmured Ambrosius, "but for how long? The army of Rome has ever been fickle – and I tell you plain: my heart is not in it."

When the protests of the men calmed a little, he addressed them once more.

"I watched Magister Aetius wrestle, day after weary day, to calm and tame this monstrous carcass of an empire – and you all know how much blood I've spilled against Rome's enemies in that cause. But, my friends, Rome is an unforgiving bitch of a mistress! She would tear the guts out of us all to preserve her rotten corpse for just one more day! And I tell you: I will have none of her! Not any more..."

Great shouts of anger rose up again at his casual dismissal of Rome, followed by more questions and pleas. "What then, Dux?" cried some. "What will you do?"

Thus, only moments into the meeting, a chaotic, rolling argument broke out around the fire. For a time he let them argue it out, resisting the temptation to intervene until he felt the vehemence of their debate was beginning to diminish. Only then did he stand up and speak.

"Peace!" he ordered and an uneasy silence was slowly restored.

"Hear what I have to offer," he began. "After that, each man must decide for himself. I'll talk freely, as comrades should: I've told you that I'm done with Rome, so I'm going home – and many of you may wish to do the same."

"Where's home for you then, Dux?" asked Stavelus, who had brought more than a score of men with him from Verona.

"Gallia," replied Ambrosius. "Because that's where I last saw my family - ten long years ago - and now I'd like to see them again. From here, I'll head north across the mountains and then into Gallia – a few of my comrades will remember a similar journey we made along that road two years ago."

"I remember the icy, sodding passes!" said Marcellus, and there were grunts of agreement from two more of his closest comrades: Varta, the Frank, and Flavius Silvius Germanus, the Burgundian.

"True enough," grinned Ambrosius, "it was pig of a climb up there – but it was the cusp of winter; this time, we'll be crossing a little earlier."

He waited for the low, doubtful murmur that greeted his announcement to die down once more.

"You are not an army," he told them, "and I am not going to rebel against the emperor. I seek to conquer no-one, but I will protect those who call me comrade. Some of you are free men, but others may, by now, already be branded as deserters. Perhaps some, like me, would prefer to go back to their own homelands; if so, then I wish you God speed and we will part as friends. But, let me be clear: if you ride with me, then you are my men. You follow my orders, my code and my ways... to the death. So, go now and tell your fellow soldiers what I've said. Those who decide to come with me will leave here in the morning at first light."

When the crowd had eventually dispersed, Ambrosius found Marcellus beside him.

"Gallia, Dux?" he said. "Is that truly where you come from?"

"It's true I was born in Gallia," said Ambrosius.

"And your father is still there?" enquired Marcellus.

"When I left, he commanded the garrison at the port of Caracotinum."

"Never heard of it," said Marcellus.

"I'm not surprised. Even ten years ago, it was shithole - half the town was more or less derelict."

"And so, of course, you want to go back there," said Marcellus with a trace of a smile.

"I have a few reasons…"

"You once told me you parted with your father on the worst possible terms," said Marcellus.

"Did I? By Christ, I'd forgotten that." It was not like him to reveal such truths. "I must have been very drunk to tell you that."

"You were," Marcellus assured him. "So why go back then?"

"Sister, mother, brothers - need I go on?"

"It's a very long time since you were there."

"Not long enough to forget them though," murmured Ambrosius.

"Will you make peace with your father then?"

Ambrosius fixed his friend with an iron stare. "I'd sooner roast his balls in a brazier…"

"Even after so long?"

"I've not forgotten and he won't have either... I tell you, Marco, if my father and I were put into the same room, only one of us would come out alive!"

"It's going to be a hell of a journey just to get there," said Marcellus. "And most of the men don't really know anything about you. All they know is your name – and your legend! Those of us, who've served with you, we know what to expect: we know how hard you'll drive us through those mountains – but they don't..."

"I know, Marco, but it's their choice. If they don't like it, then they can piss off back to Verona, can't they? Probably better if they do."

"And face execution for desertion?" scoffed Marcellus. "I doubt many will see that as much of a choice, Dux. All I'm asking is that perhaps you take it a little easy with them to start with..."

"No," said Ambrosius, "better they know the pace I set, sooner rather than later. You know this sort of soldier, Marco. They've spent half their lives in garrison towns, gambling and fornicating; their discipline's poor and they barely know how to fight. They're not real soldiers at all..."

Marcellus nodded. "Real or not, my friend, they have come here because of you..."

With a sigh, Ambrosius said: "Well then, Marco, they will soon learn to know me better."

"And what about you, Dux?" asked Marcellus. "What will you learn? Because leading so many men... it's not what you're used to, is it."

Ambrosius made no reply, attempting to shrug off the question, but it remained with him. Marcellus made an astute point: there were no orders from Aetius to carry out now; it was all down to him. Making tactical decisions was what he had always excelled at; but deciding upon a whole, planned course of action? That was a different matter – and it was a test that he had never faced before.

5

October 454, on the road north from Leucerae

When Ambrosius broke camp shortly after a bright dawn, Inga guessed that about two thirds of those who had made the journey to Leucerae decided to ride north with him. According to Marcellus, it amounted to roughly a hundred and thirty men. Despite Ambrosius' warnings, Inga too decided to remain in the relative safety of the armed column.

After the first few hours, as Ambrosius set a relentless pace, she was grateful for the luxury of a sturdy mount. Close comrades, like Marcellus, hardly seemed to notice, but some of the men soon began to drop back. While they followed the old road beside the long, finger of lake, the way was not yet too steep but even so, some trailed into the camp late in the evening and a few simply melted away never to be seen again.

She thought Dux's pace unnecessarily brutal and told him so. In response, he invited her to leave... once again. Though she heard similar complaints muttered amongst the men that evening, Dux chose to ignore them all. Yet, she had to concede that he had made them no promises and, as Marcellus pointedly reminded her, no-one was compelled to follow him – except of course the bucellarii, who were his sworn men.

When, the next day, they left the lake behind them, their route began to climb more steeply as they followed the river up into the higher valleys as far as Clavenna. From there, the serious ascent began, through the mountain passes where sheer ravines made even the horses nervous, let alone some of the men. Two of the horses slid off an icy ledge to plummet to their deaths, taking their riders with them. That night, Inga thought she would never rid herself of the sound of the animals' terrified shrieks echoing along the ravine.

Over the next six days, desertions also reduced their numbers, but Inga could see that those who remained looked fitter and leaner than when they set out. Even so, Dux did not let up until they rode beyond the pass of Cunus Aureus. It was early in the afternoon when he halted the column and the men eagerly dismounted, but their joy was short-lived, for Dux had only stopped early so that he could spend the remaining hours of daylight training the men. Despite his claims that this was not an army, it seemed to Inga that he was doing all he could to turn it into one.

"Survival is about discipline," Marcellus explained to her that evening. "Sooner or later, someone will attack us - either from fear, or because they want to plunder what little we have. Dux is just making sure that everyone knows what to expect and how to deal with it."

Still, Inga wasn't so sure. "But what," she asked, "if his harsh rule turns the men against him?"

"It won't," said Marcellus.

"Why not?"

"Because… he is Dux…" said Marcellus simply. "You were there at the caupona; you saw what he can do."

"He fought well, but he was lucky!"

Marcellus gave her a wry smile. "I suppose you need some luck to become a living legend in your twenties!"

"But luck, Marco, always runs out," she said.

"I know," acknowledged Marcellus, "but, more important, so does he…"

Now that they were deep in the mountains, she was glad that Ambrosius had at last given up trying to persuade her to leave, though every day she asked herself why, by the eternal gods, she stayed. Though she tried to earn her place in their company by helping to prepare the campfire or by cooking, nothing she did earned her any plaudits from Dux. He expected all the men under his command to be more than proficient in such activities and besides, he had Canis and several other servants to carry out the most menial tasks. Canis and Calens, a man with many potions, had, she discovered, both been freed by Ambrosius the previous year, though they chose to remain in his service. She wondered why. However much she looked for admirable qualities in him, she saw little to justify the devotion he received. The man could fight, but so could thousands of others; everything about him was hard and relentless.

The passage through the mountains was a far cry from the Veronese brothel where she had spent the past several months. She suspected that every mile took her closer to her homeland, yet somehow it seemed further away each day. At first several of the men had shown a keen interest in her - perhaps something in her manner told them where she had been employed. But Dux warned them off – perhaps with the best of intentions but with the inevitable consequence that they all assumed she was his whore. The irony was that the skills she had acquired in the brothel seemed of no interest at all to Ambrosius. For a time she wondered if he preferred the company of men; yet, on the few occasions when they were close, or touched, she sensed some reaction there… and it was certainly not revulsion.

In an effort to understand the strange Roman better, she made it her business to get to know some of his comrades. One in particular, a young Hun named Uldar, was easy to befriend. As a relatively recent recruit to Dux's bucellarii, he was, like Inga, still trying to earn the trust of the rest. Proud of his martial skills – as young men so often were – he took much pleasure in showing her how to use his bow. Though, from his flushed face and nervous touch when they stood close together, it occurred to her that archery might not be the chief reason for Uldar's enthusiasm.

However, the more familiar she became with those close to Ambrosius, the more distant and taciturn he seemed to be in her company. Most of the time her continued presence in the camp just seemed to irk him and she, in turn, grew tired of his cool demeanour and the unyielding regime of the camp.

"You work the men too hard," she observed one evening, as she handed him a bowl of thin stew.

"It's bad enough you're still here," he complained, "don't start telling me how to manage my command, or I will personally throw you off a high ledge."

Her response to his grim reply was a bleak smile, briefly meeting his hooded, grey eyes with her own. Then, leaving him to eat alone, she went to sit on the opposite side of the fire, beside Marcellus.

"I thought once that there must be more to him," she grumbled, "but he's just a brute - and a cold brute, too."

"Dux?" said Marcellus, glancing across at his friend. "I suppose he can sometimes seem cold..."

"Is he always so... grim?" she asked. "Is this what it's always like?"

"What?" Marcellus, usually such a good listener, appeared not to have heard.

"With him? Is it always like this with him, Marco?" she repeated.

"Dux?"

"Yes, Dux! Of course: Dux! Who do you think I'm talking about?"

Marcellus, ever the diplomat, could be very irritating at times, she thought.

"Ever since I've known him," said Marcellus, "he's always been... plain-spoken and direct – but that's what we like about him. You know where you are with him."

"Well, I don't!" muttered Inga. "I don't know where I am with him at all!"

"But that's your own fault!" declared Marcellus. "He freed you, gave you money and told you to go - free as an eagle – and what did you do?"

"Well, I stayed but-"

"Exactly, you stayed!"

"But he freed me, Marco," she groaned. "He bought me and freed me! So why does he treat me like shit?"

Marcellus frowned at her. "Did you think you were special?" he murmured.

"Yes, so though he told me to go, I thought he must want me to stay. He'd paid good money for me! So I stayed, but then, by the time I saw how little he actually cared for me, it was too late. We were already in the mountains and there was nowhere else I could go. And now, I tell you: I think I was better off in the Veronese brothel…"

Marcellus made no reply, but she could see that he had something he wanted to say.

"Say it," she hissed at him. "Go on, say it!"

"It won't please him to see us whispering with our heads together, like conspirators."

"What do I care what he thinks? Nothing I do pleases him anyway!"

As she got up to leave, he took her hand. "Inga, none of the others ever stayed, so he just doesn't know what to do with you."

Staring at him in the flickering light, Inga said: "What do you mean: 'none of the others?'"

"All I'll say is that you are not the first girl he has bought and freed from a brothel…"

"He's done it before?"

Marcellus nodded. "At least seven times, including you – to my certain knowledge. So, there you are thinking how special you must be to him, and I'm afraid the truth is: you're not."

"But I don't understand; why does he do it then?"

"I don't know," said Marcellus, with a nervous laugh, "nor do I want to - and nor should you. It's time you learned to simply accept him as he is – or leave."

Inga gave a slow shake of the head. "You'd think I'd be able to read men better than that, wouldn't you?"

∞ ∞ ∞ ∞

Ambrosius stared across at Inga through the fire. Why was she still here, he pondered? It was annoying. The previous whores had just given him their thanks and left - some more swiftly than others and a few wearing puzzled expressions, but at least they had all left! Inga, by contrast, remained with him – or at least, within reach of him. It had taken him by surprise and he knew it was only a matter of time before it caused trouble among the men. They all thought that she was his whore. How long would it be before they asked to rent her favours from him?

Though he trusted Marcellus to watch over her, yet... that was another cause for concern. Day by day, he watched his friend growing ever closer to the girl – not that it was his business, since she was free to choose her own companions. Yet, he couldn't help feeling disturbed by their easy way with each other. There was an intimacy between them that he had never achieved with anyone – man or woman. If his early life had taught him any lessons at all, it was to trust no-one. As a soldier he trusted all his comrades – they would have his back in a fight; that much he knew. But beyond basic survival, that was when trust became complicated; because the moment you trusted someone with your thoughts and secrets, or with your troubles and cares, then you placed your soul in their hands. When someone knew you that well, it could only lead to trouble.

Part Two: Friends and Enemies

6

October 454, in the mountains on the road north

With temperatures dropping by the day and any sort of forage in scarce supply, the journey through the remaining mountain passes grew ever more arduous. Though hunting parties went out daily, their meagre kills were too little to satisfy the hunger of so many. Nevertheless, Ambrosius drove them on, pinning all his hopes on finding food when they reached the foothills. Two years earlier, when he had passed through the town of Centum Prata, it had still been prosperous and, despite the lack of a Roman military presence, it was very much a hub for local trade.

Each evening, they made their camp just a little lower, until eventually they entered a long valley which led them past several lakes and, for the first time, they found themselves in low-lying lands. Expecting their arrival in the richer lowlands to raise the spirits of his men, Ambrosius was stunned by what he saw when he led his company down onto the plain. The once-rich farmland which lay around the settlement of Centum Prata was now just a wasteland of unploughed fields, burnt out buildings and butchered livestock.

The town itself, where Ambrosius still hoped to find provisions, had been so ravaged by raiders that it had nothing left to offer. He learned of warring bands who had struck fear into the townspeople, as they scoured the land for the same dwindling resources. As they rode through, the local folk, perhaps understandably, viewed them with a mixture of suspicion and trepidation. Worse still, their subsequent hunting expeditions in the surrounding plain yielded almost nothing.

Amongst his exhausted and hungry followers, Ambrosius felt the growing resentment as keen as a knife's edge, but he had no answer except to push the weary column on even harder. Further along the shore of the lake, he knew there were forested slopes which might offer more game. After another, especially cold, October day, when they camped in the trees above the lake, the mood around the campfires was murderous. Making his customary rounds, Ambrosius found that few had a good word to offer and several even turned their backs upon him. But most just built up their fires as high as they could and took refuge under their skins and blankets.

Around his own campfire, it was a different matter, for these were his elite bucellarii. Aside from the Frank, Varta, and Marcellus, who were close and constant advisers, all the others lived only for the struggle. Thus, however hard their journey was, such men, having followed him to almost certain death countless times, would remain steadfast. Riding hard on starvation rations before fighting a bloody encounter came as easily to most of them as breathing and shitting. Yet, even for such men, there would be a limit and, this evening, though they made no complaint, he sensed something there, unspoken - a reserve, hovering beneath their nightly banter.

"Centum Prata was a shithole," observed Varta, glancing across at him.

Ambrosius frowned back. Varta had been with him from the start of it all - recruited by Aetius to fight the Huns in Gallia. Though he loved Ambrosius like a brother, Varta could always be relied upon for a regular dose of misery. His skill with a spatha was only surpassed by the depth of his pessimism.

"Everywhere's a shithole now," declared Germanus, the Burgundian, whose gloom often exceeded even Varta's. If Germanus had ever laughed, Ambrosius reckoned he must have missed the moment.

"Give me some good news, Onno," he said, with what he hoped was an encouraging smile.

"You give me some, Dux," replied Aurelius Marianus Onnophris – universally called Onno - "and I'll be sure to pass it on to Germanus..."

The Egyptian's glum response was out of character for a man who only ever sought solutions to problems. When even Onno was depressed, thought Ambrosius, then morale must be very low indeed.

"Perhaps we'll have to get used to this," said Ambrosius, "If a thriving place like Centum Prata is on its knees, what has become of other places?"

"Most likely torn apart, like this place!" snorted Marcellus.

"Aye, that's about the word for it. Torn apart... so, Onno, there is no good news. This place used to get fat from the merchants who travelled the road to Gallia, trading the fruits of nearby Raetia. But then Raetia was a fertile land - rich with grain and vines - now, it's damned near barren… so no-one's getting fat off it! There's nothing here for us; all we can do is push on through as fast as we can."

"That'll go down well," murmured Marcellus.

It was only when he smiled across at Marcellus that Ambrosius noticed for the first time that Inga was not with him. His smile must have quickly become a scowl.

"Dux?" said Marcellus.

"Where's Inga?" he asked.

"She's around; she was here… not long ago, fussing over the empty bowls," said Marcellus. "I think she must have taken them to the lake to wash."

"You think?"

"I'm fairly certain," replied Marcellus.

"On her own?"

"Well, I suppose… unless Canis, or Uldar, went with her."

But Ambrosius could see that his servant, Canis, and the young Hun, Uldar were on the far side of the fire. "How long ago?" he asked.

"Not long, Dux," said Marcellus. "But no-one would dare touch her."

"No-one among us, Marco," said Dux, "but there are others in these parts – and we've seen their handiwork already…"

"I'm sure there's no need to worry…"

"Did I say I was worried?" growled Dux.

"I'll go and look for her then, shall I?" asked Marcellus, for once letting his exasperation with Ambrosius show.

"Let's not heap any more attention on the foolish bitch!" snapped Ambrosius.

As usual, whenever he spoke about Inga, the words spilled out more roughly than he intended, so, to escape the startled looks of his comrades, he stood up and abandoned the flickering circle of light to go and look for her.

Damn the girl! Why had she gone to the lake alone when any of his sworn men would have gone with her? At first they had been dismissive of her – to them, she was just another in the long line of the Dux's freed whores. But, on the journey through the harsh mountain passes, her tenacious spirit and sheer hard work had won their respect. So much so, that now these hardened veterans doted upon the girl. Even he had to admit that she had more than pulled her weight, especially in helping Calens treat the sick and injured – of which there had been more than enough in the mountains. Gaining acceptance within the bucellarii was not easy, but he had to concede, Inga had managed it.

With a soft tread he walked down the slope through the trees where they had made their camp for the night. Marcellus had advised clearing a broad swathe of trees around the camp, but for one night, Ambrosius reckoned that if they simply built up their fires and showed their strength, it would suffice. The strip of forest would also provide some welcome protection from the cold winds. In any case, he reckoned that it would be a very reckless group of bandits who would take on a hundred or so heavily-armed Romans soldiers.

Close by, dead leaves crunched under a booted foot and he stood still. More footfalls sounded, no more than a few yards away, heading up towards the campfires. He turned his head, hoping to catch sight of Inga, but what he saw was several columns of men, moving in single file. He froze, knowing he had not yet been seen; then, slowly, he reached for the hilt of his spatha; but of course his sword and belt were still lying by the camp fire. With a silent curse, he eased out his knife.

Peering through the trees, he studied the shadowy figures as they passed and, to his astonishment, saw that they were Romans. Like his own men, they were well-harnessed – yet, he could not imagine how a detachment of the army could still be stationed in such a remote area – unless they were fellow renegades, or even deserters? The other possibility, of course was that they had been sent after him by Petronius Maximus, but it was scarcely credible that Maximus would pursue him this far.

There could be no doubt, though, what these men intended. While Ambrosius had detected their approach by chance down on the forested slope, those sleeping around the campfires would have heard nothing. No cries of warning from his sentries meant that they had been taken down first – so these men were well-organised.

Knowing he could delay no longer, he eased back behind one of the broader trunks and bellowed aloud: "To arms! To arms; defend the camp! To arms!"

At that moment, every attacker's eye would seek him out but only for that instant. After that, they must attack the camp or lose all advantage of surprise. When, as expected, they ignored him and began to hurry forward up the slope, he started to creep around to their rear, readying himself to strike. With his gaze fixed firmly upon the last man, he did not see Inga, crouched down beside the track. When he stumbled over her, she yelped with pain and the pair rolled in a tangle into the undergrowth.

"Be still!" he told her, but still she cried out, so he clamped his hand over her mouth.

For a moment she struggled against him, still quivering in his grasp.

"It's me!" he told her, removing his hand.

Though she ceased struggling, she wept nonetheless. "I know it's you!" she hissed at him, "but your blade's cut me!"

"By Christ! Where?" he said, releasing his hold upon her.

"Right leg, high up! You careless shit!"

"How bad?"

"I'm wet with blood!" she cried.

But he heard only the angry shouts of his men, as they fought to repulse the sudden, night assault.

"I have to get back to the camp!" he told her. "Stay here and press hard on the wound until I get back."

"You're leaving me?" Her voice betrayed her terror.

"I will come back!" he assured her.

With a shake of her head, she groaned: "Go on then, you cold bastard…leave me out here…"

Though he hated leaving her, bleeding, he could see no other choice – a commander had no choice, or so he told himself, as he left her and raced back up the slope.

Charging into the camp, he saw that the attackers were even more numerous than he had feared; they must have come from all sides, silently cutting down every sentry in their path. But, however many they were, they would find his bucellarii the most severe of tests. Though they were primarily horsemen, his sworn men were proficient killers in any situation. When he arrived, he found them fighting in pairs, back to back - each pair beside another so that there were always four men supporting each other. He had not the slightest doubt that the bucellarii would repulse the attack on their part of the camp but, of his other recruits, he was less certain. Despite the training he had instigated, many of the men with him had never been front-line soldiers. Already cold, hungry and low on confidence, they were now forced to defend themselves at night, against an unknown enemy in a bleak forest – and it was not yet even the depths of winter.

"Uldar!" he shouted, pointing back down the slope. "Inga's hurt – near the lake. Onno, go with him!"

The youth, his bow in hand, scrambled off into the forest followed closely by the Egyptian, while Ambrosius turned his attention to the mêlée before him. Only when he came face to face with one of the attackers, did he remember that he still carried no spatha. Without breaking stride, he deflected a sword thrust with his knife blade and seized the opponent's sword arm at the wrist. Avoiding a swinging shield, he cracked his boot down on his opponent's knee. Wrestling the spatha from his grasp, he slashed it down the man's back before turning to plunge it under the arm of another adversary. But there, his newly-acquired sword became firmly lodged.

Fuming, he kicked the dying man aside and snatched up a fallen shield. Careless of his own safety, he swung it hard at any of the intruders who came within his reach. Smashing the boss into one opponent, he stabbed him in the groin and sought out another victim. With a wild and reckless rage that he had rarely known before, he dispensed ugly death until he could find no more enemies to kill. Flinging aside the shield, he stood unmoving, as he tried to make sense of the fire-lit scene.

Varta and his best fighting men, having repulsed the initial charge, were already on the counter attack, battering the enemy back into the trees. Elsewhere too, the clamour of fighting was beginning to subside as some order was gradually restored to the camp.

"Varta!" he roared, "Find me one of them out there - a live one!"

The burly Frank set off at once, and at the same moment, Uldar returned, with Onno carrying Inga.

"She alright?" asked Dux.

"No!" snapped Uldar, "she's not! She's near dead!"

Struggling to recall any previous occasion when the young Hun had even raised his voice to him – let alone in anger, Dux let it pass.

"Calens!" he ordered, "see to Inga!"

"You left her out there to die!" cried Uldar, as Onno kicked aside a corpse to lay the girl down by the fire.

"I had to get back here!" shouted Ambrosius, irritated that he was obliged to defend his actions - and to a mere boy?

Onno looked none too pleased either. "She deserved better, Dux," he said gruffly.

"I think I've stopped the bleeding!" cried the Greek. "But... just look at her – look how pale she is!"

Ambrosius winced to look at her, for even in the flickering light, he could see she had the pallor of death upon her.

"Well, is she going to live or not?" he demanded.

"Just leave me to work on her, Dux!" Calens retort was curt. By God, even his servants were chastising him! They should have been thanking him that any of them were still alive!

"Haven't you got someone else to kill?" raged Uldar.

"Aye, you, boy, if you answer me thus again!" grumbled Ambrosius.

But he took the Greek's advice and hurried off to assess the damage inflicted by the attack. What did the youth expect him to do? Defending the camp was more important than the life of any one individual; he would expect no more consideration himself. Every soldier understood that – and, though Uldar was young, he should have learned that too by now. But then, of course, whatever Inga might be, she was not a soldier.

Joined by Marcellus, Ambrosius passed through the camp and what he saw filled him with despair. There were more casualties than he had hoped for, despite his warning shout, some had been slaughtered before they could even reach for their weapons – and a host of others were left with hideous wounds.

"Too many, Marco," he lamented. "Far too many…"

As he went round, he did his best to help bind up wounds and restore shattered morale, but he could see defeat in their eyes – and often, accusing glances, as he moved among them.

How had he ever imagined that he could lead these men safely to Gallia? When so many had followed him to Leucerae, simple pride had puffed him up. He was Dux – the unvanquished - a man fêted by other men. What did he care about the emperor, or Rome? Both were finished; but what he hadn't understood then was that he too was finished.

"I've been playing at this, Marco," he murmured. "Over these past years, all I've become is a butcher of men. That's what I'm good at: killing them, not leading them."

Marcellus, usually so sanguine, made no reply but trailed dutifully behind him as he made his way back to their campfire.

Inga was lying swaddled in furs close to the heat – a good sign he hoped.

Uldar looked up at his arrival, still none too pleased by the look on his face.

"She's not dead then?" asked Dux, resting a hand on Calens' shoulder.

"She should be, Dux," replied Calens, "losing that much blood… she still might pass in the night."

"Well," said Dux, sitting down beside him, "it's as well that there's not much night left then, isn't it? I thank you for your skills, my friend, but I fear you are much needed elsewhere. Uldar, go and help him."

Uldar gave him a nervous nod which, before the Hun set off across the camp, was acknowledged by Ambrosius – the mark of a truce between them.

Soon after, Varta returned, bloodied, but alone. "Couldn't take one alive, Dux," he said, "but have you seen their shields?"

He tossed the shield he was carrying onto the ground by the fire. Ambrosius nodded, for the coloured design of red and green was clear for all to see. They all knew the markings well enough.

"Scutarii Prima," murmured Marcellus.

No more words were necessary because now they knew: among their assailants, some at least had been despatched by Valentinian III – or by Petronius Maximus in his name. After they had sent half a dozen of their best men to kill him, Ambrosius had hoped there would be no further pursuit, but the shield told a different story for it belonged to one of the detachments Puglio had brought to Verona.

As a tribune of the Schola Scutariorum Prima, Puglio could only have been despatched by the emperor – or someone acting in his name. But why, wondered Ambrosius, would Heraclius, or Petronius, bother to pursue him any further than the mountains? What did they have to fear from him? He had renounced Rome forever, but then perhaps they did not believe that. God knew, the empire's history was littered with emperors who initially declared no interest in the office! Perhaps they were just taking no chances with him.

If Maximus and Heraclius had their own ambitions then the weak emperor would not last very long. Of the two, Maximus would surely triumph and perhaps, if Maximus thought Ambrosius might seek revenge for the death of Aetius, then he might well try to ensure that he never had the opportunity.

"I also found a few of these on the dead," said Varta, passing his leader a handful of bright gold solidi. "It seems someone is very eager to see us dead."

Examining one of the coins closely, Ambrosius murmured: "Fresh from the mint at Ravenna. Any sign of Puglio?"

Varta gave a dismissive shake of the head.

"Did we break them, do you think?" asked Ambrosius.

"I doubt it, Dux. I'd say the losses were about even; so, they could be back…"

Eventually the camp subsided into an uneasy peace, but no-one slept - least of all Ambrosius, who had a decision to make. His entire strategy had been found wanting because the whole point of taking the difficult, northerly route over the mountains from Italia was to discourage pursuit and keep out of trouble. Well, on that score, he had failed spectacularly. Though they had resisted the assault, he knew it would not be the last for, if the imperial guard had followed him this far, they were not going to give up so easily now.

Over the coming days, his column would be even more vulnerable than before. Not only had his effective fighting numbers had been reduced by about a third but now, encumbered by their wounded they would not be able to outrun the mounted scutarii. Indeed the following morning they were obliged to return to Centum Prata to acquire two more wagons. After that, pausing only long enough to bury their dead in the cold ground beside the lake, they continued along the road west.

Though Ambrosius would have preferred to turn and face Puglio's scutarii in open battle to put an end to the pursuit once and for all, he would be gambling all their lives on the fall of the dice. Perhaps his opponent, Puglio, had reached the same conclusion, for he seemed content merely to shadow them for mile upon mile. But Ambrosius knew that he could not leave it thus – he could not leave their fate in Puglio's hands.

In the next town, Vindonissa, they managed to purchase some desperately needed food and, soon after leaving, found better fortune in their hunting. For the first time in weeks, his men had full bellies and when they set off again, they did so with bright eyes and smiles upon their faces. The road to Vesontio followed a forested river valley but, whilst it was a relatively easy ride after the trials of the mountains, the valley narrowed in several places. With Puglio close behind them, there was always the risk that he might try to outflank them to set up an ambush. If he did so, there would be little warning and no hope of escape.

Ambrosius resolved that somehow, before they reached the town of Vesontio, he must gain the upper hand. If he did not have the numbers to destroy the scutarii, he must harry and hurt them enough to discourage them from pursuing him any further. To do that, he would need to know a great deal more about his enemies and that called for the services of his Spaniard, Xallas – an excellent tracker and a man who knew how to keep himself well concealed.

"Xallas," he ordered, "drop back and keep an eye on our friends coming up behind us. I want to know all there is to know about them: numbers, weaponry and so on. Take Uldar with you, it'll do him good - and his bow might come in handy if they see you."

Xallas raised an eyebrow, which was his understated way of pointing out to Ambrosius that his task would be easier without the youth.

"He's young," conceded Ambrosius, "but he has to learn skills like yours – and he's hunted since he was a boy."

"He still is a boy," complained Xallas.

7

October 454, on the road to Vesontio

For several hours Xallas waited with Uldar among the trees, until Puglio's cavalry arrived and swept past them. Following them without being detected was not going to be easy for the scutarii were no fools and Puglio would have posted outriders to screen their flanks and rear. Unwilling to take any unnecessary risks before nightfall, Xallas ensured that the pair kept their distance, contenting themselves with noting merely the number and fitness of Puglio's men.

The gruff warrior from Baetica and the brash, seventeen year old Hun were not natural companions and the older man struggled to disguise his disdain for the young archer. For the most part they rode in silence until Xallas could no longer contain himself.

"You should never question your leader," he grumbled.

"What?" said the youth, who intent on the scutarii ahead of them, was paying little attention to his comrade.

"You should not have questioned Dux over Inga," Xallas told him.

"Oh, that," groaned Uldar. "Well, he was wrong to leave Inga to die in the forest."

"No, he wasn't," replied Xallas. "He served the interests of all – not just one."

"But that one was just a girl…"

"Yes, exactly that," agreed Xallas. "The girl works hard enough, but she will always be a girl who is no warrior. She has chosen to live with soldiers but, if she rides with Dux, then it must be on his terms, not hers."

"I'm teaching her how to use my bow," said Uldar, his youthful enthusiasm shining through.

"Why?" scoffed Xallas. "You surely don't imagine she could actually use it in battle?"

"Well, I don't know, it's not so much weight to draw-"

"You're a fool, boy! She's just a freed whore is all she is. I like her well enough, but she can never be one of us."

"She can fight – even Dux said that!" insisted the youth.

"Scrap for her life, perhaps, but he didn't mean really fight," laughed Xallas. "She's hardly bucellarii, is she?"

"I think he-" Uldar stopped speaking when Xallas raised a silent arm in warning.

"Shit! We've allowed ourselves to get too close!" hissed Xallas. "Women are always a distraction! Puglio's column must have stopped for the night so, we must go softly now…"

Darting into a stand of trees, they halted their mounts and waited - out of sight perhaps, but far from safe…

Cursing his own inattention, Xallas knew that they had wandered far too close to the enemy column. He had allowed his disapproval of the young Hun to lure his mind from their task and, as a result, they now found themselves trapped near the scutarii camp. Since they could not get past it to re-join their comrades, they would have to withdraw a safe distance and prepare themselves for a cold night. Though Xallas did not doubt Uldar's bravery, he was worried by the youth's inexperience.

"Do only what I do," breathed Xallas. "We'll walk our horses away from the scutarii… slowly; but keep a sharp watch; there may be one or two behind us."

Uldar, gripping his reins more tightly, gave Xallas a nervous nod which did little to reassure him. Picking his way with the utmost care, he tried to follow a course which would retrace their steps. A good strategy, he decided, unless of course, some wily scutarii had already picked up their tracks in the muddy ground. After some minutes of crossing and re-crossing the woodland trails, Xallas came to a halt, with sigh of resignation.

"I fear they're all around us, Uldar…"

"So, what can we do?"

"We must wait, but we can't be taken, boy, you understand why?"

"They'll want to know where Dux is heading…"

Perhaps the callow youth possessed a little sense after all, decided Xallas. Then another thought struck him. "At least we don't know exactly where Dux is heading," he said, "so at worst we can only tell Puglio he's heading for Gallia – and that's a big place!"

After a slight hesitation, the youth nodded.

"Shit!" said Xallas. "Do you know something more, boy?"

Uldar said nothing for a moment and then confessed: "I overheard Dux telling Marco when we set out… he mentioned a town-"

"Well, don't tell me!" warned Xallas. "You should keep your ears closed, boy – as well as your mouth!"

"I wasn't trying to listen!" he protested.

"And for the love of God, keep your voice down!" whispered Xallas. "Now, I think it's best that we get you as far from here as possible listen. Do you think you can find your way back to Dux?"

"Yes, but how, if they're blocking our path?"

"I'll grab their attention for a while," said Xallas, "and, when I do, you ride fast – you hear me?"

"Yes, but-"

"You mustn't be taken alive, Uldar!" insisted Xallas. "I'll draw them off and you ride as fast as your scrawny little Hun arse can take you! You understand?"

Wild-eyed, Uldar appeared anything but confident and, just for an instant, Xallas considered killing the boy there and then. If he did so, there would be no risk to Dux and the others. But… the lad was so young and so full of life that even the veteran, Xallas, could not bring himself to do it. He had to give the youth a chance to get away.

"As soon as you hear them after me," he instructed his young companion, "you ride hard and you don't look back!"

Greeted by an unconvincing nod from Uldar, Xallas gave a shake of the head. Urging his mount forward, he began to weave a ragged path through the forest, hoping his movement would draw any nearby scutarii towards him. Though it worked exactly as he hoped, he decided to take no chances and began to fling abuse at his pursuers. Beyond that, he could only pray to the gods that the young Hun was already riding for his life back to Dux.

Eventually, of course, they would close in upon him but, since Xallas had never liked the scutarii, he expected to take a great measure of satisfaction from killing as many of the jumped-up bastards as possible. First though, he must choose his spot. Wrenching at his rein, he wheeled his horse and bent down to snatch a throwing spear from the bundle tied to his mount, only to abandon the idea when he discovered that the nearest horseman was already too close.

Ducking under a low branch, he glanced back at the chasing riders and reached the grim decision that his time with Dux had come to an end. Growling his favourite curse, his hand flicked to his belt and in one easy movement he took out a knife to hurl at his oncoming opponent. The blade flew true – well, true enough. Anywhere but the breastplate was his target, for anywhere but the breastplate usually drew blood. That evening was no exception and the wounded rider sheered away, but there were plenty more – and Xallas only had so many sharp objects to throw…

A thought struck him: perhaps, he could do rather better… perhaps he could take out Puglio himself. With a squeeze of his legs, he urged his nimble horse forward again, heading deeper into the forest, with a spear now clutched in his right hand. Somewhere close by there would be a clearing where Puglio's men would be throwing up a rampart for the night. Catching a glimpse of light through the ill-clothed trees, he followed the brightening glow to the camp. If he could get inside, he would no doubt find the tribune soon enough.

Just before he reached it, a rider hurtled at him from his left flank and Xallas released the spear with practised ease. The sharp point tore through the man's shoulder, twisting him off his mount with a cry of rage. God's balls, thought Xallas, as he reached the makeshift camp; what a disgrace! Dux would have flayed his men if they produced such shoddy work. Two men stood either side of the open gateway but both fell swiftly – one to a spear thrust and the other to the last of the Baetican's throwing knives. Once inside the camp, he darted his horse in and out of the pools of light, casting his remaining spears one after another until all were gone… but Puglio had not yet appeared.

With a broad grin of anticipation, Xallas slid from his horse onto the leaf-carpeted ground, clutching his shield. Stirring up such a hornet's nest, he had no doubts about the outcome. Hardly had he drawn out his spatha, but they came at him all at once, hacking with swords and stabbing with spears. Xallas was clever, strong and fast, but he was not Dux, or Varta; he would not keep such a swarm of enemies at bay for long.

"Alive!" bellowed a voice. "I want him alive!"

Puglio! But could he get to the tribune before the other scutarii cut him down. It never occurred to Xallas to surrender, for he could well imagine what Puglio would have in store for him. Then he heard a cry from the gateway and his head dropped to his chest in despair.

"I'm coming, Xallas!" cried Uldar. "I'll get you out of here!"

8

Ambrosius' camp on the road to Vesontio

It was well into the evening and his newly-established camp had only just quietened down. This time his preparations were thorough for, after the debacle at Centum Prata, Ambrosius ensured that this time his camp was sturdily constructed and well-guarded. While most men were settling down to sleep, he gathered his closest comrades around him. Inga, who was still recovering from her leg wound, remained apart and, for a moment, he considered leaving her there. But then, remembering how she had befriended young Uldar, he relented and let her limp in to join his inner circle.

"Xallas and Uldar aren't back yet," he told them, "and you know what that means."

"They're dead, or taken," observed Marcellus. "But neither of them knew where we're going, Dux, did they?"

"No, you were the only one I told," confirmed Ambrosius.

"Well…" murmured Inga.

Ambrosius shot her a warning look, for he had not allowed her to be present to express any opinion, merely so that she understood what was happening.

"You know different?" he enquired.

Flinching in the face of his icy frown, she said nothing.

"Speak up!" he said, with a sigh, "for I'll get no peace till you say whatever's gotten into that head of yours."

Still she hesitated, which convinced him that whatever she knew ought probably to be heard.

"For God's sake, Inga, tell us!" he ordered.

Unused to addressing them all, her eyes wandered from one face to another until they returned to stare at Ambrosius. "I was with Uldar," she said, "when you told Marco where you were going…"

For a moment, no-one said a word, until Ambrosius got to his feet and headed for his tent. "Marco!" he called, "bring her with you!"

Inside the privacy of the tent, he motioned crossly for Inga to sit – but only so that she could rest her injured leg.

"Are you telling me that Uldar knows where we are going?" he asked.

When she nodded, he felt the sinews tighten and knot across his belly.

"So," he said, "if he heard, then so did you. What was it I said to Marco?"

"You said you were going into Gallia-"

"Everyman knows that much!" he growled at her.

"You said you were going to… Caracotinum…"

"Gods! I should cut off your damned ears!" cried Ambrosius. "And how many others have the pair of you told?"

"No-one, at least I haven't - and he wouldn't!" she protested. "Uldar's loyal to you - he would die first!"

He had no doubt now what had happened, or perhaps was still happening, to his missing comrades. Taking Inga by the shoulders, he put his face only inches away from hers.

"Uldar," he said, "may well die but, before he does, he'll tell Puglio everything he knows while his body is slowly cut away, piece by tiny piece..."

Grim-faced, he stared into her weeping eyes as his words struck home and reduced her to a sobbing, shivering shell.

"Take her out of my sight, Marco!" he said.

∞ ∞ ∞ ∞

It was a risk, going after them; but even more of a risk, not to find out whether his pursuer knew his destination, or not. So, leaving the camp under the command of Marcellus, he rode out with only Varta, Germanus and Caralla with him. He hoped the four of them would be enough – three for stealth and then Caralla, because... well, because no-one else among his bucellarii could do what Aurelius Molinus Caralla could do.

Some of the others probably wondered why he did not simply take them all and attack Puglio in force. Certainly, he was tempted but, given their bitter experience the last time they fought in the forest at night, he decided it was a risk he could not afford to take. Instead, he hoped that a few chosen men might sneak into the scutarii camp undetected and discover whether Uldar had revealed what he knew. On that score, Ambrosius had no illusions; Xallas was tough enough to hold out forever and did not in any case know where they were going, but the young Hun was a different matter altogether. Ambrosius feared that the young, untested Uldar would not last without revealing his secret.

If they found their comrades still alive, they would try to get them out without alerting the camp. If something went wrong, then he would have to use Caralla... and it would not be pretty... Tethering their horses some distance from the scutarii camp, Ambrosius sent Varta and Germanus into the woodland shadows, where the light from the camp's torches scarcely penetrated.

"Find me a way in," he ordered and then squatted beside a tree to wait alongside Caralla, who, he assumed, never even contemplated dismounting. His heavy cavalry horse stood motionless, only the occasional twitch of an ear betraying how alert the animal was.

How many times had they done this over the years? One mission blurred into another now and only the climate provided a few clues: the baking heat of the Parthian frontier, or the biting cold of the forests north of the Rhine in winter. By Christ, there were so many places in the empire where he would never be welcome again!

A bird call through the trees made Ambrosius smile, remembering how he and Varta had perfected those calls when they were stills youths in Gallia – boys desperate to become men...

"You know what to do," he told Caralla and, with only a curt nod, he moved off on foot towards the scutarii camp. Caralla would close in a little further and then wait, but Ambrosius offered up a silent prayer that they would not need him.

Using hastily-felled trees the scutarii had marked out a rough camp, but Ambrosius saw that they had made a poor job of it. Simply by prising apart a handful of logs, Varta and Germanus had easily gained entry to one of the camp's darker corners. By the time Ambrosius slid in beside Varta, Germanus had already located the captives on the far side of the sprawling camp. The Burgundian led them to where they could see the two prisoners bound fast to stakes hammered into the ground.

Though Xallas and Uldar were both still alive, neither looked in the best of health; but it was the young Hun who caught his leader's attention. Slumped forward and only supported by the leather ties which bound him, the lad seemed almost devoid of life. Clearly he had borne the brunt of the torture – hardly surprising, for Puglio would have expected less resistance from the younger man.

Examining the youth's battered face, Ambrosius grimaced when he saw that one eye had been gouged out. Elsewhere on the bare torso there were further outrages: slices of skin removed here and there, a right arm that dangled, broken, and a hand missing two fingers – a hand, he knew, that would now be useless to the young archer. Hung around Uldar's neck, as a final humiliation, was his finely-crafted bow. With his body mutilated beyond forbearance, the lad had done all that Ambrosius could possibly have asked of him – and more. If, after such terrible torture, he had succumbed, it was no disgrace.

With stern countenance, Ambrosius scanned the area around the captives. Three scutarii stood guard – suitably alert, but stationary so that to free the two men, they would have to silence all three guards at the same instant. To do so in the open, under the glare of torchlight – albeit faltering torchlight – would be difficult, perhaps impossible. If they had the slightest stroke of ill-fortune, the whole camp would be roused in moments.

A sudden stirring drew Ambrosius' eye: Xallas stretched his legs and strained at his bonds. Though he gave no indication that he was even aware of their presence, his abrupt movement could not have been an accident – or could it? Perhaps the fellow really was simply easing the stiffness in his joints.

Sliding his knife from the sheath at his belt, Ambrosius gestured to his two comrades. Swift and silent, each crawled into position, ready to strike the moment their leader attacked. Ambrosius paused, taking in the usual sounds of a camp at night: the muttering of men who could not sleep and the occasional snort from a restless horse.

Pressing a hand down upon the soft, muddy leaves, Ambrosius began to edge forward, but the closer he got to his prey, the more he realised that they could not easily approach the three men at once without at least one of them being spotted. Only if all three guards were facing away from their assailants, could they possibly succeed – and that was never going to happen.

Just then Xallas began to groan and attempt to wriggle free. Ambrosius shook his head in quiet admiration of his comrade and grinned as each of the guards turned towards Xallas. Since his wily comrade had made the unlikely possible, Ambrosius seized the moment and darted forward from his crouched position, knowing that Varta and Germanus would be moving at the same instant.

As one, the bucellarii struck and, in a breath, the three scutarii were dead – throats sliced through by men who had done it countless times before. Freeing Xallas was simple enough, but Uldar's wounds meant that every time they moved him, he was in excruciating pain. In the end, Ambrosius decided to pick the youth up in his arms.

"My bow!" croaked Uldar, for Ambrosius had tossed it aside in his haste.

While Varta retrieved the bow, Xallas picked up a spear from one of the guards. Together, they retreated to the place where they had entered the camp, but in the darkness, the weary Xallas stumbled over a sleeping figure, who cried out in alarm. Within moments the camp was in uproar and they found their way out blocked.

Though clearly taken unawares, the scutarii were quick to launch themselves at the intruders. Seeing there was no escape by the way they had come in, Ambrosius changed direction to head for the gate.

Xallas hesitated. "There are even more men by the gate, Dux!"

"I'm sure there are," replied Ambrosius, "but it's where we need to be!"

Lunging, as he ran, at any man who stood in his path, he was only a dozen yards from the gate when his small band was forced to stop, hemmed in on all sides by a forest of spears and swords. With a smile of triumph upon his face, Puglio stepped forward from the crowd and the angry, rasping voices of his men dropped away into silence.

"Good rescue, Dux," murmured Xallas, with a rueful grin.

Standing very still, Ambrosius stretched out his arm so that the tip of his spatha pointed directly at Puglio.

The tribune nodded. "Defiant to the end, eh, Dux?" he said, with a dismissive laugh. "Well, I'd expect nothing less;

but to think I was worried about having to cut my way through all your men just to get to you. Is this all you brought with you?"

"Not quite all," said Ambrosius. "There's one more."

"One?" cried Puglio. "Just one?"

"One," repeated Ambrosius, "but, you know, tribune, I think that one might just be enough…"

As Puglio grinned at his trapped opponent, savouring the moment, his men began to get restless. Roughly dragged from their sleep, all they wanted now was a swift end to the night's disturbance. Then they felt it; every man there felt it… and their weary, angry faces became furrowed with doubt, for it was as if the very ground beneath their feet was trembling.

Puglio tore his gaze from Ambrosius, eyes scanning the dark forest beyond the limit of his torches. With a shake of his head, he took a pace closer to Ambrosius, but hesitated as soon as he heard it: a sound like a dozen great hammers pounding into the earth. He did not look scared, simply bemused, by what he heard. But, by the time realisation dawned on the tribune's face, the sound had become flesh. Not a dozen hammers, nor even a dozen horsemen, but just one. It was one man upon a horse, but yet, it was more than just man and horse… it was a beast.

"Cataphracts!" Puglio yelled the warning.

No, thought Ambrosius, just one cataphract: Aurelius Molinus Caralla, a renegade who, in his native Britannia, had once served in a whole regiment of cataphracts.

As the great monster burst out of the night forest, black and gleaming in the flickering torchlight, the scutarii stood transfixed. The two men at the gate died as the rider swept through it, bones cracking under the murderous hooves of the massive stallion. Two short, lead-weighted darts thudded into other men flanking Puglio.

"Varta!" yelled Ambrosius. "The horses!"

Leaving his three comrades to shield the wounded Uldar, Varta sped out of the fort's gateway.

While his mighty horse, draped with scale-armoured cloth, turned aside spear points with ease, Caralla drove his long, heavy lance at half a dozen scutarii before abandoning it, like a giant stake, through two writhing bodies. Men bounced off the horse, as they attempted to carve their spathas at the rider's legs. All in vain, for Caralla too was sheathed in mail. After that, the rest knew what was coming and, losing all interest in their prisoners, they scattered.

As the armoured stallion cantered around the dimly-lit camp, the iron blade of Caralla's spatha chopped at fleeing flesh and severed muscle. But worse, far worse, was the carnage inflicted by the beast's drumbeat hooves which splintered bone as if it were glass. Twisted bodies were left groaning on a carpet of bloody leaves, crying out for mercy – which never came.

Craving a chance to end the contest once and for all, Ambrosius searched for a glimpse of Puglio. But, with a quiet curse of resignation, he was forced to concede that the tribune was far too experienced to risk himself in some heroic, futile, gesture. He would be out there somewhere, in the shadows, doing something – but what? And where was Varta? It seemed like hours since the Frank had gone for their mounts, though Ambrosius knew it could scarcely be minutes.

Only when an arrow thudded into the ground by his foot, did he learn what the tribune had been doing. On the far side of the camp, several figures emerged from the darkness.

"Caralla!" he roared, pushing Xallas and Uldar closer to the gate.

In a moment, Caralla was there, slowing his horse to a walk.

"Archers!" Ambrosius told him, flinching as an arrow grazed Caralla's shoulder and flew away into the night.

Though he could not see Caralla's face for the chain mesh which hung over his helm, Ambrosius knew it would reveal little emotion. With only a slight nod of his helm, the Briton positioned his stallion between the archers and his comrades. Ambrosius feared that Caralla would want to do more than just stand there, but he did not rule Caralla – at least, not at that moment. Once in the fight, the heavily-armoured warrior did as he pleased; he fought in his own way - but forward, always forward. It made him vulnerable because Ambrosius knew that it would only take one fine shot, or one lucky arrow, and the cataphract, for all his armour, would fall just like any other soldier.

The next arrow snagged in the metal plates of the horse's armoured skirt and perhaps it cut the beast slightly for it raised its front hooves and crashed them down again. Without warning, Caralla gave the stallion its head and, snorting and snarling, it surged forward. As it charged, the great horse made a fearsome noise, unnerving even Ambrosius, who had heard it a dozen times before. Loosing only a few more arrows, the archers fled into the trees.

By the time Caralla returned, leading a couple more horses, Varta was back with their own. Knowing that both Caralla and his mount would be exhausted, Ambrosius was anxious to make good their escape before the scutarii could regroup. Strong though Caralla appeared, every massive blow he delivered cost him dear. Before the scutarii could regroup, Ambrosius was anxious to return to the relative safety of their own camp.

"Come!" he ordered. "Don't forget they still far outnumber us!"

A swift glance at Uldar told him the lad would be too weak to ride unaided – for only Xallas' strong arm was keeping him on his feet.

"Take heart, lad!" Ambrosius told him. "The worst is over - Calens will soon have you fit again!"

"Hold him while I mount, Germanus," said Xallas.

But Uldar stared at Ambrosius. "I told them, Dux!" he cried, weeping. "I told them all… I betrayed you – betrayed you all!"

Xallas now mounted, reached down a hand. "No man could have withstood what they did to you, lad," he said. "There's no shame in it! Now come, Germanus will help you up and you can ride between us. We won't let you fall."

But Uldar pulled away from them. "Don't you see: I've already fallen!" he cried, lifting his bow and reaching for his quiver. But, of course, he no longer had a quiver, nor fingers to put an arrow to the bow. In despair, he stumbled back towards the camp anyway, shaking his bow at a few scutarii who were beginning to creep forward once more.

"Uldar!" commanded Ambrosius. "Come back!"

But before they could gather up their young comrade, the youth was plucked from his feet and hurled back against Xallas' mount.

"No!" cried Ambrosius, as they snatched up the lad's lifeless body and sped off into the night, with only bitterness in their hearts..

"God is cruel," muttered Ambrosius, as he rode.

One fine shot, or one lucky arrow, was all it took...

9

On the sombre ride back to their own camp, Ambrosius – like all the rest – kept his dark thoughts to himself. Later, there would be questions – and unpalatable answers, no doubt; but for now, they were grieving. Over the past few years, serving Aetius, there had been losses, for death was the hazard of every soldier. But, considering what they did and where they did it, there had not been so many. Even so, Ambrosius remembered each one; but this felt somehow different. Perhaps it was Uldar's youth, or the brutal torture he had endured before he died, or perhaps it was simply that he fell at the very last moment when his safety seemed assured.

Because it suited their mood, they rode slowly – more slowly than was safe – yet no pursuit came. It was as well, for both Caralla and his horse were exhausted – and the stallion's work was not yet finished for it must carry its heavy load a few miles further yet. As they rode, the Briton peeled off the thick surcoat which covered his chain mail and tossed it to Germanus. Inside his remaining layers, Caralla was slowly cooking to death, and Ambrosius knew from experience that the cataphract would also be liberally covered with broad, ugly bruises from the blows he took – blows which appeared to have no effect, blunted as they were by padding and armour. Yet, they took their toll. The cataphract might have avoided a mortal wound, but he was still made of flesh and blood.

When they finally passed into their own camp, Ambrosius hoped to arrive unnoticed, but instead he found a crowd waiting. What good did it ever do, he reflected, to mill about with shit all else to do but worry? For now his stony-faced procession would spread further gloom into every man's heart. Though morale had been improving, he knew that the loss of such a popular youth could only hit them all hard. Studying their faces, his fears were confirmed at once, for every mouth was tight with anger and every eye downcast. Then he saw Inga, beside his tent, and felt the chill of her gaze. She would feel Uldar's loss more than most, and since he was not yet forgiven for wounding her, Ambrosius expected she would blame him for the youth's death too.

As the riders came to a halt, many hurried forward to assist them. Xallas dismounted first and lifted down the still corpse of Uldar from his mount, aided by Calens and Canis. Onno helped the bone-tired Caralla to dismount and two grooms waited to lead the sweating horse away. The animal, so ferocious in battle, was as docile as a lamb with the grooms, with whom he was very much a favourite.

The first to embrace Ambrosius was Marcellus who led him to his tent. Inga, without even a glance at him, left at once with Calens, to help clean and prepare Uldar's body. With a sigh, Ambrosius followed her with his eyes, before turning to toss his helmet through the opening to his tent.

"Dux?" said Marcellus.

"Once the camp has settled again," he said, "summon our comrades – just the bucellarii…"

"What about Inga?"

"What about her?" snapped Ambrosius. "She's not bucellarii – she's not even a warrior, Marco, is she?"

"No, but she is still one of us and she was a friend to young Uldar – perhaps more than the rest of us..."

"We were his comrades... but alright, I suppose she must come..."

∞ ∞ ∞ ∞

They had a tradition amongst them – his bucellarii – and like most such traditions; it began by accident, rather than design. Yet, somehow the ritual appealed to men who spent all their days lingering on the frontier of death. In its own way it had fostered a sense of growing fellowship amongst them. Now, crammed inside his tent, the men with whom he had shared the past few years, awaited the next chapter in their collective journey. His boyhood friend, Varta, sat on his left hand, with Marcellus upon his right. Germanus, Xallas and Caralla – three of his most formidable warriors – were joined by a fourth: the dark-skinned North African, Aurelius Maurus Rocca. Beyond them sat Placido, flanked as always by his two great Molussian dogs: Ferox and Patricus. Kneeling by the body of Uldar, was Calens, the Greek, while the tall Onnophris – 'Onno' – the engineer from Alexandria, stood casting a giant shadow, which allowed the sly Roman, Cappa, to remain barely visible beside the tent opening – as was his habit...

All Ambrosius' comrades were there... and too, sitting beside Calens, was Inga, who he had freed like so many others before her, but who, unlike all the others, had stayed.

99

Though Ambrosius tried to catch her eye, she studiously avoided him.

"Comrades," he began, keeping his voice low to avoid disturbing the rest of the camp. "We have lost another man - a young man, full of promise, which will never now be fulfilled. If any folk need to know of this youth's courage, let them study the wounds he bore for the sake of us, his fellow soldiers."

It was a feature of the bucellarii that some men were mourned very little – even by their comrades – but that would not be true of Uldar. Looking around at each man in turn, Ambrosius saw that the same cloak of sadness enveloped them all.

"So, we keep our tradition," he continued softly. "When one of us falls, he leaves something he values highly for one of his comrades – so that he will be honoured whenever the item is worn, or used. Since I have spoken with each of you, I know that Uldar – perhaps because he imagined his death to be a very long way off - did not bequeath anything to one of you."

The long silence that followed weighed heavily upon them all.

"Then it is in your gift, Dux," murmured Marcellus.

"It is," agreed Ambrosius, wishing that it was not. "Uldar's most prized possession was his bow – a very fine bow indeed. Every man here has told me who he thinks should receive Uldar's bow," he continued, "and since you all gave me the same name, it must be the right choice..."

He stood up with the bow of wood, bone and sinew in his hands and bent down to Inga.

Regarding the bow with obvious trepidation, she said: "It's wasted on me, Dux; a warrior should have it - surely, any of you could use this bow better than me?"

"I agree," replied Ambrosius, "several of my comrades could certainly use this bow with great skill, but they have other weapons and besides, you're the only one that Uldar taught to handle it…"

"It's true he did try to teach me, but I was a poor pupil and-"

"Would you dishonour our comrade by refusing it?" asked Ambrosius.

"No," she said and, despite her obvious reluctance, she took the bow from him. Briefly, her eyes met his, but he found only apprehension there.

After a few more moments of reverence, Uldar's body was borne away and Ambrosius dismissed all, save Xallas, Varta and Marcellus – and it was Xallas he turned to first.

"So, how much did Uldar tell Puglio?" he asked.

"He did his best, Dux… but…"

"I'm certain he did!" snapped Ambrosius. "But I still need to know!"

"By the time he was telling them anything his mind was wandering," said Xallas. "He mentioned Gallia – but Puglio could probably have guessed that much himself."

"Anything else?"

Xallas gave a troubled nod. "A place… Caracotinum…"

"Shit," muttered Marcellus.

"I tried to send him back to you, Dux," protested Xallas, "but the fool came back – to rescue me." He gave a melancholy laugh. "Poor bugger…"

So, it was as he feared, thought Ambrosius. But what would Puglio do with the knowledge he now possessed? Perhaps he might expect that Ambrosius would change his plans, once he knew that he had been betrayed? But would a tribune of the scutarii really pursue him as far as Caracotinum? The north-west coast of Gallia was a very long way from Rome – surely no-one, not even an emperor afraid of his own shadow, could possibly fear Ambrosius' presence there? Yet, in those moments at the camp, when he was face to face with Puglio, he sensed that their struggle had passed beyond simply what the emperor desired; it had become something more personal…

Was it when Puglio failed to take their camp, that it became personal? Or perhaps it began earlier, for the tribune was close to Anticus – one of those he had killed at the caupona. In the end, if Puglio chose to pursue him, he supposed that it mattered little why. For where else could Ambrosius go? No, he would do what he said he would: he would go home – and the only home he had ever known, imperfect though it was, lay on the west coast of Gallia. After that, well… that would depend upon what he found at Caracotinum.

10

Late October 454, on the road to Gallia

Early in the morning Ambrosius, reluctant to hand Puglio any further advantage, ordered the swift burial of Uldar and then broke camp. If the tribune decided to follow them, so be it; but now that his pursuer knew his destination, Ambrosius could see little point in changing his intended route. For the next few days, he led the column on along the forested valley and through the ancient towns of Vesontio and Augustodunum.

Each settlement seemed more forlorn than the last with their abandoned bastions and shrunken forts, their patched up walls and cracked paving. Garrisons were stripped bare to protect bridgeheads, granaries and storehouses. Here and there, a few proud inhabitants had struggled to rebuild and maintain parts of their once great cities, but their despair was almost tangible.

As he rode between two teetering, stone edifices, Ambrosius felt he was witnessing the death throes of the empire. Where were the builders of these great monuments? Where were the Roman giants who had conquered and shaped these places? They were, as he knew very well, long gone for he had been through Augustodunum before. Half the population now bore a striking resemblance to folk north of the Rhine, for these lands had been occupied for years by many of the Burgundi tribe - men like his comrade, Germanus. It seemed strange to hear their deep, guttural tones so far south; but that was the empire in the west for you… a jumble of broken shards that would no longer fit together.

When, in late October, the straggling column left Augustodunum and passed into Gallia on a road which would take them all the way to the western coast, the landscape at last began to change. It was blessed with plenty, as the full granaries demonstrated. He noted the warm glow in the eyes of his men but, mindful of the pursuing Puglio, Ambrosius dared not linger and instead, hurried on, desperate to shake off the imperial hounds.

Using the last of the gold coin they had liberated from some of the fallen scutarii, he bought much needed supplies to ease their passage. Yet, the presence of Rome seemed increasingly tenuous the further they travelled across Gallia. The closer they got to the coast, the more nervous many of the men became. Like Ambrosius himself, they were uncertain what their destination would bring and, as the early November frosts became harder and more frequent, they were obliged to contemplate where they might be spending the worst of winter.

How much more worried might they have been if they had been aware – as only his closest comrades were – that the tribune, Puglio knew exactly where they were going? In the flourishing heartland of Gallia, a few more of his men deserted - no doubt attracted by the rich pickings they observed all around them. Despite the protests of several of his bucellarii, for whom desertion was the worst offence imaginable, Ambrosius just let them go. Such men owed him nothing, for they were volunteers who had shed enough blood in his service and many of their comrades had already paid with their lives.

The road north-west took them past the ruined town of Juliabona – destroyed long before his birth. It was mostly overgrown now, with only a few low walls of the old town visible to testify that it had ever existed. Anxious to press on towards Caracotinum, he did not dwell upon the site for, like the rest of the men, he had already seen enough other places in decline and each was another reminder of their perilous predicament.

When he estimated that they must be about thirty miles from the sea, he halted his much-diminished column on the north bank of a great bend of the river Seine and sent out scouts ahead. But, even before his men returned he noticed the first, worrying spirals of smoke away to the west. By the end of the day, when the scouts cantered in, one by one, they warned of trouble ahead. All reported the same: the Roman port of Caracotinum was under siege by a small army.

Thus forewarned, he decided upon a more circuitous route which would ignore the valley road and instead follow a path up onto the slope which overlooked the port, so that he could assess the state of Caracotinum for himself. As they rode on, he found that some of the local farms had been attacked – indeed many had been looted and destroyed. Only then did he begin to regret allowing men to desert so easily.

"Who's attacking it?" he asked Marcellus.

"According to one of the scouts, it's the Franks."

"Nonsense!" scoffed Ambrosius. "It can't be; the man's a fool!"

"Well, he may be a fool," conceded Marcellus, "but he should know, because he's a Frank himself!"

Ambrosius knew very well that for decades, perhaps longer, a small number of Franks had settled near Caracotinum as foederati, pledged to defend the town. Some of them even dwelt inside the town itself. There were no other Franks this far south – at least there had not been... ten years before.

When Ambrosius fled from his father's house at the age of 13, it was to the Franks he went. It was they who had spirited him out and sent him to live with a family outside the walls. Had he tried to hide within the port, the locals, fearing his father's wrath, would have handed him over before he could say spear. But the Franks, caring rather less for Roman authority, took him in – aye, and fed and clothed him too. Perhaps they did it just to spite his father who was a prominent Roman official; but, whatever their reasons, it was no exaggeration to say that it was the Franks who made a man of Ambrosius Aurelianus.

But had the Franks turned against Rome now? Surely, even if they had, there were not enough of them to pose a threat to Caracotinum. It was a mystery, but if they truly were besieging Caracotinum, it was very likely that his adopted father, Clodoris would be among them. Nevertheless, he wished that the Franks had waited a few more weeks longer before flexing their muscles against the Roman port. Yet, could he blame them? Everyone else seemed to be doing it; every day a few more of Rome's remaining soldiers trickled away to become someone else's soldiers.

Here and there, a Roman commander would emerge to battle against the odds and, in his gut Ambrosius knew that his natural father, Aurelius Honorius Magnus, would be numbered among such imperial diehards. The old bastard would most likely fight to the last man to hold Caracotinum, oblivious of the fact that it would be overwhelmed no matter what he did. Yes, he decided, Magnus was just about bloody-minded enough to let the whole garrison, and all his own family, perish along with him. And into this chaos Ambrosius had delivered his comrades…

"What now then, Dux?" asked Marcellus, interrupting his thoughts.

"I suppose I'd better take a look," he replied.

He paused for a moment, remembering the continuing threat of Puglio. If he split his company in half, it would be an invitation to Puglio to strike at those he left behind, yet until he knew exactly what was happening, he was reluctant to take them all to Caracotinum.

"I'll take Varta, Onno and Germanus," he said. "That'll leave you with most of the men, Marco – just in case."

"But you'll need more than that with you, won't you – just in case?" replied Marcellus.

"Perhaps," agreed Ambrosius, after a moment's consideration. "Varta, bring two more!"

"Two? But we've already been taken unawares once, Dux," pointed out Marcellus.

"Yes, but the main threat lies behind us, from Puglio," said Ambrosius, "which is why you'll need every man I can spare. We're just going to take a look and anyway, ahead of us are only Franks and Romans – neither of which are my enemies."

"In your head, perhaps," muttered Marcellus.

"Well, they weren't my enemies last time I was here… and that's all I have to go on, Marco. Now, you make camp and take any precautions you think necessary – but be ready to move up, in case I have need of you…"

∞ ∞ ∞ ∞

Before the small advance party had ridden a dozen miles, Ambrosius caught the smell of death in his nostrils: the stench of blood – recently spilled and barely congealed. Gazing across the undulating lowlands to the west, bordering the broad river Seine, he found a landscape marred by the charred remains of several small farms. Built upon the ruins of some of the ancient ruined villas above Caracotinum, they had been thriving in Ambrosius' youth – but no more, it seemed.

"I didn't know what to expect," he told Varta, with a sigh, "but I didn't expect a burned out wasteland! By God, there was peace and plenty here when we left, Varta!"

Having stopped to inspect the first three incinerated farm buildings, he decided to ignore the rest. The gloomy faces of his comrades were enough to persuade him that nothing could be gained by doing so. Only when they reached his own father's large, but now dilapidated, villa did he stop once again. It was one of the last to be abandoned and here he had taken his first breath. His earliest memories were of the family's move into a prestigious house in Caracotinum, close by the town walls. Nothing was too good for the family of Aurelius Honorius Magnus – well, some of them anyway.

Ambrosius was the son of Magnus' second wife, Clutoriga, but once her beauty began to fade, so did his father's interest and she was discarded after the birth of Ambrosius' little sister, Lucidia. After that, his memories were darker: in that fine, new house he received his first beating – the first of very many as he recalled. Living like a slave in his own home, he was given only the meanest and most unpleasant tasks. A smile ghosted briefly across his face as he recalled that it was there too that he had smiled awkwardly at his first pretty girl, so perhaps not all his memories were so dark. But soon after that, he left, abandoning his mother and his sister to their life of continuing misery.

"Nice tower," remarked Onno.

Ambrosius looked up towards the bluff above the port where a lone signal tower stood – built long before he was born, to warn of seaborne invaders. Now its position was marked by a feathery spiral of smoke drifting upwards from its interior.

"It was a nice tower once," agreed Ambrosius, scowling at the stark edifice. "We'd better take a look, I suppose, before we head down to the port.

As they approached the turret, he turned to Varta. "You remember this place?" he asked.

"Last time we were here," said Varta, "I think the gates were still intact."

"They were," agreed Ambrosius, "I remember hiding in there… before we ran off to see the rest of the empire…"

Varta gave a weary shrug. "And now we've seen it, here we are back at this sodding place again!"

"You came from here?" asked Onno.

Varta grinned. "Probably still be here now, if Dux hadn't dragged me off into trouble!"

"You always found trouble easy enough to come by," remarked Ambrosius, "even without my help!"

"Is that a body by the gate?" asked Onno.

They rode closer and then dismounted to examine the remains of the burnt-out gateway and the single corpse beside it.

"One man obviously cared enough to fight for this place," observed Varta.

"That gate's not been repaired for years," said Onno. "Just look at the state of it. Even before it was fired, those gate timbers were rotten – hardly worth defending to the death..."

"Perhaps the fellow sought refuge here, as we did once?" suggested Varta. "But this time from the Franks?"

"You may be right," murmured Ambrosius, as he stood before the blackened gateway. Crouching down beside the body, which had been left in an unnatural position, he noted that it had been stripped of all armour. When he saw the face, he took a sudden breath and, resting a gentle hand on the bare and bloodied chest, he bent his head.

"Dux?" said Varta, noticing his commander's gesture.

"This was an execution," said Ambrosius, staring down at the fallen man.

Save a few flecks of dried blood upon the victim's face, there was hardly a mark on him – apart from the one ugly wound where a spear had been rammed through his chest. He was pinned to the base of the gate post, as if, after death, someone feared his body might steal away.

"Do you think he's Roman?" asked Onno.

"Oh yes, he's Roman," said Ambrosius. "He used to wear a cross around his neck – you can see where it discoloured his skin."

"Doesn't mean it was a cross," said Germanus, "or that he was Roman."

"It was – and he was," said Ambrosius.

Varta glanced at his commander. "How you can be so sure?"

"Because his name was Aurelius Honorius Gallo... and he was my half-brother."

Varta bent closer. "Shit! So it is," he murmured.

Perhaps confused by this revelation, the other men gathered close around their leader, in silence. It was left to Onno, as ever, to bridge the sudden chasm between the leader and the led.

"How is possible that he's your brother, Dux?" he asked.

"I told you: this is where I came from – like this poor fool..."

"So, why do you think Gallo's body has been... arranged like this?" asked Varta.

"He was left here as a message," said Ambrosius.

"Of course; that much is obvious," said Onno, "but no-one could possibly have known you would come here – except of course Puglio..."

Ambrosius stood up, though his eyes remained fixed upon his older brother's corpse.

"No, Puglio would not have known this young man's connection to me. The corpse wasn't left for me to find; it was left for any Roman to find as a signal of a different sort... and a powerful hatred lies behind it..."

"If your father's still alive, Dux," said Varta, "you know only too well that he was always capable of provoking such a feeling."

"You remember him well then, Varta," said Ambrosius.

Varta gave a grim nod. "Magnus? Oh yes..."

"The thing about my father is that he manages to stir even the most placid of men to anger. You can be sure he'll be at the heart of all this trouble - it sounds just like him."

"Perhaps we should go somewhere else," said the Frank. "He almost killed you once, Dux."

"But I'm not the untried youth I was then..." growled Ambrosius. "But for Aetius' murder, I'm not sure I'd ever have returned here.... But somehow, his death made me think of the unfinished business I left behind here."

Grasping the spear, he removed it carefully from Gallo's corpse and flung it aside. Allowing no-one else to help, he secured the lifeless body to the back of their spare horse, before re-mounting his own. Then he led them down across the slope overlooking the port and drew abruptly to a halt. In the valley below, which carried a narrow, winding river into the port, was a sprawling mass of people camped in a broad swathe around the eastern walls of Caracotinum.

"By God, they really are besieging the town," said Varta.

"I don't remember there being quite as many Franks here before," murmured Ambrosius.

As he recalled, they had established their own settlement scarcely a few yards away from the long east wall, but it had been small - hardly forty fighting men at most, along with their kinfolk. It was there that Ambrosius fled after leaving his mother; there, he found a family who cared for him and a steadfast friend in Varta – there too, he found himself. Though he was living barely a hundred yards from his father's luxurious house, he was brought up in a different world.

Since then, somehow, the Frank numbers had swelled – and recently by the look of it.

"How are there so many of them?" breathed Varta.

"After the war against the Huns, it was bound to change…" said Ambrosius. "It's changing everywhere else; we've seen it for ourselves – why should this Godforsaken place be any different."

"But… the Franks have been foederati here for a long time, Dux," protested Varta. "Why, we're virtually Romans!"

"But you're not, are you? You've always kept your own customs, dress… and Romans like my father, Magnus, just saw you as hired men - and unreliable hired men at that."

The light from the scattered camp fires reminded Ambrosius that night was closing in swiftly and, with the growing chill of winter, he decided to make camp at the ruined signal fort and approach the town the next day.

"Those in and around the town may see our fire," Onno pointed out.

"Very likely," agreed Ambrosius, "but no-one will come looking for us before morning."

"What if they do?" asked Onno.

113

"Then they'll have to wake us up!" laughed Varta.

Only later, when they were huddled around a small fire, did Varta probe his commander a little more.

"Why did you bring us here, Dux?" he asked. "I don't remember this town having many good memories for you…"

Ambrosius gave a little shake of the head. "In truth, my friend, I prayed my father was long dead. That way, I would have been able to see the rest of my family."

"Even Gallo?"

"Alright, it's true I never liked Gallo," said Ambrosius. "He resented every breath I took, but he was my half-brother – and I've another one, along with two sisters still, as far as I know."

"And your mother?"

"I don't know; could even be dead by now…"

"Perhaps Magnus is dead too – and a new Comes has brought in more Franks?"

"I don't think so, my friend. The weapon that butchered Gallo was Frankish – don't you think?"

After a shrug, Varta nodded agreement.

"So, most likely a Frank killed him…"

"What will you do about it?" asked Varta.

"Me? Not much. If I'd stayed here I'd most likely have gutted Gallo myself!" he told his friend. "He was a bastard, so I'll not fall out with our Frankish friends over it, but I would like to see my mother and little sister. So, if my father still lives, I propose to take Gallo's body to him."

Varta looked aghast. "Are you mad, Dux? Why risk it? He'll hardly be pleased to see you, will he?"

"As I said, my friend, unfinished business…"

11

Early November 454, near the Roman port of Caracotinum

After a nervous night, they set off at dawn to the port of Caracotinum, descending into the wooded river valley to follow it all the way to the town. Before long, as they approached the outlying parts of the sprawling encampment, they could smell the smoke from the Frankish cook fires. Their arrival caused women and children to scurry away to their tents; when men emerged, they had spears in their hands and scowls upon their faces. Some were mere youths, but many looked strong and, Ambrosius judged, they were spoiling for a fight with any man who looked as if he might be Roman. Yet, for the moment, the Franks made no move against them.

The smell of the food cast Ambrosius back to his youth and all he wanted at that moment was to leap from his mount and squat down at one of the fires to share bread and swap tales of youthful daring. But he was a callow youth no longer...

Glancing to his right, he stared at the north gate of the town – the only real gate through the walls since the south gate had been walled up. The river here made a sharp turn to the west until it reached a confluence with another winding stream. Together the waterways would mingle under the old fortified bridge and feed into the harbour, which was out of sight behind the high walls. As a boy, he had been told that in bygone times, water from the river was diverted along the outside of the walls so that the whole town was secured by a water-filled ditch. But even when he was last there, the ditch was dry most of the year, except on the seaward side where the incoming tide sometimes fed into it.

Studying the walls more closely, he noted that the stonework had been patched here and there. Caracotinum had certainly seen better days and it occurred to him that the small garrison would be hard-pressed to defend the whole length of the wall.

Filling the narrow plain ahead of him was the centre of the Frank encampment. Varta gave an involuntary grin and Ambrosius knew why. Aside from the numerous additions to the camp, this part had changed very little since he and Varta had left.

"Ah, shit and smoke," announced Onno, sniffing the air, "the two vital odours of every army!"

"There must be more than a hundred here," murmured Varta, meeting the gaze of many who stared at them as they continued to pick a path between the camps. Some looked puzzled, others sullen but most were openly hostile. Finally, so many blocked their way that Ambrosius decided he would have to dismount to put folk more at ease.

"They're not keen on outsiders," observed Varta.

"Especially," admitted Onno, "when some of us look like the poor sods inside the fort!"

Bringing his horse to a halt, Ambrosius dismounted and walked the mount through the milling crowd. His belligerent stallion, however, did not tolerate crowds well and snorted impatiently, as if anticipating trouble, despite Ambrosius' efforts to calm him. Yet despite his horse's reluctance, he was committed now so he urged the truculent animal right into the throng so that they must part to allow man and beast through, or risk the stamp of a vexed hoof upon their feet.

"I wish I knew what in God's name we're doing, Dux," murmured Onno.

"Varta and I are going to meet some old friends," confided Ambrosius, pressing on.

"At least, we hope they're still friends!" said Varta. "Ten years is a damned long time, Dux. And, by God, I can't say anyone looks very friendly."

Ambrosius had to agree: where, many years before, he had found succour, now he saw only a ring of flint-faced warriors barring his path. Greeting them in their own tongue gained him a small advantage as they struggled to work out who he was and what he could possibly want with a dead Roman slung over his saddle. While they hesitated, Ambrosius made for the largest tent, with his comrades following close behind. When some of those in their path recognised Varta, they froze – half in greeting; half in surprise.

At the great tent, a tight knot of Franks waited. Arrayed in a half-circle several ranks deep, they already had their spathas drawn and there, Ambrosius came to a halt. When, a moment later, he took a pace towards the tent opening, the Franks shuffled closer, levelling the points of their spathas at his chest.

Again, using the language he had learned as a youth, he addressed them in a friendly tone.

"Who commands here?" he asked.

"Who asks?" countered one of the Franks.

Studying the man for a moment, Ambrosius replied, with a trace of a smile, "You already know that, Siric; but, if you've forgotten me, I certainly haven't forgotten the boy who was always trailing around on my heels."

Though he hoped to gain their trust, his words seemed to cause only consternation and an argument broke out between several of the men who faced him.

"Enough!" he said, still smiling. "I come as a friend; but tell me, Siric, does my Frankish father still hold sway amongst your people?"

"He does!" called a gruff voice from within the tent. "Let the young bastard in, Siric; we'll have no peace till you do!"

The group blocking the entrance moved aside at once, though not all sheathed their weapons.

Ambrosius turned to his comrades. "Stay here and keep your spathas in their scabbards," he ordered. "Come on, Varta."

Inside he found the Frankish equivalent of luxury and, seated amid the furs and gold trappings and flanked by several other men, was Clodoris - the Frank he had called father in the years before he became a man.

"Greetings, father," he said, surprised at the sudden huskiness in his voice.

Giving a rueful shake of the head, Clodoris said: "The first day I saw you, I knew you'd be trouble."

"I suppose I always was…" agreed Ambrosius.

"You always were," agreed Clodoris, but he stood up and embraced Ambrosius – a warm, if measured, embrace.

Resuming his seat, Clodoris said: "You were a good son; you repaid my faith in you – until you buggered off and took my best young warrior with you."

Varta grinned and nodded to their host.

"He pestered me to let him come," protested Ambrosius.

"Of course he did! He was a restless fool - like you! And I've heard that you're in the service of Magister Aetius, no less? Yet, here you are, back in the humble place you once called home."

"I am pleased to see you in such rude health, father," said Ambrosius. "And Merovel, is she...?"

"Your adopted mother is well enough, though... I've not forgotten how hard she took your leaving... For her sake, I am glad you've returned – even if seeing her was not your purpose for coming..."

In the long pause that followed both men struggled to find the words for the next, more difficult part of their conversation.

After a glance at those beside him, Clodoris said: "You seem to have... stumbled upon your half-brother..."

"I have," said Ambrosius, a little relieved at the other man's directness. He had forgotten how blunt Clodoris could be - a blunt man, yet also a good man... and a good father to him.

"You should have left him there," chided the Frank. "He was never much of a brother to you, was he?"

Ambrosius gave a shrug, unwilling to discuss his family before several others he did not know.

For a moment Clodoris hesitated too and Ambrosius did not miss his wary glance towards the fair-haired youth who sat beside him at his right hand. For one so young, it was a place of considerable honour.

"You will know that it was a message," continued Clodoris, "for your Roman father, from some of my more… spirited comrades."

Watching the Franks as Clodoris spoke, Ambrosius noted the glare directed at him by the young Frank.

"I wasn't even sure that Magnus was still alive," replied Ambrosius.

"Oh yes, he's still alive," Clodoris assured him, stern-faced, "and he's still the same brutal bastard he was last time you saw him - only now he calls himself 'Comes' Honorius."

"Comes of what?" scoffed Ambrosius. "How can he be a Comes?"

"Is that a son's jealousy, I hear?" enquired Clodoris, with mischief in his eyes.

"No! He might be a Dux perhaps, but a Comes… that would have to come from the emperor…"

"And his power grows by the day," said the Frank. "His power - and his wealth too, for most of the coloni in these parts must defer to him; they're slaves in all but name!"

"And what is your role now?" enquired Ambrosius. "Once you used to defend the port; now it seems you're attacking it."

"Magnus has not required our service for the past three years," said Clodoris. "He doesn't want troublesome foederati anymore."

"But you still live here…"

"As you well know, we've lived here for generations!" replied Clodoris, his resentment all too plain.

"But now there are more of you – far more."

"Magnus tried to drive us away by burning some of our dwellings – and those of our folk who farmed the land. We were heavily outnumbered, so he expected us to flee. But instead, we sent for help – and some other Franks, from the north, answered our call."

Ambrosius nodded, understanding that those who dwelt further north were, in any case, being driven out of the lands that bordered the Rhine and were moving ever southwards in search of fertile land.

"But you'll also see a few others in our ranks too – folk who have fallen foul of the Comes – one way or another… So," concluded Clodoris, "now we have the numbers on our side."

"You plan to attack the fort?" asked Ambrosius.

"It's already cut off overland – the only way Magnus can get anything in or out is by sea."

"So, it's Frank against Roman now?"

"Not by our doing, Roman," said the youth at Clodoris' side. "But perhaps Rome's time is over."

Clodoris laid a restraining hand upon the speaker's arm. "You must excuse Childeric," he said. "He's a brash youth, who reminds me a lot of you at that age. But, he's right and perhaps we Franks are beginning to speak with one voice at last."

"And that voice is saying what, exactly?" enquired Ambrosius.

"Since your father expelled us from the town, he's controlled it like a tyrant – taxes are crippling the merchants

– and his rule is… severe. It's military rule and any hint of opposition is crushed. The anger against your father does not just lie outside the walls."

"So, with your northern reinforcements, you intend to free the town from its Roman… tyrant?"

"He is a tyrant, Ambrosius," insisted Clodoris. "This is one of the few Gallic ports still trading freely; we Franks have defended it for generations – we should at least be able to use it."

"What about Gesoriacum?"

"There's too much trouble up there – as there is everywhere – besides, we've lived here for-"

"Generations, I know… So, now you've laid siege to the port, what next?"

"That's still to be decided," said Clodoris, "because yesterday, to our surprise, reinforcements arrived – well-armed men too. We'd heard that the Roman auxilia had pulled back to Rotomagus, so perhaps we let our guard down and now the fort is better defended than it was."

"You'll never take it by storm," said Ambrosius. "You don't have enough men to squander at the foot of its walls."

"The walls are old and much in need of repair," replied Clodoris. "And we are making ladders…"

For a second time, the glowering youth beside Clodoris spoke out.

"You come here – an agent of Rome – and you expect us to simply tell us what to do as if you still govern here. But you don't, Roman, and very soon we'll bring down your father's cruel reign - by fire and sword!"

Addressing Childeric, Ambrosius conceded: "I *was* an agent of Rome; that's true enough, but now that Flavius Aetius is dead, I'm just another renegade…"

Childeric nodded. "We've heard the rumours… so it's true then: Aetius is really dead… Then the way is open to us…"

It was already abundantly clear to Ambrosius that, though Clodoris might have some fond memories of him, there would be other tribal leaders here who did not know him at all. Clodoris was only the head man of one Frankish war band, and some of the younger men, like Childeric perhaps, had already glimpsed more of the fading empire than just Gallia. With the death of Aetius, their desire for change would be unleashed.

"I can imagine what my Roman father has done," said Ambrosius, "and he should pay for it."

"And, rest assured he will," retorted Childeric, "when we raze his fort and slaughter all those within its walls – and the rest of Caracotinum too!"

"Slaughter?" said Ambrosius, with a slow shake of the head. "So much for helping the oppressed locals!"

"My young ally speaks in bold strokes," said Clodoris. "If the local people are with us then, of course, there will be no slaughter."

"But you can't take the port with the hundred or so men you have here. And… with winter closing in fast, Magnus knows that all he has to do is wait, with his full granaries, while this little army of yours dwindles by the day…"

A sharp exchange of glances between the Franks told him that his assessment was all too accurate.

"Unless, of course, I was to help you..." he said.

"And why would you do that, Roman?" Childeric's enquiry was sculpted from ice.

"I could offer you a swift - and much less costly way – into the fort."

"How?" asked Clodoris.

"By taking my brother's body back to his father," said Ambrosius.

"Pah! How would that help?" scoffed Clodoris. "As I remember it, your Roman father despised you so much that he forced you out, which was how you found your way to me. Why would he want to see you now?"

"He won't."

Childeric stood up. "Then let's not waste any more time talking about your family affairs!"

"Magnus won't listen to me," repeated Ambrosius. "Indeed, he might just kill me on sight - but first, he'll let me into that fort with his son's body. And, if he lets me in, I can get you in too."

"Why would you do that, Roman?" snarled Childeric. "And how could we ever trust you?"

The youth fell reluctantly silent when Clodoris raised a warning hand. "What would you want from us in return?" asked the Frank.

"Safe passage on ships for all my men, my Roman family and any others in the fort who wish to leave in peace."

"How many men do you have?"

"About forty."

"No!" snapped Childeric. "He's Roman – let him in there with another forty fighting men and that garrison will be too strong for us!"

"I'm the one taking all the risks," declared Ambrosius, "and my men."

For the first time, Varta spoke. "I stand beside Dux on this."

Childeric laughed aloud at that. "Dux? You call him Dux?" he shouted. "How is this man not an agent of Rome when even Varta, the Frank, must call him Dux?"

Ambrosius, noting the traces of doubt in Clodoris' expression too, said nothing.

"I don't call him Dux because I must," Varta spat the words at the youth, "or because he wills it! He wouldn't care if I called him 'shitcloth' to his face - but my comrades would! Why, they would ask, do you not honour a man who's saved your life so many times? So, to me - to all of us, he is Dux and whatever Dux promises, he will do."

"You can find a way to let us in?" asked Clodoris.

"We can," agreed Ambrosius. "And you will have control of the port for yourselves – with far less cost in blood."

Childeric and one of the others grumbled in protest, but Clodoris ignored them. "And what happens to your father?"

"Well, that'll be easy: either he'll kill me, or I'll kill him."

Ambrosius remembered Clodoris as a wise judge of men and their moods; now the Frank chieftain searched the faces of the men around him and even Ambrosius sensed their reservations.

"My young friend, Childeric, has a point," said Clodoris. "I can't allow you to take all your Roman-trained soldiers into that fort. Whatever you say now, you might only be adding to those who would defend the fort against us."

"I never asked to take them all in," replied Ambrosius. "Let me take a dozen or so of my most trusted comrades. The rest can remain here – as surety of my good faith."

"But yet," said Clodoris, "I suspect that even twelve of your best men would make it much more difficult for us to take that fort…"

"If I take any fewer, then my task will be near impossible!"

"It's folly to trust him at all!" snarled Childeric.

"A dozen – or nothing at all," said Ambrosius. "Or… my forty men will have to fight their way through your army to get to the fort."

"Then you'll all die!" cried Childeric.

"Perhaps, but so would very many of your own! I'm offering you another way – an easier way - to get what you want: my father dead and the Romans out of Caracotinum."

"Go with your friend, Varta, and the rest of your comrades," said Clodoris. "Take some refreshment, while we consider your proposal."

∞ ∞ ∞ ∞

"Whatever Clodoris decides," murmured Varta, when they were outside the tent, "we'll be betraying a Roman garrison. Some of our men won't be happy about that – especially Marco."

126

Ambrosius sighed. "True, but then… when is Marco ever truly happy, eh? We'll be giving the garrison a chance to escape - if we can find a few ships in that port. The only real obstacle is my father, for he won't allow his men to surrender the town without a fight. If we work with Clodoris, we can help everyone out of this mess."

"You think we can rely on the Franks?" asked Varta.

"I don't think Clodoris would betray us, but others - youths, like Childeric – just might. Clodoris represents the past: foederati in service to Rome; Childeric gives them a glimpse of a different future, independent of Rome. If the Franks have to choose, I have a feeling they might choose Childeric…"

"But he's hardly a man yet!" said Varta.

"We'll see," said Ambrosius. "It's not so long ago that we were his age, is it? And do you remember how confident we were – how dismissive we were of other, older men…"

When Varta made no reply, Ambrosius gave him a rueful smile, for it was clear that the Frank remembered those days all too well.

127

12

It was late in the day when Clodoris finally gave his decision to Ambrosius, confirming his initial doubts about how far Clodoris held sway over all the Franks. Though the Frank leader agreed to the proposal, he stipulated that Ambrosius must take an escort of no more than five other men. It was a blow, but, if he wanted to get into Caracotinum, he would have to agree to those terms. Any further argument might cause the Franks to withdraw their consent altogether.

Though Ambrosius accepted the condition with good grace, he had already sent word to Marcellus, earlier in the day, to bring up the main column. When Marcellus eventually arrived at dusk, it was a relief to have all his men in one place again. Childeric, for one, was quick to declare his displeasure at the arrival of forty more Romans – even more so when Ambrosius set up camp on higher ground than the Franks.

Though Marcellus' men and horses were dog-tired after their ride, they had encountered no problems and seen no trace of Puglio's pursuing scutarii – which was at least one mercy. When Ambrosius was finally able to sit down and explain to the exhausted Marcellus what he intended to do, his friend – as Varta suspected - was strongly opposed to the whole notion. But Ambrosius would not be thwarted, refusing to countenance either any change or delay to his plans.

"We can't waste time, Marco!" he insisted. "Puglio must be close upon our heels by now! Our best hope lies in getting into that port, finding a ship and escaping with anyone who wants to come with us."

"Yes, but at the expense of how many Roman lives?" protested Marcellus.

"Any man in the garrison, who wants to join us, can do so," Ambrosius assured him. "Clodoris has already agreed to that."

"Aye, any man who's still alive once the Franks have torn through the town!" retorted Marcellus. "And when you say we'll 'find' a ship, I assume you mean commandeer one?"

"It's no more than we've done before, Marco!"

"But before, we had the authority of Magister Aetius!"

"So it was alright to steal a ship if Aetius said so."

"Yes, because we were acting lawfully!" insisted Marcellus.

"Lawfully? Look around you, Marco. Too much has changed - where is the rule of Roman law now?"

"Where?" breathed his friend. "I'll tell you where! It's in that fort over there, Dux – that's where Roman law is. And if you attack it, or betray it, then you're just helping to destroy what's left of Rome."

"If my father, Magnus, represents Roman law," declared Ambrosius, "then Caracotinum is better off without it!"

"That's not up to you to decide," murmured Marcellus.

"You've voiced your opinion, Marco – and I understand your objections – but it's all arranged," Ambrosius told him. "Onno and Caralla will go up the estuary tonight and into the port by the south gate."

"How? Do they even know where they're going?" demanded Marcellus. "And how will they get in? You make it sound so easy, but stealing a ship can't be that easy or it would happen all the time!"

"We've done it before!"

"That was different!"

"There'll be plenty of distractions…"

"If, by distractions, you mean the cries of the innocent inhabitants of the port of Caracotinum, then I'm damned sure you're right! The Franks will run out of control - Franks that we will have let in!"

"Clodoris says that all the Franks want is control of the port – God's teeth, Marco, they used to live in that town! Don't forget that! They lived inside those walls, bought goods and, for all I know, shared the same whores as any Roman! Their loyalty as foederati was rewarded only with expulsion! They only seek to reclaim what they lost when Magnus threw them out."

"You've seen what I've seen, all across the western empire, Dux; these Franks are part of all that's going wrong with Rome…"

"Listen to me, Marco: the longer it takes these Franks to find a way into the port, the more likely they are to sack the place. This way, I can get my family and some of the garrison out alive. And – in case you've forgotten - we are being pursued by a man who will not give up – a man who has your precious Roman law on his side!"

"You truly believe this is what we must do?" asked Marcellus.

"If we don't get out of here, Marco – as fast and as far as we can – we are all dead men … dead men!"

Marcellus nodded. "I know that, Dux," he said. "It just feels wrong, that's all."

"Then you must make your mind up, my friend. God knows, of them all, you've earned the right to choose your own path. So, if our ways must part here then so be it, but we will part friends. You have a choice to make…"

Marcellus studied the face of his commander and friend. "You swear to me that you'll do all you can to spare Roman lives?"

"You don't need me to swear it – you know I will," replied Ambrosius. "I'll go in late tomorrow afternoon with Varta and a few of the others. By then, Onno and Caralla should be busy acquiring a ship -"

"Just the two of them?"

"They're not going to storm a ship, Marco, just make the arrangements… and besides, two men will pass unnoticed."

With a sigh, Marcellus gave a nod of assent. "Well, let's do it then, but I should go into the fort with you."

"No. If we're to succeed, I need you out here, commanding the rest of the men – because they'll follow your lead. In the morning, as soon as the fort's breached, you must get the men through the north gate as soon as you can after the first Franks go in. You'll have Placido with you – and the dogs - but you'll have to leave all the horses. It's a pity, but we've no choice."

"Even Caralla's stallion?"

"Yes – and before you ask – he already knows."

"Then we'll join you?"

"Yes, we'll meet outside Magnus' house, which Clodoris tells me is now called the palace – where our esteemed Comes has his headquarters – it's the large building right in your path after the gate. But if we're not there, don't wait; take all the men down to the old harbour, find Onno and make the ships secure. Remember, if we have ships, we have an escape route. You understand? Ships are the most important thing."

"I understand," agreed Marcellus.

"About one thing you are right: I don't trust some of the younger Franks. Though Clodoris will keep order, he'll not be the first Frank to reach the harbour. By the time we get there, I expect there'll be some young bucks causing trouble – so watch yourself."

"And what if you don't get as far as the palace – what if Magnus kills you on sight?"

Ambrosius smiled. "Then all the decisions from then on, my friend, will be yours…"

"What about Inga?"

"Inga?" For a moment Ambrosius was disconcerted by the question, but he should not have been for he had noticed how close Marcellus and the girl had become over the past weeks. "She'll go to the port with you, of course. Now, go and get some rest – and some food!"

Marcellus acknowledged his acceptance of the plan with a curt nod and went to join the rest of the men as they consumed a late, and very sparse, meal.

Turning around, a relieved Ambrosius saw Inga emerge from her nearby tent.

"Did you hear our… plans?" he asked.

"Difficult not to, as you chose to discuss your… plans outside my tent," she pointed out.

"How much did you hear?"

"I heard that Marco doesn't like your plan," replied Inga.

"So, I assume you agree with him?" said Ambrosius.

"No, why would I?" she grumbled. "I'm not Roman! What do I care for the lives of a few Romans in this town?"

"I thought that you and Marco…"

She gave a shrug and turned to go. "I've stopped caring what you think, Dux."

Another dart of cold steel… "Have I done something to offend you?" he asked.

"Perhaps you should just leave me behind with the horses and other beasts of burden…"

"Why would you even think that I would leave you behind?" he asked, puzzled as always by her reaction "Do you want to stay behind with the Franks then?"

"No," she cried. "Why would I?"

"But?"

"Not today, Dux; please, not today…" she said, already striding away from him into the twilight.

"Come back!" he called after her, but it seemed it was easier to persuade Marco than it was to win over Inga. Somehow, that girl always managed to drag the worst out of him.

With a sigh, he considered letting her go off alone, but it was a cold night and around their makeshift camp, loitered a hundred idle, young Franks – no doubt just hoping to come across a girl like Inga. Her presence alone would most likely cause a riot amongst them, so he set off after her, but she moved so fast he lost her in the forested area on the higher ground towards the coast.

Standing on the edge of the trees, glaring down upon Caracotinum, Ambrosius was the embodiment of frustration. Why was he wasting his time chasing after a Saxon whore? Though, of course, she was no longer a whore and he had never actually asked her whether she was Saxon or not. Of course, she was also a freedwoman – though, since he had bought her freedom, she had given him nothing but trouble.

For a while longer, he stumbled around in the forest and since darkness had fallen, it was foolish. He should return to the camp instead of chasing after a girl who cared nothing for him. As he wandered aimlessly, his annoyance festered into resentment. How was it that she did not appreciate all that he had done for her?

Close by where he stood, a young girl cried out. Was it her? He wasn't sure – damn him, he ought to know the sound of her voice by now! Her next squeal was answered by a young man – most definitely a Frank by his accent – and the girl shrieked again but, irritatingly, he was not sure whether it was Inga or not.

On a whim he moved swiftly towards the voices and coming upon the pair suddenly, found them wrestling upon the ground. At once he stepped in to haul the young Frank off the girl and fling him aside. At once, he saw that the girl was not Inga; and when she screamed, he realised that she had been an all too willing participant. When her male companion came at Ambrosius snarling with outrage, he was torn between apologising and defending himself. As it turned out, he achieved neither, for the youth knocked him down and snatched the girl's hand to steal her away. For a few moments, Ambrosius simply lay there on his back, contemplating his folly – until he became aware of her, leaning against a tree, observing him.

"How long have you been there?" he growled at her.

"Long enough," said Inga.

"I thought the girl was you…"

"It wasn't."

"Clearly…"

"I think you may have ruined their evening…" she said.

"They'll get over it. But you, as usual, have strayed into a place that a young girl should not go alone."

"Perhaps because – as usual – alone was what I was trying to be!" she retorted.

"Where were you then?"

"Watching you."

"Before that."

"I've been watching you since you started following me," she told him.

"I wasn't following you," lied Ambrosius. "I came up to observe the port from a better view point."

"Yes, I'm sure there are a hundred reasons why you might be here…" Sauntering towards him, she said: "Why start worrying about me now?"

"What do you mean? I'm always worrying about you!" he replied.

"Oh, was that what you were doing when you stabbed me in the leg?"

"That was an accident! I would never set out to hurt you!"

"Or when you left me to bleed to death?"

"I sent Calens to you as soon as I could – and you didn't bleed to death, did you?"

"Only because Calens can work miracles!"

"I did what I had to do... for my men!"

"Oh, yes, because it's only your men that matter, isn't it?"

"Just because I freed you, doesn't mean I have to protect you - you're not my woman!" he said. "And Marco's so fond of you, he'll always protect you."

"Marco?"

"Yes, Marco! He is fond of you, isn't he?"

"Yes, he is," she said, smiling for the first time.

"Well, Marco is the best of us," said Ambrosius, "you can trust him."

"I don't need you to tell me that!"

"Come," he said, offering her his arm, "let me at least take you back to the camp..."

For a moment, he thought she would heap yet more humiliation upon him by shunning his arm, but she took it and he led her slowly back through the forest. Even he was having difficulty finding the best way back to their camp now that night had fallen, for it was many years since he had been up on the forested high ground. Though the glow of campfires showed beyond the trees, most of the fires belonged to the Franks and he had little desire to stumble upon any more of them.

When there was a sudden rustling in the undergrowth ahead of them, he felt a tremor run through Inga.

"Just some night animal," he murmured, to allay her fears.

"A night animal? What, like a boar?" she enquired.

"Could be," he said, "but he'll be more interested in slashing lumps out of the earth than us."

Even so, he regretted that he carried only his long knife with him. A good sharp spear would have been useful, for boars could be unpredictable at the best of times – though of course, it was by no means certain it was a boar at all...

"Let's give the beast – whatever it is - a little more space, shall we?" he said, guiding her away from the noise – but also, unfortunately, further away from the distant fires.

As they veered away, the noise of the animal seemed to follow them, keeping its distance as if following a parallel course.

"It'll just be scared of us," he told her, as her grip on his arm tightened. Had she realised yet, he wondered, that they were being stalked - and not by any boar?

"If it's so scared then why isn't it running away?" she whispered, her fingers digging into his forearm.

Abruptly Ambrosius stopped and faced her. "Just now, you're hurting me more than the damned beast. So, stay calm!"

Trembling, she tried to break away from him, but he wrapped an arm around her. "I won't let any harm come to you," he said.

"Won't you?" she cried. "I thought that once - until the last time we were in a forest together."

He took her by the shoulders, forcing her to look at him. "Will you never forgive me for that? Why is it always that moment you return to? Why do you not remember when I defended you against so many?"

"You were defending yourself, not me!" she retorted. "You didn't even know my name! I might as well have been a wall hanging!"

"Is that what this is about: me noticing you?"

"You freed me, but I was nothing to you-"

"I never claimed that you were!"

"I'll always be a whore to you – freed or not!"

"No! You've become one of us!"

"One of you? One of your band of killers, do you mean?"

"If you think so little of us - we, who have defended you, fed you and kept you safe - why do you stay?" he asked.

"Oh, do you want me thank you, Dux, for not raping me? Should I grovel? What a lucky girl I am to be with such a fine group of men!"

"By Christ, I don't understand you at all," he murmured.

From behind them came a low growl.

Inga blinked. "That wasn't a boar," she whispered.

"No," he said. "Stay behind me - and don't… run."

Very slowly Ambrosius turned around to face the animals, for he knew well enough what was hunting them. When the howls began, he felt her pressed hard against his back, clinging to him. The wolves were grey shadows against the darkness, scarcely visible even when they moved and there would be a pack of them in the hunt. There had been wolves all along the river valley when he was a boy, but perhaps the noise and smell of the Frankish encampment had driven them onto the forested slopes by the coast. In which case, these wolves might just be a little too hungry to ignore.

"We're going to back away from them, towards the campfires," he said.

"But what if they're all around us?" she whispered. "Because that's what wolves do, isn't it? You can't kill them all…"

"Turn around," he instructed, "keep hold of my arm and lead us away, but watch where you tread – now would not be a good time to stumble..."

But Inga had not turned – indeed she had not moved at all. "They're going to tear us apart, Dux, aren't they?"

"With luck, they'll leave us alone – after all we're not small children-"

Inga gasped, gripping his arm even more tightly. "My little brother was taken by wolves…"

"I'm sorry, but I won't let them hurt you. They're just hungry – like the rest of us. Now turn around."

Still she did not move, but pressed her breast harder against his back, her heart pounding as she held fast to him.

"If we stay here, Inga, then they will attack us," he said, easing out his long knife. "They're waiting to see what we do; but they won't wait forever…"

"I can't move," she breathed. "Wolves… I can't face wolves…"

He watched the beasts carefully, trying to catch sight of them all; he reckoned at least three, but there could be more – and, he knew, there could be half a dozen more… Still, no need to worry about any others - these three would be more than enough… While he watched them, the wolves too studied their prey and what they saw must have filled them with longing.

"Inga, if I turn my back," he told her, "they will come at us."

"They'll attack anyway," she muttered. "They always do – if they're hungry enough."

Over the years he had seen many frozen by fear – both men and women – and almost every one of them died because of it. Fear alone was enough to kill you. Their only hope was to stand up to the beasts in the hope that the pack would seek food elsewhere.

"You have your knife?" he asked.

"I can't fight a wolf, Dux," she muttered.

"Turn around," he growled at her. "Keep hold of my hand and take out your knife. Then, when you've done that, say a swift prayer to whatever god you believe in – and start walking!"

"I can't!"

"Do it!" he ordered. "I didn't free you just so that you could be torn apart by wolves!"

He felt the ferocity of her embrace ease a little until her right arm dropped away from his shoulder.

"Gently," he said, as she began to turn. "Lead with your knife in your right hand and guide me with your left – and don't look back unless I let go of your hand…"

So, they began to move, at first only by tiny steps, a few inches at a time, her hand held fast in his. A yard covered, two yards… and then five… But the wolves too were moving.

"Are they following?" she gasped.

"They'll follow; we just need to keep them at bay till we get closer to the camp."

But, wolves were clever and, after a dozen yards or so, they began to close in. Though he had managed to coax Inga much further than he expected, her hand was beginning to slip in his grasp as sweat formed a greasy barrier between them. However tightly he tried to hold her, the constant movement contrived to break their hands apart. With a cry of despair, Inga came to sudden stop.

Reaching for her hand, he heard the gasp of relief when he grasped it once more.

"Be calm," he urged her. "You're doing well, just keep going."

"I can't!" she cried.

"You can, Inga! You've been doing just fine."

"No, I can't... because there's a wolf blocking the way!"

Risking a glance at the nearest trees, he told her: "Step two yards to your left – and stop by that oak."

"But-"

"Just do it!"

To his astonishment, she did, but by the time they stopped under the oak, the wolves were neatly arrayed in a circle around them. A closer look at the oak told him that in the darkness he had made a fatal mistake: the lowest branches were not as low as he thought – and certainly not low enough. With a sigh, he knew they would find no escape at the oak tree; they would have to make their stand against it.

The wolves, now only a dozen yards away, were edging in for the kill. Well, he reflected, it was no shame to be killed by a hungry wolf.

"Keep your back against the tree," he told her. "I'll be in front of you."

"It had to be wolves…" she murmured.

"Have courage and, when I fall, use your knife; by then, it might be enough."

"It won't," she whispered, "and comrades shouldn't lie to each other…"

"You're more than a comrade to me …"

"Will they all come at us at once, do you think?" she asked, holding her blade out to protect his flank.

Eyes focussed on the closest, largest wolf, he replied: "I don't know – biggest first, I'd have thought, but I'm not sure wolves have rules about it…"

The wolves began growling and snarling – not a good sign.

"Don't let them rip out my heart, Dux," pleaded Inga.

Ambrosius lifted her hand and kissed the back of it – even when there was no hope, he thought, a little reassurance couldn't hurt.

"What was that for?" she breathed.

"I'm just… glad I'm with you…" he said.

"Well, you picked a great time to tell me that…"

Abruptly the growling stopped, and the largest grey wolf leapt at Ambrosius.

13

Early November 454 in the evening, at Dux's camp near Caracotinum

Warming himself by the welcome fire, Marcellus looked around at the ring of familiar faces – an incomplete gathering of course, because Onno and Caralla were off purloining a ship! Dux was not there either, though at times like these he often preferred to spend some hours on his own. More surprising to Marcellus was that Inga was absent, for he had grown accustomed to her presence beside him in the evenings and he had to admit that he missed her.

"Where's Inga?" he asked Calens, but the Greek offered only a shrug by way of answer.

"Do you think she's alright?" he persisted, but even Calens, who was fond of the girl too, seemed to lack any interest in discussing her. The Greek had a certain look in his eyes which Marcellus knew all too well; for Calens, poorly equipped with the skills of war, always dreaded the night before some action. It had become his habit to fortify himself with one of the many powders he carried in his physician's bag. Sometimes Marcellus wondered whether the habit was already an addiction – still, Calens was the only physician they had, so they could hardly take his powders away from him…

Since no-one else seemed interested in Inga's absence, Marcellus decided to go for a stroll around the camp. She could, of course, be in her tent but a swift visit there confirmed that she was not, so he wandered around the camp, feeling bereft. Unable to hide his feelings for her, he knew that all his comrades must have noticed – even Dux. It was hard to be near her sometimes – yet even harder, as now, to be apart from her.

And all the while, she had eyes only for Dux, who being an indifferent bastard at the best of times, had probably not even noticed. But Marcellus had; he saw how she watched Ambrosius. The harder Dux pushed her away, the quicker she came back for more. Though Ambrosius was his friend and bitterness was not in Marcellus' nature, he could not help but resent how things were. Could she be with Ambrosius now? He thought it unlikely.

As he walked the camp perimeter, nodding a greeting to some of the weary soldiers he had brought in earlier, he noticed that a few of the Franks too were sharing their campfires – mainly older men, no doubt relating tall stories of their many exploits. In the shadows, away from any of the fires, he noticed a figure standing alone and, just for a moment, Marcellus assumed it was Ambrosius – who frequently loitered close to the men to get a sense of their mood and morale. But as he walked closer, he saw by the fellow's dress and hair that it was one of the Franks.

"Good evening, friend," said Marcellus, thus requiring the watcher to step forward a little into the glow of fire light. "What brings you to our camp?"

The Frank smiled - the assured smile, Marcellus recognised, of a leader of men.

"I am Childeric, a prince among the Franks. I was just curious to meet a few more Romans."

"And how do we Romans look to you?" laughed Marcellus.

Childeric smiled again. "You look too few…"

Marcellus noted that, though the smile remained, it carried no warmth. "Too few?" he said.

"You have no women in your camp – or boys either! What sort of Romans are you? Not much like others I've met.

Stung by the Frank's rudeness, Marcellus retorted: "We have women in our camp!" But instantly he regretted taking up the challenge, for in truth, though there had been several whores during their long journey across Gallia, there was only one young woman in the camp.

"I don't see any," said Childeric.

"Well, our women are not a matter for you, in any case."

"Are we not allies?" asked Childeric. "Do allies not share? I could trade you several of our girls for yours."

"Our camp is not a slave market for whores!" chided Marcellus.

"You Romans are always the same: what's ours becomes yours and what's yours is still yours…"

"Time you went back to your women-rich camp, friend," growled Marcellus.

"I did see a girl here, earlier," murmured Childeric.

"Have you nothing better to do than spy upon our camp?" cried Marcellus.

"Couldn't help noticing her, the way she moved, the swing of her hips-"

145

"That's enough!" snapped Marcellus.

"Why, is she your woman?"

"No!"

"There was much fire in your denial, friend," grinned Childeric, "but perhaps she is just the camp whore…"

"I said, you should leave," said Marcellus.

"She must be very busy if she's the only one…"

"She is not a whore!"

"Strange. She had the look of a whore to me," replied Childeric, "and, believe me, I'm something of an expert when it comes to women. I know: perhaps she's the personal whore of your Dux, Ambrosius Aurelianus! And you are his faithful dog… protecting his property…"

Before he knew it, Marcellus had taken a pace forward and reached for the hilt of his sword; but, just in time, he checked himself.

"Wouldn't look good, would it?" said Childeric, "Frank and Roman allies scrapping with each other, the night before they go into battle together?"

Angrier with himself than Childeric, Marcellus forced a thin smile. "Yes, we both have a fort to storm tomorrow," he conceded, "so let's put off the fighting till then, shall we?"

"There'll be more than enough fighting for you in that town, Roman," warned Childeric, giving Marcellus a curt nod before stepping back into the trees.

How can such a villain be our ally, thought Marcellus? Not for the first time that evening, he began to doubt the path his commander was following.

14

7th November 454 in the woods east of Caracotinum

When Inga's terrified scream punctured the night, even the wolf seemed distracted. Nevertheless, it continued its lunge at Ambrosius, planting its forelegs onto his shoulders as its keen teeth reached for his throat. Wrestling with one hand under the animal's slavering jaws, he plunged his long knife deep into its chest. But only when he felt the warmth of its savage heart blood pulsing over his hand, did he sense the wolf's fury begin to abate. After a few more moments, Ambrosius was able to wrench the blade free, and let the heavy animal fall, stone dead at his feet.

Undaunted, the rest of the pack continued the attack, with two springing at him at once. Even as he impaled one in the throat, the other closed its jaws upon his arm until it felt the impact of Inga's blade, yelped and leaped aside. But the respite was brief for, as he suspected, there were several more wolves and now they attacked as one. Cutting and slashing at them seemed to have little effect as the ravenous animals ignored their wounds.

A cry from Inga prompted him to thrust his knife across into the exposed flank of a wolf that was savaging her arm. With a howl of rage, the beast turned to meet his attack and he watched with pride as Inga plunged her knife into the wounded beast's neck. Again and again she stabbed

147

it, screaming at it in her own tongue, until the bloodied animal at last shied away, cowed, but still snarling at her.

A brief glance at Inga revealed that she had suffered some serious wounds to her arm and side. If they stayed where they were, the wolves had all night to wear them down. A bloody death for both of them would be inevitable.

"While they lick their wounds, we must move," he told her.

"No," she said, shivering and pressing back, wild-eyed, against the sturdy oak. She had done more than he imagined she could, but now, at last, shock was beginning to overwhelm her blind courage.

"Inga! Listen to me!" he urged. "Your scream was loud enough to wake the dead – someone will come looking – and the closer we can get to the camp, the more chance there is of them finding us!"

But she just clung to him while, a few yards away, the wolves began to howl again. Though they were cowering for the moment in the trees, they would not remain subdued for much longer.

"We won't get another chance," he said gently. "We've driven them off; if we leave now, they might give up. We've been damned lucky so far, but we have to move!"

She was weeping as she told him: "I can't do it, Dux; I don't trust my legs to hold me up, let alone run…"

With a sigh, he turned his back on the wolves and wrapped both arms around her, wincing as his savaged left forearm grazed the rough, oak bark. Hugging her to him, he whispered into her hair: "I won't leave you and I won't let them have you either… So, come with me…and, if you fall, I'll carry you."

Before she could succumb to paralysing fear once more, he pulled her away from the tree and hauled her in the general direction of their camp – though, in truth, any camp would do now: Frank or Roman. At first she could only stumble alongside him, grimly hanging on; but then she seemed to rally a little, as if finding some belief. Even when he dared to break into a run, her legs seemed strong enough to keep pace with him.

He was taking a terrible risk, for a single careless step would bring the pair of them down. Cold reason reminded him that the remaining wolves would still be desperate for a kill and their best chance of feeding that night was the two they were pursuing. But soon he could see the camp fires – scores of them - and hardly any distance away at all.

"Wolves! Wolves!" he cried out, hoping to alert the camp, and was at once rewarded by answering cries. Relief coursed through him as they ran and he squeezed her hand, feeling a fierce pride in this brave girl that he had pushed away for so long. The next moment, the wolves thundered into them, knocking them off their feet and wrenching Inga's hand from his grasp. Breath knocked out of him, he rolled in the undergrowth but managed to recover in time to throw himself across Inga.

Lunging up with his knife, he stopped one animal, but three more came at them together. Teeth gripped his leg and he lashed out with his boot - pleased to hear a yelp, but by then his knife had been torn from his grasp. Another beast was tearing the clothing from his back as he fought to cover her body with his. She was screaming, but whether from pain, or dread of what was about to happen, he could not tell.

Though he had faced death many times, he had never done so in the arms of someone for whom he cared. He had sworn that he would not let the wolves rip out her heart so, if the beasts wanted her, they would have to tear him apart to get to her. When one of the animals finally managed to sink its teeth into the flesh of his side, he cried out in agony and Inga twisted around to look up at him.

"I'll see you… in the afterlife," she said, as he wrapped himself around her.

Then another wolf leapt onto his back and a wave of pain swept over him.

Part Three: Caracotinum

15

Early November 454 in the night, on the estuary of the River Seine

"We should have done this at first light," grumbled Caralla. "I can't see where I'm going! We could be trudging around in this evil-smelling shit all night!"

"Not if you carry on making all that noise!" hissed Onno. "Because the damned Franks will find us soon enough!"

"I'm more worried about sinking into this marsh, never to be found again – by anyone!" complained Caralla.

They were heading for the south gate of the town – or at least what had once been the south gate. According to Dux it had been walled up many years before – even before he left the town - because there were too few men to defend two gatehouses. After the expulsion of the Frank foederati, Onno reckoned they must have struggled to defend even one gate.

"Keep going," he said, now up to his knees and struggling to lift his leg to take the next step through the mire. He had to admit – though he wouldn't to Caralla – that it was damned hard going. All the same, by risking the marshes, they should escape the notice of the Franks – as long as Caralla could keep quiet, of course.

"Anyway, we haven't seen any Franks yet," moaned Caralla.

"That's rather the idea, my friend."

"Aren't they all camped at the north gate?"

"Not according to Dux, no," replied Onno, pausing to rest for a moment. "Apparently a few are watching the disused south gate in case some of the garrison sally out to outflank the Franks."

"Can they sally out if it's blocked up?"

"Who knows?"

Onno could not imagine why the small garrison would want to sally out anywhere just at that moment, and he was more worried about attracting the unwelcome attention of any Franks who might be close by.

"It's damned cold," moaned Caralla.

"It must be warmer than Britannia though?"

"In the north perhaps," agreed Caralla, "but I was always in the south..."

"I'll make a note of that," said Onno.

"Why?"

"You never know, I might end up there sometime..." said Onno vaguely.

"Not if you've got any damned sense!" said Caralla.

"What's wrong with it then?" enquired Onno.

"Don't get me started – and anyway, about that south gate. If it's bricked up, how are we supposed to get in?"

"Dux told me how."

"Oh good," sighed the Briton, "that'll be handy then, if we ever get out of this lot!"

According to Dux, the south gate had been very poorly bricked up and, years ago as a boy, he had found a way through it, enabling him to come and go freely from the walled town. What concerned Onno was whether the defenders had discovered Dux's private entrance during the intervening years and repaired it. If they had, he and his unhappy comrade would be stranded outside the wall. And, if they were still there at first light, they might struggle to explain their presence to the besieging Franks.

Just as he was about to offer some encouragement to Caralla, there was a muted curse from in front of him.

"What is it?" he gasped.

But only a groan emanated from the darkness in front of him.

"Caralla?" he murmured.

Where they were, on the fringes of the estuary marshes, there was not a glimmer of light from the town to help them find their way. Onno could not even see Caralla – or for that matter anything else. Plunging a leg forward into the mud, to try to close up to his comrade, he was at once immersed up to his chest. Desperate not to cry out, he flailed his arms around aimlessly for a moment, until he managed to calm himself down.

"Don't move so much," advised Caralla, just ahead of him. His despairing tone suggested that he had done so and slid deeper into the marsh as a consequence.

"I know, I know," agreed Onno, "it only makes you sink deeper... I am an engineer, you know... Can you move to your right, closer to dry land?"

"Already forgotten what dry land's like," groaned Caralla, but a few moments later he said: "It's all right; I'm on firmer ground now. Give me your hand."

"Where in the name of God are you?" whispered Onno, peering into the utter blackness.

It was a shock when a strong arm reached out and seized him by the shoulder – but also a blessed relief. Just then, despite the Briton's never-ending complaints, Onno was very glad to have his powerfully-built comrade with him. Slowly they hauled each other out and squatted where they were for a time, recovering. Onno counted himself – among other things - a seasoned warrior, yet when he emerged from the cloying marsh, he found he was trembling all over.

Once rested though, and with their confidence restored, the pair set off inland, with a stiff, cool breeze on their backs, which felt all the colder since they were both now covered with a thin layer of wet mud. Soon they stumbled upon – or, more accurately, fell into - the main channel from the estuary which carried ships into the harbour. Narrowed by the outgoing tide, it was also, fortunately, not very deep and, although they were further chilled by the experience, at least it washed off some of the stinking mud.

Walking alongside the channel, they were encouraged to find that they could actually catch a glimpse of some of the town walls, for lanterns burned at the twin towers which marked the fortified harbour entrance. Following the channel towards the lights, they could soon make out the south wall of the port looming ahead, illuminated along its length by dull pools of light from torches on the rampart.

Keeping to their right, they found they were crossing marshland again.

"Make straight for the wall," said Onno. "That, at least, must be built on a sound footing!"

Thankful not to have disappeared into the marsh, they made careful progress towards the wall but, before it, lay a shallow ditch into which water steadily seeped from the marshes. The ditch, Onno had no doubt, had once been much deeper but it was still an awkward obstacle.

"We'll walk alongside it until we reach the old south gate," said Onno.

"If you say so," agreed Caralla.

The south gate was easy to find, even in the scant light provided from the rampart torches, because its two curved towers were still there, thrusting out at them. As expected, closer scrutiny revealed that, where there should have been a timber gate between the towers, there was now only more stonework.

Glancing around the area, it did not take them long to pick out a small band of Franks who were some distance away, huddled around a blazing fire – a luxury for which Onno briefly considered it might be worth shedding some blood. But instead he turned his attention back to the stone wall in front of him.

"Forget the Franks," he told Caralla. "They're far enough away not to trouble us - as long as we're quiet."

Praying that the instructions Dux had given him would lead them straight to the hidden point of entry, he started to cross the ditch.

"I've been in latrines that smelt better than this," murmured Caralla, "and it's very damp."

In some places, the ditch was firm, but in others a boot could sink in up to the knee, as Caralla demonstrated several times.

"Don't look too close at what you're stepping in," advised Onno, hearing the crunch of bone under his foot.

"I can't see anyway," muttered Caralla. "Shit!"

"That too…"

After a few unpleasant minutes, they clambered to the base of the wall.

"What are we looking for?" enquired Caralla. "If we could just see…"

"We can feel our way," said Onno. "Now, Dux said: go to the left hand side of the gate way and count up to the third course of stones. Two of the stones in the middle of the course can easily be prised loose. So, from the outside we should be able to push the pair of stones in and then once we've clambered inside, we can just put them back in place again."

"Sounds far too easy," lamented Caralla, "and Dux is relying on a memory from a long time ago… Those stones could have been repaired any time!" Caralla's gloom was almost tangible.

Working his way around the curved stone face of the left tower, Onno ran his fingers over the stones of the blocked-up gateway, counting to work out the ones for which he was searching. It was always the same when a gateway was blocked up; everyone knew it was never as strong as a normal wall. Often the work was carried out in haste under threat of an attack – and frequently by those whose masonry skills were very limited. It was also invariably – as in this case – nowhere near as thick as the original wall.

Though he quickly worked out which stones he wanted, no matter how much he heaved and strained, he could not shift either of them. After a while, his comrade applied his superior strength but also to no avail.

"I think I got one to move a bit," said Caralla, "but, I tell you, if those stones ever came out, they're not shifting far now. They must have rebuilt this section..."

For a while they simply squatted on their haunches, contemplating the blank wall while Onno considered whether he had counted wrong and traced the outline of each individual stone again, until he was satisfied there was no mistake. Then he tackled the stones again but to no avail. As Caralla said, if they had been loose once, they were no longer loose now.

"God's hands!" said Onno, staring at the unhelpful wall in disbelief. "We can't get in here – but there's no other damned way in…"

"Yeh," groaned the Briton. "Well, we're truly buggered then, my friend, because we can't stay here much longer! By Christ, the stench alone will kill us! But… you don't suppose Dux has forgotten which stones it was, do you? I suppose we could work our way along a bit and feel for any other loose stones."

"It's worth a try," agreed Onno. "We've got nothing else to do!"

They did not know how many hours remained until dawn when they would be immediately visible to both the besieged Romans and the besieging Franks. So, they had nothing to lose but, as they explored the base of the wall, water began to splash around their boots.

"Shit!" muttered Onno.

"But it was dry a moment ago!" declared Caralla.

"The tide must be on its way in now. It's an estuary; the tide comes in fast and feeds into the harbour channel," explained Onno. "It must come some way along the ditch too, I suppose."

In no time it seemed, the water was lapping at the lower stones of the wall preventing any further attempt to find loose ones. The two men waded back across the ditch back to what passed for dry land and sat down.

"What now then?" asked Caralla.

"I don't know; I truly don't know," replied Onno. "But Dux was quite clear: all depends on us getting hold of a ship or two by this time tomorrow."

"Then we'll have to return to Dux and tell him we couldn't get in. We'll have to go in the north gate with Marcellus and the rest."

"That won't give us time to find a ship, will it?" argued Onno. "We need to be ahead of everyone else – not behind them! By tomorrow we'd be stuck in the chaos with the rest of them!"

"But what then? If there's no way in…"

"We'll just have to find another way – and we've only got a few hours before it'll be light!"

16

November 454 in the early hours, at Dux's camp

Ambrosius was in his tent, though with no recollection at all of how he got there. Beside the bed where he lay, an oil lamp illuminated a small heap of bloody linen cloths on the ground. He was lying on his stomach but his back felt as if it was on fire – then he remembered the wolves, every single moment of their attack until he died… because, yes, he felt sure he should be dead.

A fingertip brushed the back of his outstretched hand, a gentle reassuring touch, but he could hardly move.

"Inga?" he murmured, but if she was there, she said nothing and he lapsed into sleep once more.

When he awoke again, it was still dark and the lamp still burned. In its light this time, stood Calens, watching him. Even in his weakened state, Ambrosius could see that the physician looked most displeased.

"How did I get back here?" asked Ambrosius.

"You were lucky…" said Calens. As so often, the Greek's tone was brusque and dismissive – except it seemed rather more so than usual.

"Some of my men found us?"

"No, guess again…"

"You really are a miserable shit at times, Greek… I'm not in any fit state to play guessing games! Now tell me why I'm so very lucky!"

"Because the brave young girl who was with you fought to keep you alive even as the wolves tore at her."

"Did she… did the wolves… take her?"

"No, we all heard her screams and then your cries of wolf, but it was a couple of Franks who reached the pair of you first, with Marcellus and Germanus close behind, or so they tell me. The Franks got to you just in time and brought you up here, waking me from an unusually deep… slumber… Without them, you would certainly have fed a pack of wolves by now."

"Inga… she's not dead, is she?"

"She should be, Dux; she should be – and I dare say when she comes round, she'll wish she was…"

"What do you mean?" Ambrosius tried to get up, wincing with pain despite a determination not to show his discomfort. "Where is she?" he demanded.

When Calens shifted his gaze beyond him, Ambrosius remembered the featherlike touch in the night – perhaps he had not imagined it. Struggling up onto his haunches he turned to see another bed a yard away from his.

"Christ's sword," he muttered. "I promised to keep her safe…"

"Well you did a piss poor job of it!" observed Calens.

"A piss poor job of it, Dux," corrected Ambrosius, eyes fixed upon the girl - the beautiful girl, most of whose face and torso were now swathed in linen bandages.

"It looks terrible," he murmured.

Reaching out for her hand, he gave it a gentle squeeze, as he had done when they were cornered by the wolves. But this time there was no answering pressure against his fingers. He swallowed deep, raging silently at himself. Far from keeping the girl safe, he had almost got her killed.

"Cheer up, Dux," said Calens. "It's not as bad as it looks with all those bandages."

"But she's not responding to my touch!" he cried.

"That's because she's been given half my sack of powders!" said Calens. "Marco insisted!"

"You mean she's so drugged she can't feel anything?" said Dux.

"That's sort of the idea, Dux…"

"Being able to feel is good," growled Dux, "it reminds you that you're alive."

"You'd better rest," said Calens. "If what Marco tells me is true, you're going to need a lot more salve on those wounds to your back."

"They'll be alright," he murmured, still unable to drag his eyes away from Inga.

"Staring at her won't change anything," declared Calens, his expression solemn and unforgiving.

"Get out!" snapped Ambrosius.

"I need to put some-"

"Get out now, Greek, and take your salves with you!"

Calens, clearly shocked at Ambrosius' sudden vehemence, retreated hastily from the tent.

Ambrosius was still holding Inga's hand as he slid from his bed and knelt beside hers.

"I'm sorry," he murmured, closing his eyes and resting his forehead on the bed beside her breast. "I let you down, Inga – after all these weeks, I let a few sodding wolves take you…"

When her hand squeezed his, it felt like a lightning strike. He returned the slight pressure and she pulled his hand towards her breast. Her eyes were two dark, glistening orbs cut in the bandages. He could hardly look at her, so swathed in linen cloths. She opened her mouth to speak but no sound came out, so she took her hand from his, touched it to her lips then rested it against his. For a long time after that, he held onto her hand until she slid into unconsciousness again.

Returning to his bed, he lay down once again on his chest and fell asleep. Only a moment later, it seemed, Marcellus shook him gently awake.

"You had us worried for a while," said his friend.

"Don't tiptoe around it, Marco," he said. "You at least can be honest with me."

"Very well," said Marcellus, "You're damned a fool – why did you let her leave the camp?"

"By Christ, it was Inga that ran off - I only went to see her safe!"

"You didn't manage that though, did you?"

"Don't you start! But, no, you're right: I didn't. How is she now?"

"Not great, but Calens says she's looking better this morning. But, she's hurt, Dux and she lost some blood…"

"Damned Greek! What does he know? She's lost blood before – and she's a strong girl! There's no-one stronger!"

Marcellus smiled at him, but it was a bitter smile. "Pity you didn't notice her strength sooner…"

"I noticed," retorted Ambrosius. "I just didn't know what to do about it."

"For such a brave, inspiring leader, Dux, you're sometimes a complete fool…"

"You won't hear me arguing about that. Go and fetch Calens for me."

"He's taking a rest, Dux," protested Marcellus. "He was up with the pair of you all night!"

"I don't care, Marco. He can sleep tonight – unlike me! So get him up!"

"But Dux…"

"Just get him here," said Ambrosius, scowling as he climbed stiffly from his bed to begin dressing.

Marcellus lingered by the entrance. "Do you want some help?"

"What I want is Calens here… now!"

"As you wish," agreed Marcellus, with a sigh.

He could do without everyone sighing too, thought Ambrosius, as he bent down to her. Though she looked peaceful, he knew that Calens would have given her the strongest potions he possessed to spare her as much pain as possible. In fact, the more he reflected upon it, the more he decided that it explained her show of affection during the night. For the first time it occurred to him that perhaps the poor girl hadn't even known it was him.

Calens stumbled through the tent entrance and fell headlong. "What's happened?" he cried, scrambling to his feet. "Is there a change?"

"No, there isn't – by God, how could there be any change when you've stuffed her full of your vile powders? I know what you use those for, you little turd! And, even if there had been any change, you, the so-called healer wouldn't have seen it because you weren't here!"

"Marco sent me to get some rest…"

"I want you by her side all the time!" ordered Ambrosius.

"I don't think she'll wake yet, Dux; better she sleeps for longer anyway. That way she'll feel no pain, I assure you."

"Because you've drugged her?"

"Of course, Dux. The pain of her injuries was just too great to bear."

"How would you know?" grumbled Ambrosius. "When have you felt any pain? Don't forget, I've seen you put dying men out of their misery before. Trust me: she had better wake up again, or she'll be your last ever patient!"

"But if she stirs now, she'll be in agony, Dux!"

"Hear me, Greek: don't give her any more of your sleeping draughts."

"I can't do that, Dux; I just can't let her suffer. Nor will I!"

"You will do as you're told, Calens! She is not some dumb beast to be lulled towards death."

"But-"

"She's a warrior!" he said savagely. "She's proven herself! She's one of us! If Caralla came to you with half his belly hanging out, would you simply put him to sleep forever? No, you damn well wouldn't! You'd tell him to swallow his pain and you'd do whatever you could to restore him – whatever agony you put him through along the way."

He took Calens by the throat. "She deserves the same! She fought like one of the bucellarii – so you will treat her as one!"

164

When Ambrosius released him, Calens, visibly shaken by his commander's onslaught, murmured: "I understand, Dux."

"Do you, Greek?" snarled Ambrosius. "I hope to God you do, because I can't be watching over you all day. So you just make sure that girl is alive and awake by the time I go into the fort this afternoon! Is that clear?"

"Yes, Dux," said the Greek. "Couldn't really be… any clearer…"

17

November 454 in the late afternoon, at Caracotinum

So here he was, attempting to gain entrance to his father's fort - with only treachery in mind - and it was a strange, thoroughly unsettling, feeling. As he approached the north gate, he was appalled at how tiny his force was – just the six of them. He would get inside – of that he had no doubt - for they were too few to be attacked for no reason and too many to be ignored. To the Franks who watched them ride out, they might seem Roman, but to his father, the horsemen would look more like renegades, or deserters. It was true enough that his hardened soldiers, with their unconventional dress and their array of weapons gathered from across the empire, hardly resembled Roman soldiers much now.

"Try to look as Roman as you can," he instructed them as they neared the gate.

"I am Roman!" declared Cappa. "Unlike most of you illiterate barbarians, I was actually born in Rome!"

"You weren't born," said Rocca, "you crawled out of a Roman sewer." And the retired gladiator, Rocca, knew the seedier parts of Rome better than most.

"You don't look very Roman these days, Cappa," added Xallas. Ambrosius had to concede that the soldier from Baetica looked more Roman than any of them.

"I'll have to rely upon my natural charm then," laughed Cappa.

"Then we are all in very deep shit…" remarked Varta, causing the rest to laugh.

"Quiet!" snapped Ambrosius, suddenly feeling a chill in the air. Though he rarely felt the cold, this afternoon was different: dark columns of cloud marched along the estuary from the sea, threatening the town with storms, or at the very least, heavy rains. In truth, it seemed cold enough for snow. And then, there was the solid block of ice in his heart, for Inga had not awoken before he set out. Unable to speak to her, he thought about taking out his pain on Calens but then who would care for her?

"Remember what you're here for!" he scolded his men, dragging his own attention back to the task.

"Yeah, patricide followed by suicide," grumbled Cappa.

And Ambrosius, preoccupied by the memory of Inga, lying pale as death, could find no fault with Cappa's grim assessment.

Before they were within thirty yards of the fort, they were hailed from the rampart atop the gatehouse and Ambrosius thrust aside the image of the wounded Saxon girl.

As it turned out, the initial exchange of greetings went rather better than he had feared. To demonstrate his good faith – or, Marco might argue, to better disguise his betrayal - Ambrosius led forward the horse with his brother's body laid over its back. Assuming that those inside were aware of Gallo's absence, they could hardly reject the return of his body even if they might have reservations about those who were returning it.

As he anticipated, none of the defenders was keen to leave the safety of the fort at the day's end to inspect a corpse, so they opened their gates to allow the band of men inside. The soldiers of the Roman garrison were watchful, every eye and sharp weapon pointing at the small party as it came to a halt twenty yards inside the gates. Turning to scan the rampart behind him, Ambrosius found his father, Comes Aurelius Honorius Magnus, staring down at him, stony-faced. With a wave of the commander's hand, the gates were shut tight once more.

Leaving his men still mounted, Ambrosius climbed down from his horse - awkwardly, for the wounds of the wolf attack were still fresh and raw. Taking down his brother's corpse, he held it out to his father.

"I return my brother, Gallo, to you… father," he said. Loud, so that there could be no misunderstanding; so that all present would know that he too was Magnus' son.

There was a gasp from the soldiers in the street around them, most of whom would have been unaware of his close connection to their commander. If, like Ambrosius, they had looked up at Magnus they would have seen no trace of emotion in his father's face: neither regret, nor sadness. When Magnus finally descended the steps to the courtyard, Ambrosius walked towards him in silence to lay Gallo at his feet.

Without even a glance at Ambrosius, Magnus cried out: "Arrest them all!" and, after only a moment's hesitation, the soldiers closed in, spears stabbing towards the newcomers.

Though Varta, Germanus and Rocca drew out their spathas, Ambrosius shouted: "Lay down your arms! We're Romans; and we'll not shed the blood of Romans! Soon Magnus will see that and he'll release us!"

With much show of reluctance, his comrades surrendered their weapons and dismounted, whereupon they were, to their obvious disgust, stripped of all their armour. If his plan failed, Ambrosius knew that neither he, nor any of his close comrades would leave the fort alive, but then they would all die somewhere… for such was the true soldier's fate.

∞ ∞ ∞ ∞

When Ambrosius came to, he ached all over. His chin was especially sore – that would be from the blow his father landed moments after his arrest. Clearly the old bastard still had a bit of iron left in his fist. Even so, Ambrosius was surprised that he was still experiencing the effects of it: a kind of permanent dizziness, as if he was swinging in mid-air. When he opened his eyes and looked about him, he realised that he actually was swinging in mid-air, imprisoned in a small, wooden cage, suspended from the outer wall of the rampart.

Thinking back, he scarcely noticed the small cage the morning he first rode into the Frank camp. At the time, his attention was focussed more upon the Franks than the walls of the Roman fort. Now he had an excellent, if unlooked for, opportunity to examine both wall and cage. Stripped almost naked, he could see, even in the fading daylight, why he ached all over. So many cuts and bruises… but then he

169

recalled taking quite a beating from staves on the way to his tiny, hanging prison. That, added to the injuries inflicted by the wolves, was more than enough to make him feel very sore indeed, especially when the raw gouges on his back chafed against the rough-hewn wood used in the cage's construction.

Peering up to the nearby rampart he saw two guards loitering a few yards away with their backs to him, leaning easily upon their spears. He turned around to look out towards the Frankish encampment stretched out below, and watched as the evening fires began to flicker into life. Directly beneath him lay the fort's exterior ditches, replete with all sorts of debris including the remains of animal carcasses – at least he hoped they were animals... He didn't like the idea of landing among those...

What, he wondered, had become of the five men that he had brought in with him? If they were still alive, they would make their move during the night. If they were not, then everything would rest upon him alone but he swiftly banished that thought from his mind. Much was going to depend upon quite a few folk in this great scheme: his men, yes, but also the Franks - and Marcellus too. Though, either way, in the end their fate would hang on whether Onno could find suitable ships... So many parts were there to his strategy, he began to doubt it had any chance of success at all.

Clodoris would keep his word – of that, Ambrosius had no doubt – but it was not Clodoris he was worried about, for it was young Childeric who had been chosen to lead the Frank assault. The presence of the brash youth worried him. He was one of a new breed among the Franks

– but not just among Franks, for Ambrosius had encountered many such young men across the empire. Rome and its armies held no fear for them because, when they looked at Rome, they saw an old and weakened matriarch, near to death and ready to bequeath her riches to any who were strong enough to wrestle their way to the front of a long queue of mourners. Childeric aimed to be one of the beneficiaries of Rome's demise.

Only the falling sun helped Ambrosius to judge the passage of time and it seemed to take an age for it to slink below the roof line of the fort and disappear behind him. When it did, his cage was plunged into the gloom of twilight until the glow of the Frank fires below illuminated him a just a little against the wall. Though he must have presented a tempting target, not one Frank launched any missiles at him. Perhaps then, after all, his father was right: he was more Frank than Roman.

All along the rampart, as daylight faded, torches were lit. The two guards watching over him suddenly straightened their stance and turned to glare at their prisoner which gave him ample warning that his father was approaching. Magnus waved the soldiers away as he came to a halt on the rampart beside the cage. As stiff and aloof as ever, he was just as Ambrosius remembered him: unyielding in every conceivable way.

"Did you kill your brother?" asked Magnus.

That he could even ask the question spoke volumes about their relationship. When Ambrosius did not deign to answer, he added: "Or perhaps was it one of your friends among the Franks?"

Ambrosius, usually so calm and measured, wondered at how easily this man had already begun to rile him.

"I found my brother just as you see him," he said. "I'm sure some of the Franks did kill him – but that's hardly surprising, after what you've done to them."

"The Franks have become much more trouble since you left years ago," said Magnus. "Oh yes, I know you lived among them once, though by now, I thought – I prayed even - that you would be dead."

Ambrosius spread his hands in apology. "Sorry to disappoint you father, yet again, after all these years. But, if it helps, I made similar prayers about you… and yet, here you still are."

"So, assuming you were long dead," said Magnus, "that is what I told the imperial tribune who arrived two days ago."

Ambrosius could only pray that the sudden, mortal despair he felt had not changed his expression.

"Imagine my surprise," continued Magnus, "to learn from this tribune that, not only were you still alive, but that he was pursuing you on charges of murder, sedition and treason!"

"The imperial scutarii," murmured Ambrosius, understanding now that the heavily armed Romans whose arrival had surprised Clodoris, were not reinforcements at all but Puglio's men. By racing on ahead, the tribune had made excellent use of the knowledge he had gained from poor Uldar.

"Yes, amusing isn't it?" said Magnus. "When your friends, the Franks, trapped the scutarii in here, the tribune was distraught. Of course, the last thing he expected was that you would be stupid enough to enter the fort. He was worried about being shut up in this little backwater of ours, but now… well now, he seems so very pleased that he was obliged to linger here."

"Where are my men?" asked Ambrosius.

"Your men?" scoffed Magnus, with a look of disdain. "They're a disgrace to Rome; they don't even try to look Roman!"

"Well, I did ask them to try…" mused Ambrosius, "but the imperial guard only want me, so why don't you release the others?"

"If the emperor doesn't want them, they'll be executed – I'm sure some charge will spring to mind – perhaps: pretending to be soldiers of Rome…"

"Those men *are* soldiers of Rome and they've fought for Aetius across the empire!" declared Ambrosius.

"Perhaps they have, but Aetius, so the tribune informs me, is dead – also a traitor to his emperor - and you, his fellow conspirator, are to share his fate. They wanted to take you back to Rome, but I interceded on your behalf."

"You did?" Ambrosius looked up in genuine surprise.

"Yes, I wanted to make certain you were dead," said Magnus. "So they're just going to take back your head! The rest of you, I will take pleasure in burning – or perhaps scattering your entrails for the dogs."

"As always, your paternal love overwhelms me," replied Ambrosius, through gritted teeth.

"Paternal love? You lost all claim to that when you ran off to live with the damned Franks!"

"You can't lose what you never had…" said Ambrosius.

"Sometimes," said Magnus, glowering at him, "when the branch of a tree is rotten, you just have to … cut it off. How I thank God that I still have another son!"

When his father turned to pace away along the rampart, Ambrosius called after him. "Will you free my men? I ask only that."

Without breaking stride, Magnus replied: "So that they can fight against me? Not a chance. Say your last prayers, boy - the tribune seems rather eager to proceed. I don't think he'll wait very long…"

With his father's words echoing along the rampart like an epitaph, Ambrosius sat down to contemplate his predicament. On the rampart behind him two torches allowed the guards to saunter back and forth without stumbling over their own feet. Since his father had left, the pair lost interest in him and engaged instead in a lengthy conversation about the dexterity and artistry of the fort's slave girls. Only when their conversation abruptly stopped did Ambrosius look up and gasp – for he was looking into the eyes of his mother – at least, a younger version of her. She was so very different, so very much older... his little sister, Lucidia.

When she waved the soldiers away, they retreated, albeit only a few yards. In the harsh and flickering light it was hard to be sure, but she looked well enough. The torchlight glow imbued her features with a certain… ferocity, but perhaps it was the great, untidy bundle of bronze hair that flowed about her face.

"Sister?" Threading his arm through the bars of his cage, he reached for her hand.

"Why did you come back?" she demanded, spurning the outstretched hand.

"I suppose I thought it was time I saw you all…"

"He'll kill you, you fool," she said, her tone a little softer, "but you must know that. Wasn't that why you left us?"

"You don't know how it was…"

"I know well enough how it was!" she spat at him, shaking her head so that the wisps of angry hair seemed to fly around her in a way that reminded him even more of their mother.

"After you left, she never stopped telling me how badly you were treated, how father could never see you as his son – only as a rival to his first born, Petro. I heard all that from the age of five – day after wretched day. She told me how loyal you were and that you would come back for us one day. But then, over the years, I began to wonder. I began to ask myself why, if you were such a great son and such a great brother, you did not take us with you when you left? Do you know, every day she expected you to come, but you never did, did you? I suppose you just… forgot about us…"

"It was she who told me to leave!" he protested. "She told me to 'go – and never come back.' Those were her words!"

"You did little else she told you to do – why start with that?"

"Is she…?"

"Dead? Oh, yes, long dead," replied Lucidia, "but still singing your damned virtues to her last breath. By then, I could have strangled her myself!"

Shocked by her bitterness, Ambrosius could think of no response.

"Did you?" she snarled at him. "Did you just forget us?"

"No, I always wanted to save you both…" But that was a lie and she knew it.

"If that was the case, then you wouldn't have waited ten years to do it!" she cried. "You can't save our mother now! It's too late for her - and too late for me too. Soon I'll be wed to Gaius - one of father's aides, who's been drooling over me since I had nipples worth a second look."

"That isn't going to happen!" he told her. "It was enough that our mother was…"

Hesitating, he looked up to find her studying his face.

"Our mother was… what?" murmured Lucidia. "She told you something… what did she tell you, that she didn't tell me?"

With a sigh, he nodded. "She didn't intend to tell me. I heard Magnus arguing with her, shouting at her. I went at him, fists flailing, but he just swatted me aside with the back of his hand, as he bawled at her to 'piss off back to the… brothel where he found her.' I didn't really take in what he was saying until I looked at her face and saw the shame written there. She couldn't look at me…"

"How did she keep that secret from me all those years," breathed Lucidia, "even in her last days?"

"That's why I left," he told her. "It was never because of Magnus – though Christ knows, I hated him even more after that - but I could put up with his beatings. No, I left because my own mother simply couldn't look at me. I didn't see it - slave, whore - what did matter, I thought?

176

They're just words. She had always been my heroine...
fighting against the odds to make a life for herself and for
us. But the words mattered to her... and once I knew..."

"Well, I suppose her shame will live on in me then,"
groaned his sister, "when I'm whored out to wed Gaius."

"No," protested Ambrosius, "because you; I can still
save!"

"Hah! Says the condemned prisoner in his little
cage..." mocked Lucidia. "I should go. Petro will be
looking for me."

"Ah Petro... How is our older brother?"

"Poor man – half-man, really... Petro is still struggling
to meet our dear father's monumental expectations."

"Petro was always kind to his little brother," he said,
"at least when father wasn't there. I always loved Petro..."

For the first time she smiled, perhaps at some memory
long forgotten. "He's looked out for me too – as much as
he could."

"And Florina?"

Lucidia's smile vanished at the mention of her elder
half-sister.

"Florina? What can I tell you about Florina? Just that
she is the same frost-hearted bitch that you left behind.
How our father wished that she had been a son... but, even
so, he's taught her all he knows about power and
manipulation. And she uses every scrap of it – more than
even he knows... Our father is a cruel and vindictive
bastard, but every man in this port knows that the one
person you don't want to cross is Lady Honoria Florina."

Guilt swept over Ambrosius, as he contemplated for
the first time the bleak household in which he had

abandoned his mother and sister. Reaching out again for her hand, he was heartened when she took it in hers.

"Soon, I'll be free, Luce," he said, "and so will you."

"It's a long time since anyone called me Luce," she said, "but I'm not five now and I don't believe any more that you can work miracles. Pray for a swift end, brother..."

"I think it's a little early for that, Luce," he said, lowering his voice, lest the nearby guards should hear him. "Are you still where we used to live?"

"Hah! The palace, he calls it now! Quaint, isn't it?" she groaned. "It's no longer a home, but the place where father's clients come to bend the knee and fawn upon him! And yes, I'm still in the same tiny chamber as before - when I was five!"

"Then go to that chamber now and wait there. I'll come for you soon."

Lucidia stared at him in disbelief. "Why is every man in my family either a fool, or a bully?" she cried. "Listen to me, brother, there's nothing you can do but make your peace with God, for there is none to be made with our father…"

"Believe me, sister, I am not the boy that left here," he told her, "and I swear that I will get you out of this town."

"Out? There are Franks all around us! I'm safer in here – and to go where? Where in God's name would you take me, brother?"

"I've an arrangement with the Franks-"

"What!"

"And I've more than just half a dozen men. We'll take a ship and we'll get out of here!"

"A ship?" she breathed. "But, where to?"

"Britannia, our mother's homeland!"

"Britannia?" she hissed at him. "What in God's name do we know of Britannia? Whatever our mother remembered was from long ago – and it's well known that Britannia now is in an even worse mess than Gallia! Believe me, I'm better off here! Now, I have to go – I've spent too long with you already!"

"But-"

"There's nothing for you in Britannia, brother – and there's certainly nothing there for me! From what we've heard here, there's nothing there for anyone. God knows, I'd sooner leap off a cliff into the sea!"

"No, listen to me! I've been thinking about it a lot; we could find our true roots-"

"Stop it!" she hissed at him. "Our roots are shallow, and they lie here at Caracotinum. And, as for our mother, who knows where her roots lie?"

"Did she never say anything to you about Britannia?" he asked.

Pulling her hand away from his, she glared at him. "In the last weeks of her life, she talked of nothing but you – and I can tell you, at that time, I did not remember you fondly, brother!"

She swept away, leaving her damning words lingering in the air beside him. And, for the first time, he saw that, however many whores he bought and freed, he would never be able to free the one that mattered.

18

November 454 in the early evening, at the Bucellarii Camp

In the gloomy interior of their absent commander's tent, Marcellus and Calens stood watching over Inga.

"She seems worse now," breathed Marcellus. "She seems so... distressed..."

Calens shrugged. "That's because I've stopped dosing her with mandragora wine."

"But, why in God's name would you do that?"

"Because Dux more or less told me he'd kill me if I carried on giving it to her..."

"What? The callous bastard!" cried Marcellus. "Hasn't he damaged this girl enough? At least we have to give her some peace!"

"Dux doesn't want her to die, Marco."

"Well, I don't either, but at least she deserves something to dull the pain! Surely you told him that, didn't you?"

"I did, but he said I'd given her too much... and now, I'm beginning to think perhaps he was right... When she came in, she was bleeding so much - and I wasn't quite... myself..."

"You were out of it!" said Marco, glaring at him.

"Perhaps," said Calens. "And I gave her some opium... as well as the mandragora-"

"Well, you need to give her some more – you can see she's wracked with pain!"

"I can see she's restless, Marco," murmured the Greek. "But I think Dux was right: I need to let her feel her injuries and then – if she needs it – I will give her something to relieve the pain. I believe the mandragora has helped to stop the bleeding and her wounds are drying out. This girl is young, Marco – and a quick healer."

"But, look at her; she's squirming in her sleep!" pleaded Marcellus.

"Dux said she's proven herself to be a warrior – and, despite my worst fears, I think perhaps he has judged her better than you or I."

"Hah! Not very likely!" said Marcellus. "Dux knows almost nothing about women! And what about when she finds out how scarred she will be?"

"The point, Marco, is to let her decide for herself," replied Calens. "We'll let her body and her spirit decide. She must decide whether she can live with who she is now…"

"But by tomorrow at dawn we need to be ready to embark on a ship, for God's sake! How will she cope with that?"

"She's surprisingly strong, Marco," said Calens, "so perhaps we should use what little time remains to work out how we can convey her safely to the port."

"Pah! This is nonsense!" cried Marcellus. "Am I the only one that cares about her?"

With a shake of his head, Calens watched Marcellus storm out and then went to Inga, who was still shivering and moaning. Yet, she was not, as Marco believed, writhing in agony. If he was any sort of judge, her condition was more settled than it had been. When he took her hand, her eyes flew open.

"Dux?" she muttered.

"No, just Calens," he replied.

"Oh, where's Dux?"

"He's in the-"

"-fort…" she said softly. "Yes, I remember…"

"How do you feel, Inga?"

"Like I've been… ripped apart – it hurts to move my lips… how do I look?"

"Bandaged…" replied Calens gently.

"By the gods, I wish I'd seen him again, just once more…"

After that, she drifted into a restless sleep once more. Though he could not be certain yet, he reckoned that when she awoke again, he would need some warm broth to give her…

There was a flurry of movement outside and the tent opening parted to allow one of the Franks inside, escorted by two of Dux's men.

Calens nodded to the guards and they left, but the young Frank had eyes only for Inga.

"You were one of those who found her and her companion," said Calens, "and brought them to me."

"Yes, I'm Caranis," said the Frank. "Will she live?"

"Yes, she will – thanks to you."

Caranis nodded. "That's good! You must know that I serve Childeric and he is no friend to your Dux. But still, I am pleased that she lives."

"But we are all on the same side," said Calens.

With a frown, Caranis said: "We are not... all... on the same side; take care with her when you enter the town tomorrow."

"What do you mean?" asked Calens.

"I mean take great care – both with your enemies and... your allies..."

By the time Calens understood what Caranis was telling him, the Frank was gone. Heaving a weary sigh, the Greek went to find Marcellus again, knowing he would have to burden him with yet more troubles.

19

November 454 in the evening, outside
Caracotinum's south gate

By dawn, unable to effect an entry through the south gate, the two bucellarii were forced to concede defeat and seek a hiding place to wait out the long hours of daylight. They settled for a patch of reeds on the edge of the estuary marshes. It was cold, damp and thoroughly unpleasant but there was nowhere else. They were tempted to declare their presence to the Franks and try to work with them, but Onno thought the risk was just too great. If the Franks decided to take them back to the main camp, he could not imagine how he would explain to Dux why they were not at least still trying to get him a ship.

Watching the dozen or so Franks amuse themselves on the shore passed the time for a few moments, but Onno and Caralla found that there was a limit to how much excitement a Frank pissing contest could create. They sensed that the Franks themselves were as bored as they were, especially when a minor, but bloody, skirmish broke out which left one man dead and another bleeding profusely. Perhaps chastened by their loss, the Franks settled back into idleness, for they too were waiting out the hours until the dawn attack.

"I have an idea," said Onno abruptly. "In the night, we could swim along the channel to the port entrance and into the harbour that way. Can you swim?"

"No, of course I can't swim," retorted Caralla. "Why would I need to swim? I've got a damned great horse to do my swimming!"

"Well, you won't have him much longer," remarked Onno.

Caralla frowned. "No, I suppose not. I'll miss that evil bastard…"

"So you can't swim?"

"No."

"I suppose at low tide it's probably not that deep," said Onno.

"Probably?" echoed Caralla.

"If we could wade along the edge of the channel – at least as far as the entrance towers…"

"Then what?"

"Then I suppose you'd most likely drown..."

They fell silent again, devoid of any other ideas.

"The Franks are quiet now at least," observed Caralla.

"Stay here; I'll take a look," said Onno, glad to find an excuse to move his stiffening limbs.

On his knees, he crawled across the scrub land that bordered the marshes and crept closer to the Frank camp. As he did so, he became aware that the Franks were actually not very quiet at all – in fact they were a lot noisier than before. The reason became apparent soon enough: reinforcements had arrived and not empty-handed either, for he noted with interest that half a dozen or so roughly-made ladders were now stacked at one side of the camp.

So, it appeared that the Franks were not willing to rely solely on Dux to get them into Caracotinum. They were planning an assault of their own on the south wall, more than likely at dawn when the most of the town's garrison would be summoned to defend the breached north gate.

At once Onno considered stealing one of the ladders, but the difficulty of doing so under the noses of so many Franks, seemed too great. Nevertheless, when he returned to Caralla he brought with him a few ideas at last.

"We could follow them over the wall," said Caralla. "Wait for them to attack and then use one of the same ladders."

"We could, but that would be far too late!" said Onno. "God's breath! We're supposed to be finding a ship now; now, Caralla, not at dawn tomorrow!"

"Well, what else can we do?" demanded Caralla. "Even if we steal one of the ladders, we can hardly use it in daylight, can we? We might as well surrender now!"

"I agree that, whatever way we choose, we can't move before this evening," said Onno.

"But that will mean seeking a ship at the dead of night," cried Caralla. "What ship's master would even let us aboard to talk at such an hour?"

"We're going to be desperate, my friend. I fear that talking may not come into it much... One thing is certain: we've got to get into that port tonight! Either we swim, or we steal a ladder and climb. All our comrades are depending upon us; so, whoever chooses to stand in our way, they cannot be allowed to stop us. "

∞ ∞ ∞ ∞

By evening, when the Franks settled down to snatch a few hours' sleep before their dawn attack on the town, they numbered more than twenty. Though sentries had been posted, none was awake when Onno and Caralla paid them a nocturnal visit. Creeping through the low scrub, they found a slumbering camp – or so it seemed. Once at the outer limit of the encampment, the two Romans made for the pile of ladders. With a final glance at those closest to the stack, Onno went to take one end while Caralla went to the other.

"Who are you?" a husky voice slurred from the far side of the pile of ladders.

Dry mouthed, Onno leant over to find one of the young warriors staring back up at him.

"We're to join your attack tomorrow," whispered Onno.

"But who are you?" repeated the Frank.

"We're on your side," Onno soothed, as he and Caralla lifted the ladder from the top of the stack.

"Noooo….wait," groaned the Frank, lurching to his knees. "Who are you, though? You look sort of Roman…"

With a sigh, Onno put down his end of the ladder as the worried Frank tried to stand and swayed with the effort of it.

Catching the man as he fell, Onno rapped the poor fellow on the back of the neck to be sure and then laid him on the ground.

"Finished?" hissed Caralla, still bearing one end of the ladder.

With a curt nod, Onno seized the ladder again and the pair hurried away towards the wall, stumbling in the dark with every few steps they took.

"Where to?" gasped Caralla. "It'll be too soft near the old gate."

"The problem is, my friend that the further away from the docks we are when we go over the wall, the longer it will take us to get to the ships," said Onno.

"But we can't go up too close to those Franks," added Caralla.

"Let's just move!" said Onno. "Anywhere where the ditch is firm will have to do!"

As they hurried across the open ground, Onno felt a few raindrops, which was all they needed! Planting the ladder, they leant it against the wall as gently as they could. Knowing one of the guards might spot the ladder at any moment; Onno gripped his knife between his teeth and started to climb up. Beneath him he felt the timber give a little as the mighty Caralla began to follow him up. The horseman, he knew, would be nervous, for this was not his sort of activity. Onno couldn't suppress a sympathetic grin as he climbed: poor old Caralla - unable to swim and not comfortable with heights, his sweaty hands would be slipping on the wooden rungs. It was just as well the fellow rode better than any other man he knew.

Reaching the top of the ladder, Onno took his knife in his right hand and poked his head above the parapet to squint along the rampart. Pulling back for a moment he was aware of a heavily breathing Caralla coming up close behind him. Though they had chosen a dimly-lit section of the rampart and the nearest guard was a long way along the wall, Onno was still concerned. If they were seen on the rampart at all, they could so easily be trapped up there. There was almost certainly a flight of steps close by at the gatehouse, but there they might also encounter some of the garrison.

"You going?" wheezed Caralla.

Onno leapt softly down onto the rampart, took a pace to the right to allow room for his comrade to join him and then crouched down low. Caralla thudded onto the rampart, his greater weight making the timber boards shudder.

"That should give everyone fair warning," said Onno.

"Where next?" asked Caralla.

"Quickest way down," hissed Onno, setting off towards the nearest tower.

Though he expected the tower to be heavily guarded, he was relieved to discover that it was empty – both of stored weapons and armed men. It was cold, dark and abandoned… It seemed that the garrison really was terribly depleted in both men and resources. Nevertheless, they exercised much caution as they made their way down a stair which Onno knew must lead to ground level. At last, they were inside Caracotinum.

According to Dux, they ought now to be in a small, walled enclosure originally intended to house the garrison which protected the harbour itself from attack. Several yards away a flickering torch illuminated enough to confirm that Dux's recollection had been correct and Onno gave a sigh of relief. Though the rain was coming on heavier, he thought it might work to their advantage when they were caught out in the open, as now.

"To work then, my friend," he said, feeling optimistic for the first time that night. "Let's get ourselves onto the town docks, shall we?"

"No," growled a voice close by. "Let's not."

A figure stepped out into the wavering pool of torchlight, followed by another and then two more.

"On the bright side," muttered Caralla, "I think we're soon going to be out of the rain…"

20

November 454 in the early hours, in the barracks at the north gate

Fingers clenched around an iron bar of the gate, Varta waited with the rest, while Cappa worked at the lock.

"Is it open yet?" demanded Xallas, for the third time.

"No, it isn't!" hissed Cappa, not even troubling to glance at his comrade. "It'll be done when I tell you it's done!"

"God's hammer! Let him work!" grumbled Varta. "Or it'll be dawn before he gets it open!"

"He said it would only take a moment," Xallas reminded his comrades.

"There, it's done now," announced Cappa, "so stop complaining!"

"We need our weapons, Varta," said Rocca. "Without them, we've no chance."

"We can make do with borrowed weapons for now," snapped Varta. "All that matters now is getting to the north gate!"

Standing ready beside the door, Varta waited for the guard. The fellow was more reliable than most gaolers and sure enough, after a few moments, he strolled around the corner to check on his prisoners. The iron gate swung open fast, cracking the guard on his chin. Catching him as he fell, Varta dealt him another blow and tossed him inside the cell.

One by one, the others shuffled out into the stone-walled passage.

Reaching the barracks courtyard without any alarm, they paused for a moment, each man seeking his own place of concealment. Varta was pleased with what he saw: only a handful of torches still burned, giving them just enough, but not too much, light. Dux had told him that the garrison was undermanned, so there should only be a few men left in the barracks – hopefully asleep. The north gate itself, however, might be a different matter.

"You know what to do, lads," said Varta. "So be swift - swift and silent... and try not to kill the local soldiers. Germanus and I will free Dux and join you back at the gate. By then our Frankish allies should be making their way in. Oh, and we could do with a few more spears – if you should come across any."

He nodded to Germanus. "Come, my friend, let's free the caged animal, shall we?"

A simple plan, reflected Varta, but the trouble with all simple plans was that they were often equally simple to foil. Once the alarm was raised, they would have to fight for their lives – and somewhere, very close by, would be the imperial guard and their tribune, Puglio. The latter had already paid them a visit in the cells, unable to disguise his triumph. But, Varta suspected, Puglio might still be wondering where the rest of Dux's small army was.

He permitted himself a silent smile for Puglio himself had in fact saved them a deal of time searching for their imprisoned leader. In his eagerness to gloat, he had told them precisely where and how Dux was caged. They might have spent the rest of the night in a fruitless attempt to find him in a cell somewhere; as it was, all they had to do was search the rampart walls.

With Germanus following close behind, he moved with stealth up the steps to the rampart. From the courtyard below he heard only a few grunts as guards were rendered unconscious. Then he concentrated on carrying out his own task with equal effectiveness. Approaching the two men posted on the walkway, he began to chuckle aloud.

The guards swivelled at once to face him and Germanus.

"What are you two Franks doing up here?" demanded one.

"I'm no Frank," grumbled Germanus.

"All you lot look the same to me," said the guard.

"We've been released now," replied Varta, moving closer, as he clapped the belligerent Germanus on the back. "So, we're all on the same side."

Taking no chances, both guards raised their spears.

"Steady, fellow!" cried Varta, his bare chest almost at the point of the spear. "We're not trying to cause offence!"

He smiled and, though the guard did not return his smile, he lowered his weapon a fraction.

Still smiling, Varta made a sudden lunge, seizing the spear just below the blade and pulled hard on it, to swing the guard around into his comrade, with whom Germanus was already grappling. In a few moments, both guards lay disarmed and out cold.

"Varta?" Ambrosius called softly from the other side of the rampart.

Peering over the edge of the rampart, Varta squinted down at him in the darkness.

"You made enough noise," complained Ambrosius.

"You want to stay in that cage a bit longer, Dux?" enquired Varta.

"Just get the damned door open!"

Clambering down onto the top of the cage, Varta cut the leather ties that held shut a small opening in the top. Then he reached down to clasp Ambrosius by the arm and pulled his leader out and up onto the rampart.

For the first time, Ambrosius grinned at him. "Thanks, old friend... but are the men at the gate? Shouldn't I be hearing the clamour of fighting by now from the gatehouse, or the courtyard? Shouldn't the Franks at least be inside the fort by now?"

Varta and Germanus exchanged a glance, knowing he was right. The simplest of plans, thought Varta...

"You'd better get down there and see what's gone wrong," ordered Ambrosius. "We're hardly dressed for combat, but take what you can from these two. I'll fetch my family and bring them down to you."

They watched him snatch up a spatha from one of the fallen guards and hurry along towards the far end of the rampart.

"Do you think he knows where he's going?" asked Germanus.

"He ought to," said Varta, leading them off back the way they had come. "I doubt much has changed since he lived here!"

When they returned to the courtyard below, they came to an abrupt halt. At first, all seemed as it should be: several guards lay on the cobbles before the gate - which stood wide open – and beside it, his comrades waited.

"Where are the Franks?" asked Varta when he joined them. "The gates are open, so where are the sodding Franks?"

"Oh, they're out there," replied Xallas. "They're sitting on their arses about fifty feet from the gate."

"What? Why?" hissed Germanus. "Why would they do that?"

After a long silence, Varta gave voice to what each of them already knew.

"Because," he said, with a heavy sigh, "their commander, that cunning, little bastard, Childeric, is waiting for the Roman guards to kill most of us before he saunters in to slaughter them. He doesn't want a share of the victory; he wants all of it... and he wants every Roman dead – including us."

"Clodoris won't allow that!" argued Germanus.

"But Clodoris isn't here, is he?" Varta pointed out. "And, though he's bound to keep his word to Dux, it might suit him rather better if Childeric does not..."

"What do you mean?" asked Germanus. "We're not their enemy!"

"But that's just it: for a lot of these Franks, we are the enemy: men paid by Rome and in the service of Rome – and we're in their way..."

"But we're trying to leave!" protested Xallas.

"So what do we do?" asked Rocca.

"We'll have to give that little shit no choice – force him to come in now!" said Varta.

"I'm a simple man," grumbled Xallas. "Just tell me what to do, Varta, and I'll do it!"

"God's hammer! It'll be starting to get light soon," muttered Varta.

"So?" said Xallas.

Grim-faced, Varta told them: "You want something to do? Well, go and close those gates!"

"But Marco and the others will be shut out," murmured Xallas.

"You're not actually going to close the gate, Xallas; just make it look as if you are," explained Varta. "We need the breach to happen now - before a few more of the garrison wander along to relieve their comrades, find an open gate and only us to argue with!"

Jumping up from his place of concealment, Xallas went to the gates and put his shoulder against the left hand door. Rocca ran out to help and between them they slammed one half of the wooden gates shut. A moment later a spear flew through the remaining gap and clattered across the courtyard.

"I think we've got their attention," remarked Varta, nodding in satisfaction.

Now Childeric would have to advance on the gate, or risk losing access to the fort altogether – a disaster which he would find most difficult to explain to Clodoris.

"As soon as we're sure the Franks are actually coming in," said Varta, "we'll go for Dux and his family. Then, with luck, the Franks and the imperial guard will fight themselves into a bloody tangle! And by then, Marco will have brought up the rest of our comrades."

"They're running to the gate now," reported Xallas.

"Thought they might be," murmured Varta. "Come on then, lads, time to move. We don't want to get caught between them."

With an impressive lack of subtlety, the Franks roared as they attacked the still-open gate. Almost at once, Varta heard warning cries from along the rampart as the Roman defenders realised they were under attack. As Varta led his comrade back up the steps to the rampart, the Franks, with another mighty roar, poured into the fort. He reckoned that the sound of the attack alone would be causing considerable alarm amongst those defending the fort. Once they realised that their gate was open and wholly undefended, they would be seized by panic.

"Where now?" wheezed Cappa, unused to so much exertion.

Lethal if a knife blade in the shadows was required, Cappa – unlike all the others - was not a battlefield soldier.

"The palace!" replied Varta. "That's where Dux has gone! So, keep up!"

By the time the first of the Franks passed into the courtyard by the barracks, Varta and his friends were already racing towards the palace. Before they reached it, however, several of the imperial scutarii appeared. Clearly they had just been roused from their slumber by the sudden assault on the gate, for several were still donning their armour.

Since there was no sign of Puglio, Varta tried deception.

"We're under attack!" he cried. "Get to the gate – the Franks are already inside the fort!"

But the scutarii were not to be so easily fooled.

"We don't take our orders from shits like you," retorted one, drawing out his spatha. "Bugger the Franks! You're the scum we came for!"

Varta's face broke into a fierce grin and he growled: "Go on then: try buggering this Frank!"

Though the scutarii were tough, they were no match for Dux's men; but there were more than enough of them to hold the bucellarii up. Varta soon realised that getting past them was taking far too long – especially since, in a few moments, there could well be a host of Franks surging up behind them. In all the time Varta had served with Ambrosius, he could not recall being embroiled in such a ludicrous struggle: scutarii ahead of them and Franks behind, with a Roman garrison scattered around for good measure! Hours before, he saw the Franks as his allies; were they now his foes? Yet, one thing was certain: the scutarii were most definitely his enemies!

His fighting spirit fuelled by anger and frustration, Varta battled harder to drive back the scutarii and, when two of their number were badly wounded, the rest decided to fall back. With a shout of triumph, Varta watched them retreat into the nearby streets, allowing the bucellarii to make for the palace entrance.

"Xallas, Germanus, watch our backs as we go in! I don't want those bastards up our arses later. We have to move faster now – Dux is on his own and, with the scutarii on the move, he could be in trouble!"

21

November 454 just before dawn, in the Palace at Caracotinum

When he burst into the palace building through its ancient doorway, Ambrosius anticipated being met by Magnus' guards, but no-one challenged him. Passing through a vestibule, he expected to enter the colonnaded courtyard he remembered, but inside he came to a stunned halt, for it was a courtyard no longer. Instead he was standing in a large chamber with a raised dais at the far end and banners hanging upon the walls. Remembering what Lucidia had told him, he recognised the room at once as an audience hall, for he had seen such chambers in Ravenna and several other cities across the empire.

Here, the humble folk of Caracotinum would come to pay their homage to Comes Aurelius Honorius Magnus and thus did rich men make themselves richer still. Shaking his head in disgust, Ambrosius spat on the fine mosaic floor, before turning on his heel and heading up the main stairway. Hurrying through the first floor chambers, he searched in vain for Lucidia.

After a few minutes, he despaired of ever finding her and, abandoning all caution, shouted her name aloud. He crashed through door after door until he came to a large triclinium. Once again, the opulence of the room astonished him: such a large, formal dining room was usually the preserve of the most high-born. With its several apses and padded semi-circular couches, it must have accommodated as many as thirty diners. Small round tables bore silver platters and bowls; painted glass goblets were littered about the chamber. He gasped to see the rich hangings which adorned the walls and the mass of intricately interlocking colours that made up the stunning floor mosaic.

A moment later, he was face to face with his father who entered from an adjacent room. Around him two slaves fussed to attach his breastplate but, seeing his son, Magnus pushed them aside and drew out his sword.

"Is the attack on my town your doing, boy?" he snarled. "I should have known the tribune was right about you – a damned traitor to Rome! By letting in your Frankish friends, you've betrayed all true Romans!"

"True Romans? I don't even know what that means anymore," murmured Ambrosius.

"Pah! I don't think you ever did!" declared Magnus, "But, whatever you intended, I promise you, you'll be dead before it happens!"

"We don't have long," replied Ambrosius, ignoring his father's threats. "If you surrender to me now, I can save the garrison!"

"A few hours in that cage must have addled your mind, boy, if you think I'd surrender to you! I wouldn't give my sword to you if there were a thousand Franks inside this town!"

"All the Franks want is the port!"

"The Franks want it all, you fool!" was Magnus' savage reply.

Alerted by the pounding of footsteps along the passages outside, Ambrosius turned to the doorway and saw a fully-armed soldier - sword in hand and breastplate slick with blood.

"Petro?" murmured Ambrosius, but his half-brother, Aurelius Honorius Petro, barely glanced in his direction.

"We're being overrun, father!" he announced.

"Then get back out there and lead the fight!" bellowed Magnus. "I've a traitor to deal with..."

"There are too many, father... perhaps we should seek terms," suggested Petro, the strain showing in the high pitch of his voice.

"Terms?" Magnus took an incredulous step towards him. "You just go down into those streets and kill some more of those whoreson Franks! You hear me, boy? We're betrayed – by your precious little brother!"

"Petro!" cried Ambrosius. "There's a way out of this!"

But his brother, unable to challenge his father's iron will, had already turned away to return to the struggle in the narrow streets.

With the sounds of the battle below growing louder every moment, Ambrosius faced Magnus again. "You must give up the fort! Think of your daughters! I can still save-"

Only his warrior instinct saved him from his father's sword, snaking out at his bare torso; but, even so, he barely turned the blade aside in time.

"You think you can take me, boy?" Magnus hurled the words at him in disgust. "Think again!"

When the older man's weapon lunged at Ambrosius again, it came so fast that he failed to evade it a second time and it sliced against his unprotected side. Though the cut was shallow, it was enough to confirm what he had always known: Magnus would never yield the fort: not to the Franks and certainly not to his estranged son. Ambrosius had only tried to persuade his father for the sake of Petro and his sisters. But the brutal rebuff came as no surprise for a final reckoning with his father had been inevitable from the start.

"You aren't worthy of the rank of 'Dux'!" roared Magnus, chopping at his son's head. "You're a disgrace to this noble Roman family!"

Though Ambrosius ducked in time to evade the next blow, another followed it, arrowing at his chest; that too was pursued by a wild, venom-charged slash at his shoulder. With only a flimsy loin cloth for protection, a single mistake was very likely to be the death of him. But before he could catch his breath, the room suddenly began to fill with people.

First, Petro, with arms ever more bloodied, ushered in his elder sister, Florina; then Lucidia was propelled in by a man he had seen the previous afternoon at Magnus' side in the courtyard – his sister's would-be husband, Gaius, he guessed. Following in their wake, was a small group of frantic servants shepherded in by several members of the Roman garrison.

This then was what his betrayal had wrought; far from brokering a peace between Roman and Frank, as he had hoped, he had plunged the two sides into a brutal struggle for supremacy. If the younger Franks were not so determined to kill Romans, or if Magnus was not so intransigent, it might have been different. If…

A glance at his sister Florina gave him no encouragement for her face was flushed with anger. Staring at him with undisguised contempt, but not a trace of fear, she yelled at her father. "Just kill him and be done with it!"

"Get them all out of here, Petro!" shouted Magnus, standing off Ambrosius.

"But where, father?" cried Petro, in alarm. "There's nowhere to go! There are Franks everywhere!"

It only added to the confusion, when Puglio hurtled in with four of his scutarii.

Magnus raged at his fellow officer. "You should be below, defending the town!"

With a mirthless shake of the head, Puglio pointed at Ambrosius. "Your precious town is lost, Magnus – and all because of your own son's treachery. So, if you don't mind, I'll just remove the head I was promised and then we'll take our chances down at the harbour."

For a moment, there was an impasse: all stood staring at each other, with weapons raised; waiting for someone else to break the spell. They might have lingered there even longer had not half a dozen Franks thundered into the room to put an abrupt end to the stalemate. Unfettered by any doubts, they leapt at the Romans, their wild spathas carving though the air.

While the few garrison soldiers, aided by Puglio and the scutarii, attempted to beat back the Franks, Magnus - seemingly oblivious to his deadly predicament – launched another assault upon Ambrosius. Around the circling father and son, men butchered each other, while the women and servants cowered behind the bolstered couches, shrieking their terror. Silverware was slapped aside and glasses shattered, while the floor mosaic was decorated anew by splashes of blood.

Driven back by Magnus, Ambrosius found himself for an instant next to Puglio, who was busy bludgeoning down one of the Franks.

"You're next, Dux!" warned the tribune. "I don't care who kills you – as long as I get that big, hairy head off your shoulders!"

Ambrosius absorbed every detail of the intricate scene being played out around him. Surveying the chamber as if it was a great fighting arena, he saw at once that the Franks would be no match for Puglio's scutarii. They would put up a brave resistance but, unless they were reinforced, one by one, they would be cut down. When that was done and all distractions were removed, he would have to face his father and the scutarii alone; Puglio would no doubt be rewarded with the head he so craved.

In another part of the room, one of the remaining Franks, a young warrior no older than Childeric, managed to fight his way to where the women waited. Knowing he was hopelessly outnumbered, he probably reckoned that he could keep the Romans at bay by holding one of the high-born women as a hostage. It was a sound idea, thought Ambrosius, for if the youth could hold out – perhaps even for a few more minutes - his Frank comrades might just arrive in time to rescue him.

Casually disembowelling a servant who dared to stray into his path, the Frank wrapped a bloodstained arm around Lucidia's waist and dragged her away with him. Hastening to her rescue, Lucidia's intended, Gaius, managed to pull her roughly aside, but as she scrambled away, the speed and fire of Gaius' youthful opponent overpowered him. Slashing his spatha across the Roman's neck, the Frank was rewarded by a sudden, bright gush from his opponent's torn throat.

By the time Gaius' lifeless fingers relinquished their grip on his sword, Ambrosius was already moving. Keeping a close eye on Puglio, he retreated before another onslaught from Magnus. As he watched Lucidia attempt to crawl away across the bloodied floor, Ambrosius saw the youth once more catch hold of her. Desperate to get to her, he turned about to batter Magnus backwards, before making a dart towards the Frank.

"Leave her!" he roared at the youth, who was holding Lucidia before him like a shield. "Clodoris agreed my family were not to be touched!"

When a sudden lunge from Magnus almost killed him, Ambrosius hacked back at his father, forcing him to give ground.

"Release her!" he ordered the Frank.

"If I do, I'm a dead man!" declared the youth. "You know that!"

"Release her and I'll give you your life!"

With a shake of his head, the Frank cried: "My life's not yours to give, Roman!"

The Frank had a point because, though Ambrosius was only two yards away, he was still fending off his father's sporadic attacks. It was time to settle matters. He aimed a cut at Magnus' upper leg, wounding him. Then, in one great bound, he leapt beyond the Frank, who was thus trapped between Ambrosius and his raging father.

While her captor was distracted, Lucidia wrenched her arm free from his grasp and dropped to the floor.

"You made your choice," said Ambrosius, as the Frank, suddenly realising his peril, tried to turn to face Magnus. In his desperation to reach his son, the Roman commander chopped the Frank down with two powerful blows. Then, appearing to draw renewed vigour from the kill, he launched another furious assault upon Ambrosius, who pushed Lucidia into a nearby apse and shouted to his half-brother: "Petro! Take our sisters out!"

Without a moment's hesitation, Petro clambered over one of the couches and grasped Lucidia's hand. Guiding her to where Florina stood, with several of the servants and slaves, in the far corner of the room, Petro handed Florina his dagger and she accepted it with cool resolve, as if impervious to the bloody confusion that surrounded her.

One moment chaos echoed around the large chamber and then, as if by some dismissive, divine gesture, only one mortal contest lingered on: that between Ambrosius and Magnus. Though covered in blood where the Comes had nicked his flesh here and there, Ambrosius could see that his father, increasingly hampered by the wound in his thigh, was tiring fast. Not only that, but Magnus must have been well aware that he no longer commanded the room. After the scutarii hacked down the last two Franks, it was Puglio who held sway – and the tribune was not a man renowned for his patience.

"Put the dog down, old man!" said Puglio. "Or I will! If you take much longer, none of us will get out of this place alive!"

About that at least, Puglio was surely right for very soon the palace must be overrun. Ambrosius had never intended to be trapped in there at all; so much for getting his family safely to the harbour! With Puglio triumphant, his only hope – and it was a slim one - was to prolong the struggle with his father until Varta and the others could reach him. To do so, he would have to lessen the intensity of his blows to allow his father to make a fight of it. Sooner or later though, a man of Puglio's experience would notice what he was doing. How long, he wondered, would the tribune wait before intervening?

Drawing the murderous Magnus on, without getting himself killed, required all Ambrosius' skill since his father had no such reservations. While Ambrosius scrapped and fought to keep Magnus at bay, he glanced at Puglio for any hint that the tribune might step in. When the bitter struggle came to an abrupt end, it was a shock – not just to Ambrosius, but to everyone else in the room too.

Darting forward, Florina stabbed Petro's knife up to its hilt into her father's exposed side, forcing the blade far up into his chest. With a pitiful groan, Magnus dropped to his knees, staring up at his beloved daughter, as the blood pouring through his fingers from the fatal wound she had inflicted. Even Puglio seemed unable to find any suitable words, but all eyes were now focussed on Florina and her next words confirmed Ambrosius' worst fears.

"In the name of God, take your traitor, tribune," she said, with icy calm. "But despatch him quickly and then get me out of this butcher's yard!"

Such a formidable woman might have been admirable, thought Ambrosius, had she not just killed her own father and urged the death of her brother. A glance towards the doorway, guarded by two of the scutarii, told Ambrosius there was no way out there.

"Petro!" he shouted. "Take Lucidia down to the port! Go to the river gate and I'll find you!"

His brother, struck dumb by what had just happened, stared at Florina and then Lucidia. Seizing his hand, Lucidia dragged him away and with one final glance back at Ambrosius, they fled and the few remaining servants and garrison soldiers fled with them, leaving only Florina and the scutarii.

"Well, well," said Puglio, with a smile, "it takes a bit to surprise me, but well played, Lady Florina. I say, well played!"

"Enough talking, tribune - make haste!" Florina ground out the words in a rebuke stern enough to quell a riot.

Yet, despite the dire circumstances, Puglio seemed strangely reluctant for his long pursuit to come to such an abrupt end.

"You had a good run, Dux," he said, taking a step towards his trapped quarry.

"I've been in worse places," said Ambrosius, remembering the caupona at Ardelica.

"If you're just going to exchange fond memories," growled Florina, "then perhaps I should kill him myself!"

Whilst Puglio's attention was on Florina, no doubt studying the shape of her breasts under the expensive clothes, Ambrosius backed away from him. Pausing only to snatch up his father's sword from the floor, he set himself with his back up against the wall, ready to meet the impending attack with a weapon in each hand.

Puglio interrupted his assessment of Lady Florina's finer points to motion his comrades forward. Not all of the scutarii would survive the coming encounter – and they knew it. To give themselves a better chance, they would have to come at Ambrosius together.

"There are only five of you," cried Ambrosius, in defiance.

"Five's more than enough, Dux," said Puglio, more relaxed now, perhaps because his mission was so close to its end.

"Tell that to Anticus – remember him, Puglio?"

"What about him?"

"Six imperial guards were sent to kill me… six of the emperor's best men. Anticus was the sixth to die… and, as I said, there are only five of you…"

Knowing his words would have little effect on the veteran, Puglio, he concentrated on each of the other scutarii in turn. They were no callow youths but even so, he wondered, just how willing they were to embrace certain death? Because that was the difference really: Ambrosius had looked death in the eye countless times. It held no fear for him, because… in every battle… when he picked up his weapon, he carried the spectre of death upon his shoulder.

He was still thinking about death when they rushed him.

22

November 454, before dawn, at the south barracks in Caracotinum

"How long do you think we've been in here?" asked Caralla.

"Too damned long!" snapped Onno, trying hard not to surrender to despair. Always Dux relied upon him to push through and get the task done - and never had he let his commander down – until now. Though he had pleaded with the garrison soldiers, they had insisted upon locking the two bucellarii up until morning.

"We're on your side!" he told them but, if he was honest, he couldn't blame them, for he wasn't even sure himself that his assertion was true.

"You're in league with those Franks outside!" replied one the Roman guards. "We know - we've been watching you!"

"Do I look like a Frank to you?" he argued.

The fact was that Onno did not look much like your average soldier of the empire either, but Caralla certainly did. He had told them his comrade was a cataphract, but they had just laughed and asked him where his horse was. That jibe had not amused Caralla much; the Briton was getting quite sensitive about his damned horse.

So, as dawn bore down upon them, they were still bottled up – and they weren't even sure exactly where!

Somewhere in the southern part of the town was all Onno knew but, incarcerated as they were, and with no weapons there was not a chance of finding a ship! At dawn, the Franks would swarm into the town and they could do nothing but watch the attack unfold.

But Onno was wrong because the trouble came even before the sun rose. He had forgotten all about the other Franks – and their ladders - until two dozen of them swarmed over the south wall. At first, there was just a lot of shouting and the shuffling of feet across the yard outside, followed by the rap of boots on the steps up to the rampart, while Onno rattled the door of their cell and banged on it.

"Let us out," he bellowed, "and I swear we'll help you against them!"

"You calling to the Romans," asked Caralla, "or the Franks?"

Onno blinked and stopped banging for a moment. "The Romans, of course... I think; though, just now, anyone who lets us out of here may be my friend for life!"

One of their Roman captors, his left arm running with blood, stopped at their cell door and stared in at them.

"Did you speak truly when you swore to help us?" he asked, his eyes darting wildly about him.

"Yes, yes," insisted Onno. "I swear it! I swear we'll fight by your side!" But then, at that moment Onno would have sworn anything in exchange for his freedom.

Though the fellow clearly still doubted them, with the garrison in deep trouble, he had little choice. Reaching to his belt with his uninjured hand, the soldier selected a long key. Never had a man looked less certain, but assailed by ever closer and murderous cries from all around him, he finally placed the key in the lock.

Before he had time to turn it, a spear grazed across his back. Though his mail shirt saved him from death, he was knocked forward into the cell gate. No doubt expecting another, killing, blow to come, he clutched the key and hastily turned it. But his attacker had moved on without a second glance at the downed man who did not know - as Onno did - that the Franks would be in a hurry to join up with their comrades entering by the north gate.

Caralla pushed open the gate and between them they helped the guard up.

"Our weapons?" enquired Onno.

"Next storeroom along," gasped the wounded man.

"How many of you are left?" asked Onno, as he retrieved his knife and spatha.

"On the south wall?" said the soldier. "You're looking at him…"

"Shit…"

"Yeh, shit. Christ knows what I'm supposed to do now! I ought to head along to the barracks at the north gate."

"I wouldn't," advised Onno.

"You knew that attack was coming," grumbled the soldier.

"Yes, we did!" replied Caralla. "And, if you recall, we tried very hard to warn you!"

"You got a name?" asked Onno.

"Prosperus."

"Really?"

212

"Yes! So what are you two going to do now I've let you out?"

"We need to find a ship," said Onno.

"A ship?" said Prosperus. "What for?"

"Well, I'm not going to juggle with it!" said Onno. "What do you think I want a ship for?"

"You climbed over the wall just to get a ship so you could leave again?" asked Prosperus.

"Well, it's a bit of a longer story than that," said Onno, "but I suppose, more or less, yes. You know any ship's masters?"

"Not a single one…" said Prosperus.

"Excellent! But you can take us to the port?"

"That I can do," agreed Prosperus, "since it's not far away."

"By now some of the ships might already be heading out of the harbour," said Onno.

"Because it's getting lighter!" complained Caralla.

"Nothing to do with light," said Onno, "but a lot to do with tides."

When they ventured out of the barracks gate, they found themselves surrounded by produce gardens, such as many towns now had. In November, of course, there was much bare earth and little cultivation - though here and there makeshift pens held a few animals. As dawn arrived in all its splendour, Prosperus led them along the line of the wall to their left, past two great warehouses towards the harbour. Their view of activity along the docks was obscured by the long harbour wall. Once, Onno guessed, it had been a bulwark to defend the town against sea raiders, but the wall – like many of the buildings they passed – was crumbling and in desperate need of repair.

Only when they passed through the harbour wall, could they confirm that Onno was correct about the ships: several ships were already converging on the harbour entrance at great speed and thus in grave danger of hitting each other or blocking the channel completely. Surprised at their reckless haste, Onno scanned the whole harbour to left and right. Furthest away from him were the northern wharves which were already more active than usual with people having no doubt heard of the incursion by the Franks. Might Dux and the others be somewhere in there? But, of course, he had no way of knowing.

What was clear to him at once was that he could not get to any of the ships at the northern docks because there were already too many people gathered there. To his left, at the southernmost point of the harbour, lay a ship repair yard while, closer to him, scarcely a few yards to his right, were the southern docks where several ships were also preparing to leave. Each one was already packed with last minute passengers, so seizing control of any of those ships looked impossible. The day before perhaps – as they had intended – but not now, not amid such blind panic and disorder…

"What are we going to do, Onno?" murmured Caralla. "What in God's name are we going to do?"

"I don't know, my friend," he replied, staring at the docks, where, here and there, ships edged away a few feet from the heaving jetties which thrust out into the harbour. But even as the vessels tried to leave, scores of desperate people flung themselves at the ships, hoping to land on aboard. Most did not even reach the decks but fell straight into the churning water; a few more struck the oars as the rowers attempted to manoeuvre their vessels out into the channel.

Though Onno was distressed by the utter futility of it all, he was not a man to be dispirited for long. Dux had enough warriors among his bucellarii; hence, he valued Onno for a different set of skills, and he expected the Alexandrian to use those skills to solve problems. Well, Onno reflected, the lack of a ship was certainly a very considerable problem and, if he was going to solve it, he would have to think like an engineer, not a warrior.

23

November 454 after dawn, outside the north gate of Caracotinum

It fell to Canis and Calens to be Inga's litter bearers but, from the moment they set off, she knew that it was not a task to which the two men were well suited. After several steps, Canis stumbled and the litter came to a shuddering halt, sending a shiver of pain through her body. She seemed to feel every one of her numerous wounds, which Calens explained, was because, as the wounds dried out and healed, her already tortured skin was being stretched and torn anew.

His words did little to alleviate her discomfort which seemed worse than she remembered in those first hours when she lay in the cot next to Ambrosius. Whatever Calens was administering to her now, it hardly seemed to dull the pain at all. Nevertheless, it helped her to know that the Greek physician was with her for, lying on her back in the litter, she felt utterly helpless. In fact, she had felt nothing but helpless since the wolf attack – all the more galling since it came when she had just begun to earn a little respect – at least from some of the men.

After another awkward lurch of the litter, she cried out: "Calens, why do my wounds seem to hurt more than before?"

Calens, who was carrying the rear of the litter and was thus facing her, replied: "I suppose… your body is not so easily dulled by my potions now."

When she stared at him, he looked away, unwilling to meet her eyes.

"Calens?" she murmured.

With a sigh, he said: "Alright, Dux told me not to give you so much…"

"But why?" she said, "Why would he want me to endure this?" She was puzzled, distraught – for had he not shown that he cared for her – at least in his way?

"I think he feared that you might not…"

"Might not what?" cried Inga.

"Might not… wake up again," replied Calens softly. "He told me to give you every chance of life… that you had proven yourself… as one of the bucellarii… and should be treated as one."

As she absorbed the import of his words, she said nothing, but her first, overwhelming, emotion was relief – relief that Ambrosius cared about her enough to want her to live. Her breast filled with pride to be spoken of as one of them – one of Dux's bucellarii…

"Perhaps I should give you a little more," said Calens.

"No," she said at once, "I can manage without."

"We're almost at the gate now," said the physician. "Once we get you through the town to the harbour and aboard a ship – then you can rest properly again."

When their column reached the gates, Calens and the litter came to an abrupt halt but, after a brief pause, they lurched forward again.

"The gateway's crammed with Franks," Calens explained. "But, don't worry, Marco's forcing a path though."

Moments later, Inga saw the rampart pass over her head as they entered the town. But beyond the gates, shouts of anger and cries of warning told her that it was utter chaos.

"What's happening?" she asked, frustrated that she could see so little.

"Stay calm," Calens assured her.

But Inga could hear fighting and, whatever was happening ahead of them, she could tell that it was nothing to stay calm about. Her escort suddenly closed in around the litter, spear points facing out to left and right. At her breast, Inga gripped Uldar's bow which she had refused to entrust to any other – though she could hardly have used it.

As the litter was jostled and driven sideways, a grim-faced Marcellus appeared at her side.

"Calens and the escort will take you to the port by another, quieter, route," he told her. "I'll see you down at the harbour!"

But Inga knew Marcellus too well to accept, even in her weakened state, that all was well.

"What's wrong?" she demanded.

"We'll never get your litter through the crowd of men… and, in any case, I need to find Dux and the others. To do that we'll have to do more than just stroll down the main street. We may need to fight our way to the harbour. It'll be safer for you to take the route beside the south wall…"

She nodded acceptance, though she imagined that his casual explanation played down the actual risks they were all facing. After giving her hand a brief squeeze of encouragement, he was gone again. At once Canis steered the litter and its escort down a side alley which at first was quieter but even there, they passed small groups of marauding Franks and fleeing citizens caught up in a violent, rolling struggle. Passing three men of the town's hapless garrison surrounded by half a dozen Franks, Inga cried out: "Help them! We must help them, Calens!"

"Carry on!" Calens ordered the escort, and to her dismay, they marched on without pause, leaving the cornered men to their fate.

"We daren't stop, Inga!" explained Calens. "Since we can only move slowly, we must keep well ahead of the Franks."

"But-"

Calens cut short her protest. "It stinks of cowardice - I know that - but the fact is, the more distracted the Franks are by others, the less they'll trouble us!"

"You're buying our lives with theirs?" she wept. "But you're a physician!"

"No!" he retorted. "I'm a servant, Inga, not bucellarii… I spend most of my time stitching up men's wounds – or women's. I do what Dux tells me to do. He told me to keep you alive and safe, so that's what I'm going to do."

She argued no more and, for a time, Calens' judgement proved correct; the Franks did not follow them – as far as Inga could tell at least. All she saw, as the litter bearers and escort hurried on, was a glimpse of run-down houses and even one or two tall insulae that looked fragile enough to collapse at any moment and disgorge all their inhabitants – if they still had any - into the adjacent, rubble-strewn streets. After another fifty yards or so, dilapidated buildings gave way to open ground, which she assumed was used for growing crops.

When they passed between several buildings again, Calens called a halt to get his bearings. For what seemed like a long time, he and Canis stood in the middle of the narrow street conversing, but when they returned to the litter, they looked confident.

Picking up their burden once more, they carried on. "At the next crossroads, we'll head left," announced Calens, "and that should lead us straight the docks!"

But the Greek's initial confidence evaporated when they found themselves in an alley which simply came to a dead end at the town wall.

"This can't be right," grumbled Canis, while the soldiers of the escort darted nervous glances around them.

Inga, weary from the bruising journey, suspected that they must be close to the harbour, for she could smell the pungent marshlands, exposed along the estuary at low tide. Soon enough, the Greek too realised his mistake and turned the litter around for them to retrace their steps. Despite their confusion, Inga smiled, for she was struggling to keep her eyes open - a sure sign that her pain was at last diminishing.

It seemed only a moment later that a cacophony of snarling voices assaulted her ears. Someone, close by, cried: "By God, no!" and she was tipped out of the litter onto the street. The fall onto the cobbled surface snapped her awake as the pain returned with a vengeance. Though her natural inclination was to scramble to safety, with one hand already injured, it hurt even to drag herself a few feet. Refusing to abandon Uldar's bow, she tried to use it to support her weight and escape from the throng. In a matter of moments, the litter itself disappeared, scattered by the careless boots of an unruly crowd.

Surrounded by so many thrashing legs, her chief fear was that she would be trampled to death there and then. Though she managed to evade all the boots and crawl her way to the side of the road, she could feel her raw wounds opening up again. Only her will to survive drove her to endure the agony – aye, her will and the knowledge that Dux had accepted her as one of the bucellarii. If he truly believed her to be a warrior, then she must act like one.

Slowly it dawned upon her that they were back at the crossroads where she remembered several low walls that might just help to preserve her life. Rolling onto her left side – the one less ruinously savaged by the wolves – she used the bow and her left arm to claw her way along the street. Perhaps it might have been easier if she discarded the bow, but there would only be dishonour in that...

Dropping, finally, behind the shelter of one of the walls, she took a succession of short, shallow breaths to alleviate her distress. The urge to scream her despair was strong, but instead she propped herself against the wall and remained still, praying that no-one would notice her. The strips of clean linen, so carefully applied to her wounds by Calens, were now besmirched by every sort of the filth from the streets. So, who would look twice at someone, whose blood seeped through countless bandages? Her hiding place was not, however, a good vantage point, for she could not tell how far from the harbour she actually was. A few yards distance she might manage, but any more would surely be beyond her.

Though she could make out a few of her escort entangled in the great crowd of snarling, grappling people that stretched across the street, there was no sign of Calens. For the time being, no-one fighting for their lives in the bloody skirmish was remotely interested in her, But when the fighting stopped – which at some point it must – that's when she would be most at risk - hopelessly exposed to anyone who cared to prey upon her.

With no weapon – save a bow she could not use - and precious little strength left to wield one in any case, her only hope was that her brave escort would be able to regroup and come to rescue her. That thought sustained her whilst the struggle raged on, until one of her escort did join her. Falling down only a few yards away, Canis rolled to a halt beside her, coughing his life's blood out into her startled face.

24

November 454 after dawn, at the Comes' Palace

When facing several men in combat, a soldier had few advantages, decided Ambrosius – well, perhaps only one: whilst his opponents were obliged to co-ordinate their efforts, he was not. He could defend himself as he pleased, devoid of any pattern or design, simply because the only flesh his blades would encounter was that of his enemies. A co-ordinated, disciplined assault would kill him, but from the first, furious moment he knew that this encounter would be far from disciplined. Puglio, no doubt driven by the frustration of his long and bloody pursuit, seemed oblivious to anyone else. Thus, his desire to kill Ambrosius caused him to hamper the efforts of his comrades; he simply got in their way.

Ambrosius, who was proficient with a spatha in either hand, now wielded one in each and focussed all his attention on Puglio. Though the tribune was a handful for any opponent, Ambrosius kept him moving this way and that. As a result, his comrades - understandably reluctant to stab their own commander - were obliged to hang back a little from the fight. For several precious minutes, Ambrosius was thus able to distract his adversary until - too late - Puglio realised his error and took a pace backwards. But by then, Varta and the others arrived to unleash all the devils of hell upon the scutarii.

It was over in seconds – and Puglio, seeing his remaining scutarii being cut down, retreated to the far door of the chamber. Dragging the livid Florina with him, he fled the same way as Petro and the rest had gone.

"We need to get after them!" shouted Ambrosius, when the last of the abandoned scutarii fell.

But before they could follow the tribune, the chamber was engulfed by Franks pouring up from the streets below. Left facing them, Ambrosius lowered his swords at once and the bucellarii were quick to follow his lead. Many of the Franks, no doubt, were Childeric's men, but the rest most likely followed several other war leaders, some of whom might see Ambrosius as an ally. Seizing upon their confusion, he shouted aloud:

"The fort is yours, my friends, but Clodoris swore to allow us safe passage to the port."

As he hoped, it was a puzzled group of warriors who now filled the room, but that was far from unusual where the collaboration of several war bands was involved. Since their loyalty was to a man, they were bound to his oaths as much as their own. As a result, in no time, a dispute erupted between rival groups: Childeric's hotheads arguing that all the Romans – including the bucellarii - should be summarily despatched, while others felt obliged to honour the oath that Clodoris had given to Ambrosius. More than a few probably believed that killing the adopted son of the Frank leader might be seen as overzealous.

When the Franks' good-humoured discussion descended into abusive argument, Ambrosius and his men took their chance and left. Hard on the heels of Puglio and Florina, they fled from the room and descended back to street level, where they found the town in uproar. For the most part, the Franks were roaming utterly out of control. What a fool he had been to accept Clodoris' assertion that his people wanted only to occupy the port! Aye, occupy it and bring ruin to its Roman inhabitants! How could he have so misjudged his adopted father? Much of the actual fighting seemed already over, as looting was in full swing – and worse, far worse...

Though he had agreed to meet Marcellus outside the palace, there was no sign of his friend, or any of his men. With every thoroughfare crammed with hostile warriors and terrified townsfolk, he could not see over their heads to the streets beyond. Without the rest of his men he could not leave Caracotinum, but if he delayed now then Petro and Lucidia would be too far ahead and finding them might prove impossible. Such were the decisions, he thought, that determined life and death…

"Make for the port!" he ordered.

"What about Marco?" roared Varta, above the clamour.

"First we have to find our ship before Childeric seizes control of the whole damned town!" insisted Ambrosius. "We find the ship – and we hold it against anyone – or Marco will have nowhere to run to!"

But, even as he set off to force a path towards the harbour, part of him was cursing his decision, because he knew that not only was he abandoning Marco, but he was also abandoning Inga. Nor did the carnage he witnessed along the way, do anything to relieve his anguish. It was an easy lie to tell himself that the town's fate was inevitable, that the small garrison could never have held out for long –

even without his surrender of the main gate. Yet, all too soon, his head was filled to bursting with the wrath of men and the screams of women and children and the word they screamed was treachery.

Shutting out the unwelcome distractions, he forced himself to carry on until he reached the river which fed into the harbour. Since it was the quickest way to the port, Petro was sure to have taken it. With any luck, they would overtake his brother and sister soon after reaching the harbour. But his hopes of finding anyone – including Onno – swiftly evaporated when they arrived at the river gate which marked one end of the harbour. From there they beheld a scene of burgeoning chaos on the docks as desperate townsfolk competed for a precious place on one of the ships.

Ambrosius had expected something of the sort to happen – even without the ferocity of the Frank attack - which is why he had despatched Onno and Caralla to commandeer a vessel before panic struck. But when he saw the degree of disorder, he started to doubt whether his two men, even if they had located a suitable vessel, could possibly defend it until the rest of their comrades arrived. Even at the river gate men, desperate to escape the town, were beginning to squabble and come to blows over possession of even the tiniest river craft.

"Where now, Dux?" cried Varta.

A fair enough question: what to go for first: Onno and his ship, or Petro and Lucidia? And then there was Marcellus… and Inga. To attempt to find all of them at once would be futile, he realised.

"We'll have to split up," he told his comrades. "Varta, take Rocca and Germanus to find Marcellus and the others - Inga's litter should make them easy enough to pick out…"

He stopped for a moment because, as he stared at the seething mass of bodies stretching up towards the palace, it struck him that Marcellus could not possibly propel Inga's litter through such a vast array of hostile, jostling warriors.

"Oh, shit…" muttered Varta, who must have drawn the same conclusion. "What do you think they'll have done?"

"I gave Marcellus a rough description of the shape of the town," said Ambrosius. "They might have been forced to take a different street - most likely further east. Perhaps that's why we can't see them."

"Who are we looking for, Dux: Marco… or Inga?" asked Germanus.

Of course, they all knew there was no right answer.

Ambrosius swallowed hard. "Find Marco first," he told them. "With luck, Inga and Calens will still be with him. If not, then you'll have more men to go looking for Inga."

"As you wish," acknowledged Varta, "so where do we meet?"

"By Christ's sword!" growled Ambrosius. "Let's pray that Onno will give us a sign by then!"

"And if not?" said Varta.

"If not, meet us back here."

"It's a long way back here, Dux," said Varta. "With all these crowds…"

"Yes, yes; it is," said Ambrosius, struggling to clear his head. "Just get back down to the docks any way you can and I'll find you. But if I know Onno, he'll find a way to tell us where he is; so stay alert and watch for his signal!"

As he clasped Varta's arm, his friend said: "Don't get lost, Dux; already, this place has the smell of death about it." Then the Frank was gone, forging a path through the crowd, hurling aside anyone who blocked into his path, with Germanus and Rocca following in his wake.

With Xallas and Cappa, Ambrosius was confident that, if only he could find Petro and Lucidia, he would be able to protect them from the Franks. Standing beside the river gate, he scanned the crowds for a sight of his sister. Every moment, more folk were flooding on to the wharves and jetties in an attempt to clamber aboard one of the ships. Trying to pick out an individual was simply out of the question.

Where could Petro have gone, he wondered? He had told his brother to make for the river gate, yet he was not there. Perhaps he feared it was too dangerous to wait there for long and was holed up somewhere close by. Ambrosius tried not to consider that he might already have been cut down by the rampant Franks surging through the town. By Christ! What might they do with Lucidia? He did not to dwell upon it – for, after all, the Franks were civilised men, not savages. Yet he had seen enough already to remind him that a horde of soldiers, once let off the leash, had no code of behaviour at all.

Disconsolate, Ambrosius led the way from the river gate back into the town where they struggled through the crowd, peering at each building they passed – though more in hope than belief. They even entered one or two houses where they thought a few fleeing Romans might have taken refuge.

"We can't search every damned building, Dux!" cried Xallas.

Ambrosius replied with a shake of the head, his expression tight-lipped. No, they most certainly could not, but he knew that Petro would have gone to ground somewhere and it could not be far away.

Without warning, Cappa seized his arm. "Look there, Dux!"

Having spent his youth in the festering back streets of Rome, Cappa was a shrewd observer of men and their ways. On the battlefield he was sometimes a liability, but here in the streets, untroubled by baying crowds or bloody squabbles, he was better suited than any of the other bucellarii for what they needed to do now.

When Ambrosius followed Cappa's pointed finger, he expected to see a clutch of fleeing Romans, but what Cappa had noticed was a band of Frank warriors attempting to stave in the doors of a building set back a little from the street. They might, of course, simply be bent on pillaging one of the more luxurious-looking houses and, in the present circumstances, there was nothing too surprising about that. Yet they seemed to be meeting with some stout resistance from within and surely the average householder – even a wealthy one – would struggle to defend his home against so many heavily-armed warriors?

"I'll take a wager there are Romans in there," declared Cappa. "If not your brother, Dux, then at the very least some men of the garrison are in there. Either way, we could help get them out – and it would swell our numbers a bit."

Cappa was right: whoever was trapped there, it was in his interests to help them.

"You two want to fight your way in past all those Franks?" asked Xallas. "We'll be cut down in seconds!"

"We're not going in the front!" said Cappa. "Do you know this house, Dux?"

"No, too prestigious for the likes of me," replied Ambrosius.

Cappa nodded. "Well, I doubt it's so rich inside. You know what happens: some greasy little landlord buys up a big, old property and in a few weeks it's twenty rooms for rent!"

"So it could be a warren of smaller rooms inside?"

"Might be," said Cappa, "so we'll just have to rely on my dark skills, won't we?"

Without another word, he darted to a walled property adjacent to the house which had attracted their attention.

"What are you doing?" gasped Ambrosius.

"Getting us inside!" called Cappa over his shoulder, as he studied the aged wooden gate.

With a grin, he kicked out hard and the rotten timber splintered at the hinges into several large pieces.

"Learn from the master, Dux!" declared Cappa, pushing on past the debris.

Ambrosius and Xallas could do little but follow and put their trust in the stocky Roman as he hurried on. Keeping close alongside the perimeter fence, Cappa seemed to ghost across the property. Ambrosius could not help noticing how ill-kept and overgrown the garden was and even the briefest glance at the house itself revealed a distinct lack of maintenance. Here and there, roof tiles were either broken or missing completely. Even a short wall abutting the house had collapsed and been left where it had fallen. Such a house provided ample evidence that the decline of Caracotinum began long before the arrival of a few Franks.

Abruptly Cappa disappeared through a gap in the broken boundary fence and Ambrosius beckoned Xallas to follow.

Careful to avoid being seen by the Franks, who were still hurling abuse and battering at the door, they headed for the rear of the house.

"How do you want to do this?" enquired Cappa. "Quick, or quiet?"

"Both?" suggested Ambrosius.

Though Cappa gave a nod of acknowledgement and set to work to open the door, he did not find it easy.

"Come on, or the Franks will be inside before we are!" urged Xallas, but his habitual impatience did not appear to improve Cappa's concentration.

"It's a tough one," observed Cappa.

"Enough!" said Ambrosius. "Quiet isn't going to get us in."

Thrusting Cappa aside, he put his boot to the door and it crashed open at once.

"That's more like it!" said Xallas.

Cries of alarm from within warned Ambrosius to be cautious as he went in. Sure enough, the moment he entered the small vestibule, Petro came at him with his sword and only just pulled back in time.

"By Christ, brother!" he exclaimed. "How did you find us?"

"I have a man who makes lucky guesses," explained Ambrosius, following his half-brother into a long passage. From the passage, rooms led off at regular intervals in the area which had probably once been a grand atrium.

"How many of you are there in here?" he asked Petro, as they entered a larger chamber at the front of the building – once a great entrance hall, with tall, solid wooden doors.

"Enough," drawled a familiar voice, "perhaps even enough to see you off, Dux."

With a sigh, Ambrosius looked around the room; he had found Petro and Lucidia, with half a dozen soldiers and servants, but he had also located his dangerous half-sister, Florina, along with the tribune, Puglio and a few more surviving members of the scutarii.

"Forget our quarrel, Puglio!" he snapped. "The only way we get out of here is by fighting our way out – together."

As if to accentuate their plight, they heard the Franks begin to smash their axes once more into the heavy doors.

"Perhaps I have the numbers to kill you first then fight my way out," suggested Puglio, but they both knew that he did not.

"We have a better chance with my brother than without," argued Florina.

Though slightly bemused by Florina acknowledging him as her brother, Ambrosius pressed home her point. "There are at least ten men at that door, tribune – too many for your few scutarii."

Though Puglio still seemed inclined to debate the issue, the sudden splintering of the door must have convinced him otherwise.

"Very well," he conceded, "but once we're out of here, you'd better watch yourself, Dux."

As the Franks burst in and an axe flew past his head, Ambrosius moved closer to Petro and the few remaining members of the garrison. Pushing Lucidia and two of the servants behind him in Cappa's charge, he looked across to Florina who stood alone. If he knew his elder half-sister at all, she would watch and wait - remaining aloof until she could tell who would emerge the stronger.

When the young Franks swept aside the remains of the door and leapt at the defenders, at least a dozen warriors surged in, each one hard on the eager heels of the man before. Though he had no stomach for more bloodletting, Ambrosius raised his spatha and turned to meet the ferocious assault head on.

Part Four: Ships and Harbours

25

November 454 in the morning, in the port of Caracotinum

When he managed to tear his gaze from the chaos at the northern docks, Onno looked away to the far southern end of the harbour where, by contrast, there appeared to be hardly any ships at all.

"What's along there?" he asked Prosperus, squinting at the area towards the harbour entrance.

"Just the old ship repair yards," replied Prosperus, "but they're hardly used and, as you can see from here, there's nothing there now."

But Onno was not so sure. "You can't tell from here," he said, almost to himself. "I think I see a mast. Come on."

Hurrying along the narrow wooden strip which ran alongside the harbour wall, he came to a sudden halt when he reached the remains of the structure which lay at the extreme southern end of it. Prosperus was quite wrong about it: what faced him was wholly undeserving of the term ship repair yard – ship grave yard might have been more appropriate! Though it might once have used to build or repair vessels, it was not much more than a rubbish heap now. Several floating platforms still jutted out at right angles to the harbour wall, but the bays between them served only to collect some of the objects which had drifted into the harbour.

With some caution, Onno stepped onto the nearest of the pontoons and it seemed stable enough, but he could see at a glance that many of the others had been rotting away for half a lifetime. As he clambered from one bay to the next, all he found was floating timber debris. Here and there on the platforms, heaps of bent nails had formed small, rusting, iron humps which over time had welded themselves to the timber boards.

"Come, Onno," urged Caralla. "Prosperus was right: there's nothing for us here…"

Onno could hardly disagree, for even the mast he thought he saw turned out to be a broken one abandoned against the harbour wall. But as he turned to follow Prosperus and Caralla back to the main docks, a voice snarled at them.

"Hey! This area's private! Get out!"

Though they could hear the voice, they could not see its owner.

"Show yourself, man!" ordered Onno and at once a bald head popped up from within the carcass of a low vessel he had not even noticed at the far end of the yard.

"What do you want here?" the stranger growled at them. "This is a priv-"

"Yes, a private dock," said Onno, making straight for the man. "We heard! We're looking for a ship – are there any vessels here that might be seaworthy?"

"Piss off!"

"We're in trouble, friend," said Onno, gesturing towards the town. "Have you not seen how the whole of Caracotinum is in uproar?"

"Uproar?" repeated the fellow, in confusion. "What uproar?

"The Franks are sacking the town," Onno informed him.

When the man attempted to stand up but failed, Onno at once diagnosed his condition. "You're drunk!"

"I'm drunk?" mimicked the seaman. "You're the one talking about the sack of the town!"

With a shake of the head, Onno explained: "We need to leave soon – how about you?"

"The Franks, you say?" said the fellow, uncomprehending, as he tried to peer at the town that lay behind Onno and Caralla. By the smell of him, the man had undertaken a lot more drinking than repairing.

"What's your name?" asked Onno.

"Remigius!"

Onno regarded the scruffy Remigius doubtfully. "Caralla," he murmured, "assist dear Remigius to a standing position."

"Hey!" protested Remigius when Caralla hoisted him upright. "You dare lay hands upon me? I'm the master of this ship!"

"What ship?" demanded Onno.

"The one I'm standing in!"

Onno thought there were a few things missing from the ship – at least if it intended to cross a sea – a mast for one thing.

"Is this ship seaworthy, Remigius?" demanded Onno.

"I don't answer to you!" retorted the seaman.

"Tell me then: who do you answer to?"

"Aurelius Honorius Magnus! 'Cos this vessel belongs to him!"

"Not any more it doesn't," declared Onno. "It belongs to his son - Ambrosius Aurelianus."

"Eh?"

"Now, tell me: is it seaworthy?"

A sly smile ghosted across Remigius' face. "No. She's not… seaworthy…"

"What's wrong with it – her - then?"

"Oh, nothing," Remigius assured him. "Nothing's wrong with her."

"How then is… she… not seaworthy?" asked Onno, summoning up his last reserves of patience.

"'Cos she's a… navis lusoria!" cackled the mariner.

"Oh, good!" said Onno. "A river ship! But she could manage a trip along the coast, couldn't she?"

"Maybe, in fair weather, she could…"

"What about across to Britannia?"

"Pah! Only if you've got a death wish!" Remigius spat out his response, "but then I reckon you must have, if you want to go to that place!"

"Could you sail her there?" Onno pressed him.

"Only if I don't sober up!" retorted Remigius.

"Why is she here in the repair yard, if she's fit to sail?" enquired Onno.

"Just been fitted out with new steer boards – and a new mast," said Remigius, pointing to the mast, which Onno now saw was lying on the deck.

"It's not much use lying there, is it?"

"Pah, these ships mostly use oars anyway," he said, "which is why - without a crew of oarsmen - you ain't going nowhere!"

"Let me worry about that. Just get this vessel ready to sail!" ordered Onno.

Taking Caralla onto the dock, he said: "I'll keep an eye on him, while you and Prosperus pile up all these broken wooden bits and pieces against the far end of the harbour wall as far away from the ship as you can."

"Alright, but what for?" asked Caralla.

"Just do it," said Onno, "You'll see why later – and only dry bits!"

For a short time, while Onno helped the still-inebriated mariner to haul up and fit the mast, Caralla and Prosperus gathered all the broken spars, planks, and even a few damaged oar-blades and built an impressive heap against the wall.

"Now what, Onno?" called out Caralla.

"I noticed a brazier of warm coals over there," he replied. "Let's put the two things together!"

Pleased to see the light of understanding dawning upon his comrade, Onno concentrated on ensuring that the drunken Remigius did not let the mast, now poised precariously in mid-air, drop over the side into the water – or worse still, fall down and crack one of them on the head.

"You still need a crew," insisted Remigius, "even to launch her!"

"We'll push her out into the channel now," Onno told him. "Then the four us can get her to the nearest dock."

Remigius laughed heartily. "Know much about tides, do you?" he asked.

"As a matter of fact I do," retorted Onno, with confident grin.

"What about tidal river estuaries?" was Remigius' gruff response. "The tide's going out. You push my ship out into the channel with only four men to row and no-one to steer and we're heading out of control into the mud banks outside the harbour entrance. I may be drunk; but I'm not a shit-headed idiot!"

It seemed to Onno, that as soon as he removed one obstacle, another raced along to take its place. Glancing across at Caralla and Prosperus, it seemed that they were having little success in trying to start a fire.

"Right," said Onno. "You're the master mariner: how do we get this ship over to the jetty there to make it easier to board?"

"Put a rope on her, that's how," replied Remigius glibly.

"Fine," agreed Onno. "Then let's get it done, shall we?"

At that moment, there was sudden whoosh and a yelp from Caralla as the fire sprang to life, singeing its makers.

"Give us a hand here!" cried Onno. "Or we'll never get this mast fixed! By Christ! I only hope that when we're done, we still have some comrades left alive to take aboard!"

26

November 454 morning, in Caracotinum

As Ambrosius expected, from the first clash of spathas, the struggle was brutal. The Franks, mostly young men, were almost certainly part of Childeric's vanguard, charged with sweeping every Roman from the port. Clearly angered that it had taken them so long to force their way into the building, they were in no mood to show restraint. In such a tangled mêlée, there could be no place of safety and Ambrosius was very aware that his sisters would make fine prizes for the young Frank warriors. Though at first he tried to keep a close eye on both ladies, the struggle itself soon craved every last scrap of his attention.

Alongside him, his half-brother, Petro proved a resolute fighter, delivering blow after punishing blow with his heavy sword. Fleetingly, it occurred to Ambrosius, as he carved aside a stripling youth, that it was the first time he had ever fought alongside his brother. It might also, he reflected, be the last...

Caught in a close-quarter clash, Ambrosius twisted and turned like an eel. Though the Romans were heavily outnumbered, he remained confident that they would prevail, but the determined Franks kept coming. Soon the floor was littered with bloodied bodies and, whether living or dead, they became a hazard for the combatants. Stumbling over casualties, Ambrosius finally managed to carve himself some space and free his arms to wield his spatha. Then his opponents truly began to feel the force of his controlled fury; for Ambrosius, as ever, fought with no fear, no doubt and not a trace of remorse.

A glance behind reassured him that Cappa, grim-faced beside Lucidia, stood ready, spear in hand, to lunge at any man who strayed too close. Unruly and ill-favoured he might be, but Cappa had dragged himself from the squalid streets of Rome to claim a place among the fêted bucellarii of Aetius. And that, thought Ambrosius, as he narrowly evaded another thrust at his bare torso, was not achieved without being willing to shed a bucketful of blood.

Around him, tired men were being slain in moments, their bodies chopped apart like butchered cattle. Every man, wild-eyed and frantic, was caught up in the manic, pointless slaughter. No sooner did Ambrosius put one man down, but another hopeful adversary flew at him and a pair of pale, blue eyes glared at him from under a knotted shank of black hair. Perhaps this youth was one of those he had strolled past in the Frankish camp the previous evening, but it counted for nothing when battle came. All past ties counted for nothing, reflected Ambrosius, as he drove his spatha through his opponent's belly and twisted it free. No fear, no doubt and no remorse…

Of course, the killing came to an end eventually and, when it did, the Franks fled as suddenly as they had come; but they did not leave empty-handed. Desperate to take some trophy - to give meaning to the river of blood they had shed - they seized the screaming Florina and escaped with her in their midst.

With his practised eye, Ambrosius surveyed the room. The floor was slick with blood, and, though seven or eight Franks had been killed, the toll among the Romans was also high. A blood-covered Xallas gave Ambrosius a nod to confirm that most of the blood he wore was not his own. Petro was on his knees and nursing a cut shoulder, while the other local men had fared little better. Darting a look at Puglio, Ambrosius saw that only one other member of the scutarii had survived.

Only then did he glance down at his own ribs, and saw that he would have yet another scar there tomorrow – if he was still alive tomorrow.

From the floor, Petro cried out: "I must go after Florina!"

"Not like that, you won't!" retorted Ambrosius. "You wouldn't get to her, Petro..."

Nor did Petro's two remaining soldiers, trembling with relief that they had survived the bloody onslaught, seem keen to embark upon the rescue of the lady.

"What about you, Dux?" asked Puglio. "Are you going after your sister?"

Clearly Puglio knew little of his relationship with his elder sister, if he thought that Ambrosius would risk Lucidia to save Florina. He could hardly leave the wounded Petro and Lucidia unprotected amid all the carnage being unleashed upon the town.

"Tough decision, eh, Dux?" said Puglio. "I don't give much for her chances though, do you?"

"Ambrosius!" pleaded Petro, "You have to go after her!"

"Bind up his wounds," Ambrosius told the soldiers, snatching a cloak from one of the fallen. "We need to leave."

Despite his brother's protests, Ambrosius decided that he could not risk going after Florina – by Christ, she was more likely to try to kill him than the damned Franks were!

"She stabbed our father in the back, Petro – her own father!" he told his brother.

"I know!" cried Petro. "I saw it too, remember – it was my own damned knife!"

"God knows I hated the man," said Ambrosius, "but she's not worthy of a brother's love!"

"But we can't just leave her!" protested Petro.

"Dear, dear, what a family spawned you, Dux," remarked Puglio.

While he was speaking, Ambrosius knew that the tribune would be weighing up his chances of success if he tried to kill Dux now. But the grim presence of Xallas was enough to dissuade him – at least for the moment.

"Well if you're going, Dux, you'd better go first," invited the tribune, "but don't worry, we'll be close by – in case you find yourself in trouble… and I'll see you very, very soon."

Lucidia was staring at her brother's chest where the cloak hung open, no doubt seeing for the first time in daylight, all the recent wounds he carried.

"You have so many scars," she breathed.

With a shrug, he replied: "Only the marks a soldier bears…"

After a moment's hesitation, she pulled aside the cloak and drew her fingers over some of the rough, scarcely-closed gouges across his back. "And even some that were not inflicted by the weapons of men," she murmured.

"We need to make haste!" he said, brushing aside her concern.

One of the slaves, who had somehow managed to survive, gave his shoulder to Petro, who could not walk unaided. Reminding Cappa to stay close to Lucidia, Ambrosius led the small group out, leaving Xallas to watch their rear.

Outside the house, a chaotic and bloody scene awaited them.

"Where to?" asked Cappa.

"I said I would meet Marco," said Ambrosius, "so I owe it to him to at least try."

"But don't we need to find Onno and that pissing ship?" urged Cappa.

"Yes, but we should join up with Marco first."

"But you sent Varta and the others after Marco," protested Cappa.

"Only because I had others to find – but now we've done that, we'll look for Marco. What if Varta and the others haven't found the main column yet?"

"Marco's got more than thirty men with him. They'll be alright, I tell you!"

"And I'm telling you," growled Ambrosius, "that if Marco has to fight his way here from the north gate, every damned Frank will turn upon him and there won't be many of our thirty men left, will there?"

"But, Dux-"

Ambrosius cut him short. "We need those men, Cappa – unless you intend to row our ship all on your own! So, we try to find Marco! You lead; we'll follow…"

He did not add that there was someone else he was most eager to find… and, he supposed, he must also keep a look out for Lady Florina…

In the streets, men and women hurried away at the sight of them, while others cowered in doorways in the vain hope of escaping the attentions of their attackers. One fellow, his clothes torn and bloody, stood in the shattered remains of his looted shop, glaring at them as they passed.

"They've taken everything I've got!" he wailed.

Ambrosius seized him by the shoulder. "Not yet everything, man!" he said roughly. "But if you stand there much longer complaining, you'll lose your life too!"

"We should be doing something for these people!" cried Lucidia, eyes red with tears.

But Ambrosius pushed her on along the street to follow in Cappa's footsteps. "They're beyond our help now," he said. "We must protect our own first."

"But Rome is their protector!" she declared, her voice breaking.

"Rome, sister?" he replied. "The Rome of our fathers is long gone – it can't even protect itself…"

"Dux!" cried Cappa, pointing up the street. "I don't think we can get to Marco this way…"

Ambrosius scanned the road ahead as far as a large church and, in the distance, he saw the palace. Cappa's assessment, he decided, was prudent enough: there was just no way through, for every yard of space was occupied by Franks jostling and roaring as they broke into shops and looted their way steadily down towards the warehouses and the docks. Ambrosius knew now that he could not stop them; nothing could stop them. Only a passing desire to ransack the houses of the wealthy along their way would even slow their advance.

Constantly, he looked behind him for Puglio, but saw no sign of him - nor any of the other scutarii. Perhaps the tribune would be swallowed up by the horde of Franks; if so, he was unlikely to survive the experience. With a sigh, Ambrosius conceded that Cappa had been right from the start: there was no more time for searching – for comrades, or loved ones. There was scarcely even time left to flee. So they hurried back to the docks, where matters were even worse than before.

There was hardly room to stand, let alone move and, as they watched, two ships left the wharves, overloaded with people and with more clinging on to their oars. On another vessel, there was a running battle for control, which was preventing it from departing at all. The decks of other ships were piled so high with people and goods that the vessels were in danger of being swamped. Frantic ship masters bellowed instructions in vain above the screaming voices of their would-be passengers. All too soon the struggle took a darker turn as mariners started to toss both people and their unwelcome baggage into the harbour. In all the chaos, Ambrosius sought a glimpse of Onno or Caralla, but could not see them.

"You should have sent me to get you a ship, not that fool of an Egyptian!" complained Cappa.

"Stop moaning and keep moving!" shouted Ambrosius.

"Move? I can't pissing move!" cursed Cappa. "I can't even-"

The Roman broke off as a finger of flame flared up on the far side of the harbour.

"There!" cried Ambrosius.

"God's mercy!" cried Lucidia. "They're burning the town!"

"No! That'll be Onno!" declared Ambrosius. "And that fire is where we need to get to: right at the far south end of the harbour!"

"Hah! It might as well be Rome!" snorted Cappa. "We're stuck here, I tell you!"

"Then use your knife to persuade your way through," ordered Ambrosius.

"I could stab all the buggers," retorted Cappa, "but they've nowhere to fall, so they'd still be blocking my way!"

"It's hopeless!" groaned Petro.

"No!" cried Ambrosius, "Go right up to the harbour wall and force a path alongside it. You can use the wall to help you - press against it to force aside any folk in your way!"

Acknowledging at once the sense of his suggestion, Cappa led the way to the stone wall. Though it was centuries old and long past need of repair, it provided a way for them. Squeezing along beside it meant they had half as many folk to push out of the way. But sometimes the crowd could not be moved an inch and they were forced to clamber past over a ruined section of wall. Such moments, Ambrosius saw, were agony for the wounded Petro but never did his brother utter a word of complaint.

The further along the dock they moved, the more the mass of people began to thin out. Everyone else was heading to the centre and north of the docks where the few remaining ships were moored so, going away from the congestion, speeded their progress. Nevertheless, it occurred to Ambrosius, belatedly, that he would look very foolish if the flames he could still see close to the harbour entrance proved not to be a signal from Onno at all.

When they were still fifty yards away, his face broke into a grin of relief for he recognised the bulk of Caralla, wrestling with several others to control of a small vessel which was veering out into the main channel.

"Xallas, Cappa!" he ordered. "Run ahead and give them a hand! You too," he told the slave, transferring Petro's weight to his own shoulder.

Minutes later, they were all staring at the ship now safely moored against a wooden jetty. A smiling Onno leapt off to meet Ambrosius, who at once took him aside.

"This ship won't do!" he told the Egyptian. "It's too small - but you must know that!"

"I know it, Dux, but too small compared to what?" replied Onno, with a rueful smile.

27

November 454 in the morning, near the palace in Caracotinum

Having watched Inga's litter veer away to the south, Marcellus felt a little easier about what was to come. Already, as he led his column towards the palace building where he hoped to find Dux, he knew that they were vastly outnumbered by the Franks. All around them spears and spathas were brandished with ever-growing enthusiasm – indeed some warriors actually leapt up and down as they scoured the streets and houses for someone to fight.

In the nervous glances of his own men, he saw, not fear exactly, but a creeping unease rooted in simple mistrust of their allies. Were these men in their bright tunics, with long hair bunched strangely over their foreheads, truly their friends? Not to Marcellus, they weren't; and not to many of those who marched with him...

When they reached the palace and found no trace of Dux and the others, Marcellus wanted to stop and wait – perhaps even conduct a swift search of the building. But what he wanted soon became irrelevant, for the small Roman column was swept along in the Frankish tide. For another two hundred yards or so, it was good-humoured and all was well. Franks and Romans admired each other's weaponry, exchanged crude insults and laughed at each other's ribald jokes – as soldiers always did. Passing the

town baths, they cheerfully discussed the possibility that
there would be brothels close by. But then they were joined
by another, different group of Franks, who must have
swept first through the barracks along the north wall and
then turned back to join their comrades.

With their arrival, a dark shadow seemed to pass over
the crowd and the mood changed. Their swords and spears
bloodied, these men had clearly already seen some hard
fighting against the local garrison – who were, of course,
Roman. Now, when they found yet more Romans in their
midst, the casual banter started to take on a more rancorous
tone. Marcellus could see disaster coming but, like a man
falling from a rooftop, he could do nothing to stop it.

"Steady lads!" he warned. "Keep your order now – and
keep those weapons sheathed!"

Even if they heard him, amid the clamour all around
them, their nerves were too frayed to heed any instructions.
Even Placido's dogs – usually so disciplined – were
growling and grumbling as they flanked their master. With
their spiked collars and armoured coats, they rippled with
menace. Any moment, Marcellus thought, one of them will
snap its jaws around a nearby Frank who waves his spear
too close to Placido. And he knew, well before anything
happened, that it would only take one such rash action, by
man or dog, or one barbed word, to provoke a bloodbath.

Having missed Dux at the palace, the only other place
Marcellus could make for was the harbour. Trying to
calculate how far away the docks were, he found himself
silently counting off each yard and praying that the tense
accord between Franks and Romans would endure a little
longer. But his prayers went unanswered and all hope

vanished when a great swathe of the Frankish warriors came to an abrupt halt, without warning, thirty paces ahead of him.

As one, they turned about to face the Roman column in a manoeuvre that could not have happened by chance. Other Franks close by, he noticed, hastily sheered away from the Romans as death hurtled towards them in a blur of thrown axes and spears. Men beside him cried out, or clutched at mortal wounds as they dropped to their knees.

In vain, Marcellus flung out orders that no man could hear. Surrounded by so many, he knew they were doomed; their only chance of avoiding complete annihilation, was to form small, tight groups. Six or eight men with shields together and spears pointing outwards might just force a bloody path out of the crowded street. Bullying the nearest soldiers into formation, he all but dragged them down a side street.

"Take the blows on your shields and keep those spear points low!" he bellowed. "Strike at their bare legs – and, in God's name, stay on your feet!"

He said a lot more, hurling abuse and roaring encouragement every time an axe looped down upon them. Those who were not cut down in the first attack were quick to follow his lead for they were experienced men. But the Franks too had spears to lunge at the tight Roman groups - sometimes to no avail, but one or two pierced bellies or tore through thighs… and men fell. Wounded men had to be abandoned to their fate, as the survivors trampled away over their fallen comrades.

Though Marcellus' dwindling band of men had scrambled their way out of the clutches of the surrounding army, they were still being pursued. To break ranks and run was tempting, but they dared not risk being isolated. So, though they relaxed their formation a little, they were still a tight unit of men. Most had sustained minor wounds and a few were limping but, as long as they could walk, Marcellus reckoned they might just get to the docks.

Raging with anger and bitterness, he cursed the perfidious Franks, but also his friend – for Dux should never have trusted the Franks in the first place. It was foolish – and a folly which had now brought about the slaughter of many of the soldiers who had followed him so willingly out of northern Italy. They had put their trust in him and he had betrayed them…

But what, thought Marcellus, if Dux himself was already dead – killed by his father the moment he entered the town? Remembering the many times that Dux had been all that stood between him and certain death, he regretted his rage against his friend. The sudden ambush had unnerved him, causing dark thoughts to surface; but now he felt ashamed. Dux deserved better than that - and Dux had entrusted him with the lives of these men…

Leading the small group through a warren of narrow alleys, Marcellus summoned up some of his usual confidence. Every now and then, he was given further encouragement by the arrival of stragglers from the column who had also managed to escape the carnage. One such group was led by Placido and his now blood-smeared dogs. When several of the local garrison joined them, he soon had about twenty men with him. Even so, with Franks spilling out of every side street, their situation still appeared hopeless.

Everywhere, the inhabitants of the town were fleeing – though Marcellus could not think where they hoped to escape to. There were only two routes out of Caracotinum that he was aware of: the north gate - which was now impossible to reach - and the port itself which was where everyone was going. It occurred to him that, even if Onno had already secured a ship, he might not be able to hold it against so many. Nevertheless, as they edged closer to the harbour, Marcellus felt his spirits rise, especially when they rounded a corner and found that the central, walled dock area was only fifty yards away. The wall was old and half ruined, but it might give them a place they could actually defend if the Franks caught up with them. But the elation that put new light into each man's eyes was swiftly and cruelly extinguished.

They heard the screams first before a tide of people swept towards them - not Franks, but townsfolk – bewildered men and women whose small world was being torn asunder. Seeing the score of armed Romans, they fled towards them, mobbing them in their relief. Some folk were wounded and scarred beyond reason, but others were simply in shock. Among them was a bloodied and shivering, half-naked woman who did nothing but mutter to herself. After a few moments trying to talk to her, Marcellus gave up and told one of his men to drape a cloak over her. Though he could not undo what had been done to her, he could at least hide it from others.

Shepherding the civilians ahead of them, they continued to the port, with Marcellus determined to escort the refugees there in safety. It was not the first time he had found himself in a town on the brink of destruction, so he knew that for most folk, he could offer no reprieve from what was to come. But for these few at least, he vowed to try.

With the docks now only yards away, a small band of young Franks overtook the Romans and, though hopelessly outnumbered, the youths went on the attack. Fearless in battle, the young warriors whirled their shields around and hurled themselves at the Romans. Marcellus' men, having endured more than enough punishment earlier, were hungry for revenge. Within a few minutes, led by Placido, they scythed down their opponents, killing them all. No mercy was shown and the shaken townsfolk shrieked and spat upon the blood-soaked bodies.

Their celebration was abruptly curtailed, however, when a far larger number of Franks rounded the street corner, launching spears and throwing axes. Flying blades punched through light mail coats to bore into flesh. Soldiers and civilians alike were struck down. One woman, shielding her young son, cried out as first a spear buried itself in her midriff and then she was hacked to the ground. Staring down at his mother, the boy stood motionless. While, all around him, men snarled and women screamed, he simply stood watching the dark blood pump from her body.

Marcellus was about to snatch up the lad when a spear struck him in the shoulder and spun him around.

"Make for the docks!" he barked, snapping off the spear shaft, as he attempted to form up his men in a ragged screen to protect the townspeople.

The motherless boy might have remained where he was, had not the cloaked woman reached out a hand to grasp his and haul him away. Together, the unlikely pair shambled along with the others, with the Franks in fierce pursuit.

They're going to drive us straight into the harbour, thought Marcellus; but, in a way, that made his decision easy. With no signal of any kind from Onno, he had to assume there was no ship. Thus, he had no choice now but to make a stand with the harbour wall at his back. Better that than flee beyond the wall onto the wharves where they would be easily cut down, or driven backwards into the water. With the exhausted civilians cowering against the wall behind him, devoid of all hope, he arrayed the men he had left to face the oncoming Franks. Standing just ahead of the others, with Placido beside him, Marcellus resolved that he would fight to the death where he was.

The Franks came at a pace, roaring and bellowing, but then, oddly, their advance seemed to falter – and, to Marcellus' surprise, the great, unstoppable surge of men started to come to a halt. Only when he turned to his left, did he see why. From the dockside, the tall and unmistakable figure of Varta ambled into view, followed by Germanus and Rocca. Aside from Dux himself, it would be difficult to find three such imposing warriors. The three men nodded to Marcellus, sauntered in front of his line of men and took their positions beside him, with Placido.

Yet, thought Marcellus, they were only five men – so how could they make any difference? Varta was a Frank, of course - known perhaps to some of those now facing him and very probably a blood relative of one or two, but even so...

Taking a pace forward, Varta raised his right arm and spatha aloft. The street and the area around it fell silent.

"These Romans," declared Varta, "are... my... friends..."

At once his words caused a murmur of anger among some of the Franks and Marcellus gripped the hilt of his weapon more tightly, anticipating a rush attack. But Varta, seemingly unconcerned, continued and his deep voice quelled the crowd once more.

"Now that I've told you all... that these people are my friends, you should know that I will personally disembowel any man who threatens their safety. So, go away, and look elsewhere for your amusement..."

It would certainly be a brave Frank who took on Varta, but then there was a whole host of brave men to do so. Even with the three mean-looking men flanking Varta, Marcellus could not see how they would hold up the Franks for long.

From what he knew of Childeric, Marcellus had no doubt that, had the young Frank chieftain been there, he would not have allowed Varta's challenge to go unanswered. But no-one who was there appeared willing to answer it and Marcellus watched, astonished, as the crowd of armed men began to disperse. Though some left muttering and moaning, they did leave.

"That was a good trick, my friend," he said, as he clasped Varta's arm to congratulate him. "How in God's name did you know that would work?"

"I didn't think it would," laughed the Frank. "Mind you, Rocca and Germanus are disappointed – they would have preferred a fight!"

"Have you found Onno?" asked Marcellus. "Does he have a ship for us? And what about Dux – where is he?"

With a shrug, Varta replied: "We parted company with Dux, Xallas and Cappa a while ago. Where they are now, I don't know.

Marcellus had just begun to convince himself that the worst was over, but without a ship, all their problems would return soon enough. Suddenly, his wound seemed worse…

"So, what do we do then?" he asked.

"We're supposed to meet Dux down on the docks," said Varta. "If we keep together, we might still have a chance."

"This is all a complete mess!" grumbled Marcellus. "By Christ, we've lost half our men, Varta!"

"I see that," said Varta, with a shrug, "but we are bucellarii, Marco. We go where Dux goes and we live, or die, with him."

"Yes, but in doing so, we've brought ruin upon the whole damned town – and ourselves! It's been a slaughter!"

"I know," acknowledged Varta. "I've seen it too, but how could Dux have known what awaited us here? And do you think my fellow Franks were going to camp outside the town walls forever, Marco? They were making scaling ladders before we even arrived and the small garrison could never have held out against so many. So, if you have saved some folk this day, then you've done all you ever could have done."

Marcellus gave a weary nod, relieved at least to have his three formidable comrades with him – and then he remembered Calens and Inga…

28

November 454, on the south docks at Caracotinum harbour

Ambrosius could only stare at the boat. "A navis lusoria… is too small, Onno. I mean, that thing can't cross the channel in November – it can't cross the channel at all…"

"Well, it's the only ship we've got!" retorted the Egyptian. "By the time Caralla and I got to the docks, there was nothing else!"

"But you were the only one who knew where I intended to go," he groaned. "I told you so that you could choose a suitable ship, like a liburnia! But… this is just a river patrol boat!"

"Choose, Dux? There was no choice in it! Just ask those poor souls over there!" he cried, pointing to the northern docks. "Either we make use of this ship, or we don't leave here at all."

"Well, we can't stay here!" declared Ambrosius. "That's certain!"

"So, Dux, we'll just have to pray that we don't drown crossing the channel. Won't we?"

"By Christ," murmured Ambrosius. "How many can we take aboard?

"About thirty rowing and, I suppose a few more on the deck…"

With a heavy sigh, Ambrosius acknowledged that there was no alternative. "We'd better start getting everyone aboard," he said.

"And… by everyone… you mean all half dozen of you," said Onno. "Where in God's name are the rest, Dux?"

"Let's hope they've seen your signal fire and are on their way…"

Some of those he wanted to take with him, like Lucidia, were already frightened; what greater terrors would the sight of this tiny vessel conjure up for them? It was not built to cross the sea to Britannia, nor was it large enough to carry all his men and his family, let alone any refugees from the Roman garrison. His situation was both simple and terrible: he would be forced to leave people behind…

"When Marco and the others arrive," he told Onno, "we'll just have to go and take another ship – or some of our comrades will be swimming alongside!"

"What other ship?" protested Onno. "Take another look, Dux - a good look, because most of the other ships have gone! And when they've all gone, we'll be lucky to keep hold of this one, never mind take another!"

"You in charge of these fools then?" interrupted the ship master.

"Who are you?" grumbled Ambrosius.

"Manned a ship before have you?"

"No! Who are you?" repeated Ambrosius.

"He's Remigius, the ship's master," said Onno, "albeit a drunken one!"

"Yeh, I'm the poor sod who keeps this vessel – which, as I told your slave, belongs to the port commander."

"Onno's not my slave; and as for the port commander, well, let's say that he won't be requiring your services anymore."

"You telling me Magnus is dead?" said Remigius.

"I am."

"I don't believe you!"

"Listen, fellow: he was my own father, so trust me on this; he's dead! Now, can you sail this ship, or not?"

The master, who looked thoroughly put out by the sudden change in his circumstances, made no reply.

"I've not much time – and even less patience," growled Ambrosius. "So tell me: can you manage this ship, or not? Because, if you can't, I'll throw you off it, to make room for another of my men!"

"Course I can sail it," muttered Remigius, "just not to Britannia…"

"You'd rather stay behind here then?" suggested Ambrosius.

With a furtive glance across the harbour, the master conceded: "I suppose I might be able to do it… if you had enough rowers – which you clearly haven't!"

"We'll have rowers," Ambrosius assured him. "You just be ready to leave on my command!"

If Remigius had any thoughts of arguing further, he did not get the chance.

"Dux!" called Caralla.

Looking up, Ambrosius saw a weary company approaching and frowned. There was no mistaking Varta and Marcellus but the rest of the straggling group were scarcely recognisable as the ranks of seasoned veterans he had brought out of Italy.

"By Christ," he muttered, "what have you done with my men, Marco?"

Among the soldiers he saw several women and even one or two children - a few souls saved then. While Caralla and Cappa went off to greet their comrades and help some of the wounded, Ambrosius could only look on in disbelief from the deck of the ship.

"Dux," said Marcellus, nodding to his commander.

"What happened?" demanded Ambrosius.

"The Franks, Dux - your friends, the Franks - they happened..."

"They attacked you?"

"No, we threw ourselves onto their spear points!"

Marcellus' savage response revealed the depth of his bitterness and Ambrosius' face softened when he saw the despair on his wounded comrade's face.

"Then you did well to get anyone out alive, Marco," he said, gripping his friend's arm.

Marcellus gave a shake of the head and indicated Varta. "Without Varta and the others, we'd all be dead."

"I never thought Clodoris would break his word to me..." said Ambrosius.

"If it makes you feel any better, Dux, I don't think it was his doing - I'm not even sure he was there..."

"Then he damned well should have been!" cried Ambrosius. "Look at this broken shell of a town – its people killed, robbed or ravished!"

"You've seen it before, Dux," murmured Marcellus. "We all have..."

"True enough, but I've not had a hand in causing it before!" said Ambrosius, tasting bile in his mouth.

Staring at the faces of the survivors as they filed onto the ship, one caught his eye: a woman hunched over in a borrowed cloak, with a boy beside her. Ambrosius was still studying her when Lucidia leapt from the ship and enveloped the woman in her arms. Wincing at the sight of her, he did not follow Lucidia's example. Compassion was the last thing the woman would expect from anyone, but least of all from her estranged half-brother.

"Who is that?" asked Marcellus.

"That… is my elder sister, Florina. She was captured…"

"Dear God, Dux! I'm sorry; we've done our best but, when we found her… let's just say she had not been treated well…"

"Who's the boy?" asked Ambrosius. "Not hers, that much I know!"

"His mother was killed before his eyes – and… Lady Florina sort of… took him with her…"

Ambrosius was still wrestling with the concept of Florina showing kindness towards anyone, especially some poor, abandoned child who could offer her nothing, when a sudden thought struck him like a blow to the stomach.

Seizing Marcellus by the shoulder, he whispered: "Inga? Calens? They're not with you! Where are they, Marco?"

Marcellus bowed his head. "I was hoping they'd already be here," he said. "I prayed they would be…"

Swiftly, he explained how he had tried to protect the girl and her escort from being trapped amongst the great host of Franks.

Ambrosius nodded. "Of course, you did the right thing, Marco, as ever… but where can they be now?"

Standing up, Marcellus said: "I'll go after them at once, Dux!"

"Sit down, my friend; you're already bleeding out onto my deck; and you've done more than your share already. I'll go myself."

"Then take some others, Dux," insisted Marcellus, "because, God's breath, you're going to need them!"

With a shake of the head, Ambrosius replied: "Not as much as you will, Marco. Better I slip out there alone; you'll need every man here just to defend this ship against those who'll be trying to take it. Now, where do you think Inga might be?"

"I sent them to the south east of the town, thinking it was furthest from the Frank attack – and thus, trouble… They should have reached the docks long before us and their road should have taken them past the large warehouses on the seaward side of the town…"

"Dux," said Onno, "there was a group of Franks with ladders at the southern wall – they came over before dawn and cleared the rampart there. The litter could have run straight into them…"

Dux said nothing, unwilling to reveal his despair, but at once he leapt from the ship onto the jetty.

"You can't go alone, Dux!" protested Varta.

"You," ordered Ambrosius, "will stay here with everyone else. Keeping this ship in our hands will be near impossible once folk realise it's here – and they very soon will! Some of those aboard will be terrified and they'll want to cast off. Then they'll be angry at you for not doing so. I need you here, Varta, because I want to know that when I get back, there'll still be a ship here to come back to!"

"I see all that, Dux, but you must take at least some of us," replied Varta. "Inga will need to be carried, so you'll need someone with you and - I simply won't let you go alone."

"I'll go," offered Placido, who had been listening close by. "You know me, Dux, I'll only get bored waiting here; I'd most likely pick a fight with someone and anyway, the dogs could do with a run…"

"And I suppose I'd better go," chirped up Cappa, "'cos, to be honest, Dux, you've no hope of finding them without me."

"Very well," conceded Ambrosius, turning to Varta. "I'll take Placido and Cappa. Are you happy now?"

"Not till I see you coming back with our comrades," grumbled Varta. "And Dux, best not take too long…"

29

**November 454, in the morning on the east side of
Caracotinum**

Gently easing the corpse of Canis away from her, Inga
tried, with the aid of slow, steady breaths, to calm her
shattered nerves. If she did not, she was lost. The Franks,
perhaps supposing that she was already dead, had moved
off without giving her a second glance. For once, her
extensive wounds and deathly pallor had served to protect
her.

Steeling herself for the agony to come, she stared up at
the street and buildings nearest to her. With no evidence
that any members of her escort had survived, she had to
assume she was on her own. So, if she wanted to live, it was
up to her – just a normal day for a warrior like her, she
thought, giving a nervous giggle. Before she knew it,
however, a tear was tracing a path through the grime upon
her cheeks; then another rolled down, salty at the corner of
her mouth. She wept then, an uncontrollable river of tears
such as no self-respecting bucellarius had ever cried before.

When the moment passed, she scrubbed away the tears
with an angry swipe of her damaged hand, ashamed at her
sudden weakness. But no, she told herself, there was no
harm in a few tears – or in her case a whole torrent of them.
Because, once the weeping ended, her mind felt clearer,
sharper. She had no broken bones, so she knew she could

move well enough; only pain was preventing her from getting to her feet and simply walking away. Pain, that was all – and pain could be her friend... prodding her awake and keeping her alert.

Holding out her hands before her, she began to flex her damaged fingers, slowly at first as the ragged wounds shrieked in protest. Then she gripped the wooden shaft of her bow – her bow now, not Uldar's – and with each hand in turn, clenched her palm and fingers tight around it. She kept doing it until her hands not only became accustomed to the feel of the sinew and horn, but also the excruciating agony the movement caused her. Then, taking several deep breaths, she planted the bow on the ground, pressed her back against the wall and eased it slowly upwards until she was standing tall.

Though the torn muscles in her legs implored her to sit back down, Inga did not. Instead, using her bow for balance, she took a step forward, then another. Reassured that she had neither fallen over nor bled to death, she took a few more steps. It hurt but, in a strange way, it felt good. Step by step, she made her way along to the crossroads, passing several other unknown, wounded souls along the way.

Fleetingly, she wondered what they made of her, this walking dead girl. But it did not deter her, because she was a warrior who had found her courage. Grunting with the effort, she stopped at the corner, averting her gaze from the blood-soaked bodies that lay there. All about her were shabby, derelict buildings – it was a place without hope, she thought. Yet, as long as she could still put one foot in front of the other, she would not surrender her hope.

When she moved on again into the broader road, she could see several warehouses and, beyond them, the harbour wall, which did much to strengthen her resolve. Though still wary of encountering some of the Franks, she plodded on down the hill, encouraged by the knowledge that the docks were close now. As she passed a side street on her right hand, she came to an abrupt halt, her attention caught by a lone figure limping towards her. Calens!

Despite her weariness, she cried out and set off along the street to meet him, knowing she had more chance of survival with the Greek physician than without him. Her elation quickly evaporated though when she noticed half a dozen or so Franks coming down the street behind him. Though they did not appear to be pursuing Calens, they would surely reach him before she could – and what would they make of her?

Seeing her looking behind him, Calens glanced back and at once moved a little faster.

"Go back, Inga!" he cried. "For God's sake, go!"

It made complete sense, of course, for her to leave him and flee. If she did, she would almost certainly reach the docks ahead of the Franks, but what then? For the rest of her days, she would remember how she had deserted Calens. So she did not run, for bucellarii did not leave wounded comrades behind. Instead, she gritted her teeth and forced her aching limbs to work just a little harder. With Calens walking towards her, the distance between them closed rapidly, but the Franks too – perhaps noticing her arrival – were now moving with more haste.

She had assumed that the Greek was hampered by a leg injury, but as she came nearer she realised that the wound was higher up – in the groin, or the belly. A chill swept over her, with the knowledge that his wound might, after all, be a mortal one. When she reached him, they had only a few moments before the Franks would overtake them.

"You should have gone, you foolish girl!" Calens rasped at her. "God knows, I'm already dead!"

"Pah, what do you physicians know?" she replied simply. "But, if you are going to die, Calens, you won't die alone."

"For the love of God, Inga," he cried, "just go on to the docks… I beg you!"

Ignoring his protests, she wrapped an arm around him to support some of his weight.

"Either we both go," she declared, "or neither of us do.",

By then the Franks had drawn level with them and come to a halt. One man half-drew out his spatha, but another, staring at the wounded pair, shook his head. "They're almost dead already and they've nothing worth taking," he said. "Leave them; they're not worthy of your sword."

One or two nodded agreement and the rest shrugged their indifference, so the spatha was sheathed and they hurried on without further discussion.

With a long sigh, Inga remained still, her heart beating so hard she expected it to leap out of her breast at any moment.

"Any man who doubts there is a God, should have been here," murmured Calens. "Did you recognise him?"

"No, should I have?" she asked, helping the Greek to stand.

Calens managed a weak smile, but winced before replying. "No, perhaps not... I don't think you ever saw him, but his name is Caranis. It was he that rescued you and Dux from the wolves..."

"What?" breathed Inga.

"Yes, my dear Inga," said the Greek, "you've been saved twice - by the same man! Surely God must have some great purpose for you for, as hard as you try to get yourself killed, He just keeps saving you..." He attempted a laugh, but only choked for his pains.

Though they managed to walk a few more yards, Inga could feel that he was weakening fast and stopped to sit him down by the roadside so that she could examine his wound.

"You want to play the physician now?" he croaked at her, face paler by the moment. "Well, I can tell you: your patient will die..."

Probing the still-bleeding wound with her fingers, she explored his belly which was badly torn - too badly torn, she knew.

"I'll stay with you," she told him, gripping his hand in hers.

"Why?" he murmured. "Are you eager... to watch me die?" His voice was but a hoarse whisper.

"I won't leave you..."

"My death will be long and slow, Inga... and only you can prevent that..."

"No!" she cried.

"It's what bucellarii do, Inga," said Calens. "It's what... I've done before, for a comrade. It's quite simple: you need to... go – and I need to die..."

With a glance down at the knife on his belt, which was the only weapon he ever carried, Calens took her hand and gave it a gentle squeeze.

"Take my knife, girl – and take my bag with you, if you can carry it. There are salves… and…other things…"

Inga could find no words of solace for the man who had saved her life twice over.

"Tell me," he said, "do you know if Canis still lives?"

"I'm very sorry, Calens," she whispered, "but he fell beside me…"

"Ah… I prayed that he escaped; but never mind, if God wills it, I shall see him again before you do… now that I've made my peace with God and men…"

Though she drew out his knife, when she contemplated what he was asking of her, she froze.

"Just guide my hand," he told her, "and I'll show you how…"

"But…"

"Grant a dying man's last wish, eh?" he said, with a glint of humour in his eye even at the last.

Wrapping her fingers around the hilt along with his, she steered the point to his throat but then he passed out. At first she thought – hoped - he had simply died peacefully, but the slight rise and fall of his chest told a different story and, beneath her hands, she could feel the gentle tremor of his beating heart.

With a deep breath, she let his fingers fall from the hilt and gripped it more tightly in both her hands. For a moment, all her doubts resurfaced. She had never killed a man… yet, she could not simply let him bleed to death. In a moment of embittered rage, she thrust the blade into his neck and carved it back and forth. It seemed to take forever and her hands stung with the effort but finally blood poured forth - less than she expected but then he must have already lost so much.

For a while she lay down on top of him, utterly spent, her head filled with a miserable brew of regret and horror. She still had the murder weapon in her hands when she became aware of the tramp of feet. In panic, she sat up and glared back along the street; then she shut her eyes and slumped forward against Calens' still warm body. If she played dead perhaps these Franks too would pass by, as their fellows had done before. But this time, she reflected, her saviour, Caranis would not be amongst them.

30

November 454, near the harbour in Caracotinum

Passing through a break in the harbour wall, Ambrosius and his two companions moved swiftly towards the eastern quarter of the town. Cappa led the way, avoiding the main streets to thread his way between the warehouses adjacent to the docks. In a town which had descended into chaos, Ambrosius hardly dared to hope that Inga would be safe. He also knew that, even if she had survived thus far, she could have ended up almost anywhere. After the litter and its escort had left Marcellus, how far had it got? To find out that, he must put his trust in the skills of the stocky, taciturn Cappa.

Stalking alongside the three men were Placido's two dogs, Ferox and Patricus. Not for the first time in their acquaintance, Ambrosius was relieved to have the belligerent animals on his side, for everywhere lay evidence of slaughter and pillage.

"This is the end of the road they should have taken to the docks," explained Cappa, pointing up the street.

"I used to know this area well," murmured Ambrosius. "It's straightforward enough, so what went wrong? Most of the Franks should have been well behind them."

"Except the Franks that Onno mentioned," said Cappa, "the ones who came over the south wall before dawn. I suspect those are the ones that caused problems for our friends."

"Calens and the escort could have walked right into them," said Ambrosius.

"That'd be my guess, Dux," agreed Cappa.

"Come on then," said Ambrosius, "let's see if we can see where it happened, but keep sharp! Cappa, you concentrate on finding the litter – Placido, eyes everywhere - especially at our backs!"

Turning to the two dogs, Placido said: "Shield!" and at once the pair separated to flank his comrades.

No longer were they slipping unnoticed by privy alleys; now they were searching in plain sight. What Ambrosius noticed first – indeed, could not help but notice – were the dead. Corpses lay everywhere: beside the road, in doorways, slumped over shop tables… everywhere. Still confounded by the excesses of his Frank allies, he could not imagine how his adopted father, Clodoris, had allowed matters to get so far out of control.

Half-way down the street, they found the first member of the escort – a fellow Ambrosius remembered well – at least by sight, though he could not recall the soldier's name. How many nameless men had followed him from Verona and would never leave Caracotinum, he wondered?

"Dux!" Cappa was already moving on and had found something else. At the sight of it, Ambrosius found himself trembling – an unfamiliar sensation, though one which he had observed often enough in others. He could not remember the last time he had known genuine fear, but he knew it when he saw the blood-stained remains of the frame that had served as Inga's litter. At the mere sight of it, he recalled the light touch of her hand - the simple gesture which had conveyed so much between them.

A snarl from Ferox behind him brought Ambrosius back to the present with a jolt, as a couple of young Franks appeared from nowhere and ran at them screaming: "Death to all Romans!"

In one furious movement, Ambrosius swung around, drawing out his spatha as one of the Franks launched himself to attack. Even when the weapon lunged into the man, his momentum carried him forward impaling him further until his wild-eyed face was only inches from Ambrosius.

Glaring at the dying youth, whose thin moustache dripped with blood and spittle, he yelled: "Death to all Romans, you fool? Your people have lived like Romans since the day you were born – as did your forefathers!"

With a savage twist he wrenched out the spatha to let his assailant fall at his feet. Fuelled by wine the youth might have been - no doubt liberated from some poor inn, or shop – but the mindless assault served only to darken Ambrosius' mood further. Too slow to meet the attack of the other Frank, he was only saved by the fearless Ferox. Clamping his mighty jaws around the assailant's leg, the dog dragged him to the ground, where Placido buried a spear in his breast. After a hasty glance around, lest others were close by, Placido slapped Ferox on the flank in congratulation.

Meanwhile, Ambrosius, still distracted by his glimpse of Inga's smashed up litter, began to dread what dark deeds he might be capable of, if he discovered that she had been killed. When Cappa moved slowly on, examining the roadway and the houses they passed, Ambrosius trudged after him, motioning Placido to hang back a little further. Only a few yards on, Cappa stopped once more and turned left into a side street. Despite all that he had already witnessed, even Ambrosius was shocked at what he saw next.

A carpet of bodies clothed the cobbled street and even the most casual observer could see that both Franks and Romans lay there. Here, the escort must have been attacked and, as far as he could tell, all had been killed. A close scrutiny revealed that his men had not sold their lives cheaply, for the majority of the dead were Franks. After each one of their fallen comrades was examined, Ambrosius reckoned that the number was about right, though he was relieved to find that Calens, Canis and Inga were not among the dead.

"She sat here, I think," said Cappa, indicating a short length of wall. "Well, someone, I suppose, sat here. See, where there's a smear of blood on the stone…"

"By God, man - that could be anyone's blood!" retorted Ambrosius.

"Perhaps," conceded Cappa, "but not any of those lying in the road, eh?

Amid his bleak despair, Ambrosius grasped at the faint ray of hope offered by his comrade. Those few words from the grubby son of Rome rekindled Ambrosius' fragile hopes. "Where then?" he demanded. "Where did they go next?"

"This way - don't you think?" said Cappa, pointing at a soiled linen bandage by the roadside, "Because that is most certainly Inga's."

275

Ambrosius knelt to retrieve it, as if it were some precious necklace fashioned of gold Further along the street, he recovered another similar relic of Inga's passing; blood-blackened and filthy though it was; it was now all he had of her.

It was many years since he had been to this quarter of the town, where once he had communed with other disaffected youths. It was where he had first met Varta and come up with the notion of fleeing the town to live outside it amongst his people. Then this place had been a familiar retreat; it did not seem so safe now.

"There's nothing here," he murmured.

Yet Cappa seemed undaunted. "You give up too easily, Dux," he said. "We're doing well; we just need to pick up her trail again, that's all."

But Ambrosius, fearing that time was running too short, did not share Cappa's optimism. The longer their search lasted, the more his ship would be at risk; even a handful of desperate men could overwhelm and capture such a small vessel.

When Cappa led them back to the broader street once more, it only invited further despair. A small clutch of local men and women, their grey faces etched with misery, studied the three Romans. Though he and his comrades might appear Roman, he could well understand that few would trust them. When the citizens heard the distant roar of Frank celebration, they slunk away into several of the nearby, shattered houses. He too had heard the Franks, and exchanged a warning glance with Placido as Cappa foraged ahead again.

Where a small street crossed the main road, Cappa stopped and touched the road. "Someone was badly wounded here – not too long ago – an hour perhaps?"

"This is madness, Dux," grumbled Placido. "We're clutching at straws! 'Someone' was wounded, Cappa? By Christ, half the damn town's been wounded!"

Pointing up the side street, Placido indicated a baying crowd at the far end – no more than a hundred paces from them.

"Sooner or later, Dux," he warned, "some of those bastards are going to notice us…"

But Ambrosius, also staring up the street, did not hear him. Open–mouthed, he could not draw his eyes from a figure crouched at the side of the street midway between him and the Franks. While he watched, the woman turned around to stare behind her at the oncoming horde and then slumped back down again. Desperate to cry out to her, his lips shaped the words but his stone-dry mouth refused to utter them. Instead, he reached out to Placido, gripped his arm and stabbed a finger along the street. Then he was moving, spatha sliding out of its scabbard as he ran.

"Ferox!" gasped Placido, "Guard Inga!" and the great dog leapt forward, racing past Ambrosius, towards the girl.

Whether his boots on the cobbles alerted her, or perhaps the sound of the dog, for whatever reason, she looked up. Crying out, she scrambled unsteadily to her feet and began to hobble towards him. Willing her to move faster, he heard a sudden, single cry from the midst the Franks and they broke into a run.

She was still ten yards from him when spears began to fly – hurled wildly in anger, but still a mortal danger. Ferox, unable to protect the girl from the missiles, stood, snarling at the oncoming Franks. The instant Ambrosius reached her; he scooped her up to carry her back to his two waiting comrades. A spear flew past him and another skidded along the cobbles beside him, followed swiftly by a growling Ferox. Run straight, he told himself. Run straight and let God scatter their spears!

Against his chest, he felt her pounding heart, and her hot tears burned his neck. Perhaps God was protecting him, for he was not struck down and, accompanied by the tireless Ferox, reached the broad street without injury. Nevertheless, the Franks were almost upon them.

"We won't make it!" he told the others, coming to an abrupt halt. "Take Inga to the ship!" Passing her into Placido's arms, he kissed her hair and turned to face the Franks.

"Dux!" cried Cappa. "Don't be a fool! We'll take our chances together - as always!"

"Go! If I can talk to Clodoris, I have a chance – but with you two there, they'll just see Rome. Now get her to the ship!" he railed. "Both of you - and take the dogs with you!"

"No!" protested Inga, but Placido must have known that the slightest hesitation would get them all killed, so he set off at a run with Cappa.

Ambrosius' last glimpse of Inga was of her struggling and shrieking at him like a wild woman. Yet, as he waited for the Franks to reach him, he smiled at the thought: for, at times, she was indeed a wild woman. But, as he stood there, for the first time that day, strangely, he felt at peace.

31

November 454 at midday, on the ship in Caracotinum Harbour

While Lucidia attempted to bind up his wounds, Marcellus was lying on the ship's open deck, listening with growing concern to the argument among his comrades.

"All I'm saying, Varta," said Stavelus, "is that we should pull away from the dock – just a short way, that's all."

"This ship is not leaving that dock before Dux returns," declared Varta.

"We all want Dux to come back!" Stavelus assured the Frank. "Of course we do! We didn't follow him all the way here, just to abandon him, did we?"

"Good," said Varta, "then we're agreed."

"But… loyal though we all are to Dux," argued Stavelus, "let's not forget that he never told us to expect this whole shit storm we're in, did he? I mean, scutarii – we knew they'd come, but the further we got from Rome, the less we expected to be fighting for our lives – never mind being carved about by a host of Franks!"

"We're all soldiers," said Rocca, "What else is there for a soldier but fighting?"

"We don't all live in the hope of getting a praiseworthy death, Rocca," said Stavelus, his expression stern. "Some of us sort of intended to live a bit longer - we're not all damned, gladiatorial slaves!"

Rocca, though slow to anger, would be difficult to restrain, thought Marcellus, if the argument continued much longer. What worried him most was that Stavelus had the backing of many of the score or so rank and file soldiers who had survived this far. Though Varta, Rocca and the others could most likely crush any troublemakers, the last thing Dux would want to find when he did return was a bloodbath among his own men. Stavelus was a good, reliable soldier, but he was also very fond of his own voice. It sounded as if he was warming a little too much to the role of self-appointed spokesman for the ordinary soldier – with whom, it had to be said, Dux's bucellarii had very little in common.

The men who, like Stavelus, had given their oaths to Ambrosius in Leucerae, were used to routine soldiering and – even in these times of barbarian raids across the empire – such men expected to fight, for the most part, behind stone walls. They hoped to survive their service where, by contrast, the bucellarii always expected to face yet another impossible challenge, knowing that survival was a luxury they were unlikely ever to experience. These two groups of men had utterly different outlooks on life and, so far, they were only bonded together by their loyalty to Ambrosius. How much further, Marcellus wondered, would that loyalty stretch?

"Just remember," continued Stavelus, glowering at Varta now, "that quite a few of our lads were hacked down by those treacherous Franks that Dux promised us were our allies!"

"Hah, well perhaps if they were better fighters," grumbled Rocca, "they'd still be alive."

"Do you want to see who the better fighters are then?" cried Stavelus, incensed. "Is that what you want, Rocca?"

Realising it was all getting out of hand, Marcellus eased Lucidia aside and scrambled up onto his knees.

"Stay down," warned Lucidia. "You're too weak to even stand!"

Ignoring her, Marcellus staggered to his feet and sucked in a deep breath which hurt like hell and made him feel a little faint. Nonetheless, he was determined - despite any reservations he might have of his own – that he would keep the ship's company intact until Ambrosius returned.

"Listen!" he shouted. "All of you! Hear me!" Satisfied that he could still command silence, he continued: "We've journeyed this far together and faced death many times. We've protected each other against all threats; and now, when our unity really counts, we must not give in to fear and bickering like children!"

"We hear you, Marco," replied Stavelus, "truly we do, but look along the wharf. You can see them gathering there, whipping themselves into a frenzy, egging each other on to have a crack at us. Some know who we are and they fear us; but soon their desperation will overcome all their fears… and, if we stay yoked to that jetty, they'll kill us all and take this ship. But, if we stand off the dock a little, they can't reach us, can they? And the ship will still be here for Dux – and for all of us as well…"

"How far, Stavelus?" demanded Varta. "How far off do we wait? An arm's length - or a spear's length? Or should we stay even further out, to guard against spears and axes thrown at us? How far?"

"Well, what you said last sounds about right," said Stavelus.

"A spear throw then?" asked Varta.

"Yes, probably."

"And how far is that exactly, Stavelus? I'll tell you: it's too sodding far! Because, unless we are right next to that dock, Dux and the others will never make it aboard! Never!"

Stavelus turned away in disgust. "Well, we could have left ages ago, couldn't we, if Dux hadn't gone off to rescue his damned whore!"

There was uproar across the ship at that remark, with supporters of Stavelus echoing his words, while the bucellarii shouted abuse and rested their hands on their sword hilts.

"Peace!" shouted Marcellus, though the effort almost killed him.

To his relief, it seemed that most men were still prepared to respect his authority and at least hear what else he had to say. He must find the words to bind these men together, but he was not Ambrosius and it did not come naturally to him.

"My friends," he began.

When the spear took him full in the chest, Marcellus could only stare down at the blood spilling down his torso, until the strength vanished from his legs and he toppled over into the water.

32

November 454 in the early afternoon, in Caracotinum

It was Childeric, not Clodoris, who led the formidable-looking Franks advancing upon Ambrosius. The young chieftain did not stop until he was face to face with Ambrosius, scarcely a yard away.

"You look lonely, Roman," he said, with a grin. "Have even your friends deserted you now?"

"I thought you and I should have a few words," replied Ambrosius, "or perhaps I should talk to the man in charge?"

Childeric curled his lip in a disdainful smile. "That's just it, Roman; you are talking to the man in charge…"

"I meant Clodoris…"

Childeric gave a little nod. "Ah, Clodoris – well, you can speak to him, if you wish… but he'll not hear you… for alas, he met with a sudden accident…."

In a breath, everything had changed; Ambrosius, though rocked to the core, refused to reveal his despair and said only: "When?"

"Very early this morning," replied Childeric. "So, of course, someone had to take charge… and since I was already chosen to lead the dawn attack… the choice for my people was not a difficult one…"

Fuming with impotent rage, Ambrosius fought to control himself, knowing that Childeric was only too eager to bait him into some rash response.

"Very well," said Ambrosius, "but that's between you and your folk, not me. I've honoured our agreement and now I intend to go, leaving the town in your hands. Do you have any problem with that?"

"With you leaving?" said Childeric. "No, none at all."

"Very good then," agreed Ambrosius, relieved and surprised in equal measure.

"But…" began Childeric.

There it was: a condition… "But what?" asked Ambrosius, still seething inside.

"You may take with you only your family and your bucellarii – your sworn men. So, no Roman guards, or townspeople…or anyone else…"

"There are only a handful of others with me," replied Ambrosius.

"Even so, they must be surrendered to the new Frank authorities."

"What Frank authorities?" scoffed Ambrosius. "You've only been here a few hours!"

"Do you agree, or not?" persisted Childeric.

"Very well," said Ambrosius, deciding to put Childeric to the test. "I agree."

He had no intention of handing anyone over to Childeric and was not surprised when the young Frank looked rather put out by his prompt agreement. As Ambrosius feared, behind the youth's eyes, a darker purpose lurked.

"And the girl," said Childeric abruptly.

284

"Which girl?"

"The one you just picked up and carried off." Childeric ground out the words. "That girl!"

"What about her?"

"She stays too."

"No," said Ambrosius. "She's one of us – bucellarii."

Childeric laughed at that assertion. "No, she's not! She's not even Roman. She's just your whore! So, if you want safe passage for you and your men, you'll have to give your whore up to me!"

Struggling to restrain himself, Ambrosius took a pace forward.

"What are you going to do?" asked Childeric. "Fight us all for her?"

This prompted an outbreak of mirth from many of Childeric's followers close by, but when Ambrosius took another step, Childeric's hand went to his sword hilt. Raising his arms clear of his belt, Ambrosius showed his hands were empty of any weapon and the Frank relaxed a little.

"Come on, 'Dux'," goaded Childeric. "She's just a girl; surely a man of your talents can find another one he likes?"

Extending his right hand out to Childeric, Ambrosius said: "You know, when I first met you, I really didn't like you at all…"

Childeric nodded, clasping the outstretched hand. "Oh, believe me, I felt the same, Dux…"

"It's always as well to trust that first… feeling in the gut, isn't it?" murmured Ambrosius, as he wrenched the Frank's arm up behind his back and, from nowhere, swept a knife to his neck.

285

"Move and I'll kill you!" he announced loudly, more for the benefit of the others than Childeric. He wanted all the Franks left in no doubt what would happen to their new leader, if they tried to rush him.

"They'll butcher you," said Childeric, with a sigh, "and whatever you do now to me - or don't do – neither you, nor any of your people, will ever leave this town..."

"The thing is, my young friend," breathed Ambrosius, "I'm ready to accept death – God knows I've escaped it enough times, so I reckon I already owe death. But how about you, are you ready to be 'butchered', boy, on the point of my blade? Why, you scarcely have any hairs on your face yet..."

Several of the warriors edged forward.

"Hold!" Childeric shouted at them.

"And I've spoken to a few of the other Franks about you," continued Ambrosius, holding his prisoner tight against the knife, the sharp blade pressed to his neck. "And they tell me that there are several husbands who wouldn't be at all sorry to see your throat cut here, right now. That devil's hunger you have inside you, boy, that desire to know every woman, it'll be the death of you. It's up to you though whether that's going to be today... or not."

"What do you want?" snarled Childeric.

"Just to leave, in peace, that's all. Just to leave... Now, you and I are going to take a little walk down to the docks and we're going to leave all your men behind us."

Raising his voice, he told the restless Franks: "If any man follows us, or appears ahead of us, I'll cut your leader – and every time I even see a man even close, I'll cut him again."

One of the warriors stepped forward.

"One more thing," added Ambrosius, "I don't make idle threats…"

Scoring the knife along Childeric's jawline, he felt his captive tense from the wound. Then he began to back away, with Childeric still locked in his tight embrace, relieved that the Franks remained where they were.

"I was never very good at walking backwards," complained Childeric.

"You stumble once and I promise you, you'll be dead before you hit the ground!"

But despite the confidence he tried to show, Ambrosius knew that it was a very long walk to the ship. If he made just one mistake, he had no doubt that Childeric would seize upon it. When they reached the broad street that led down to the harbour, Ambrosius pushed the young warrior ahead of him so that they could move faster, while darting regular glances behind him to ensure that no Franks were following.

"Is there an itch in your back, Roman?" asked Childeric. "Because that's where a spear will strike before you reach your ship."

By now, Ambrosius expected that Placido and Cappa would have conveyed Inga to the ship and that knowledge alone gave him the strength and the determination to ensure that he might join them. Though it seemed to take forever, he knew he must keep his concentration. Despite the chill winter wind, both he and Childeric were sweating as both men focused upon the arm hold which was all that locked them together. It was Ambrosius who had everything to lose, for the Frank would be waiting for the slightest hint that his grip was weakening.

So slow was their progress that every moment Ambrosius feared the street would be flooded by Franks. Yet no Franks appeared – so it seemed that young Childeric's word carried some genuine power. Though he was gasping for breath and his chest felt tight with the sustained effort, he knew that Childeric too would be feeling the intense pressure of their close proximity. All the same, he was almost there: only one large warehouse and the harbour wall stood between them and the docks.

"Well, well, it must be true what they say: someday, every man's prayers will be answered."

The familiar drawl came as a body blow, not simply because Puglio was there, but because he was not alone. They must have been waiting behind the warehouse, perhaps observing his slow progress towards them with considerable amusement. Now they stood no more than twenty yards away, blocking his way to the docks.

"I take it these fellows are not your allies?" choked out Childeric.

Ambrosius did not reply.

"Release me and I'll help you against them," said Childeric.

"Now, why would you do that?" asked Ambrosius, watching Puglio and his comrades spread out to surround him.

"Because they'll kill me as well," gasped Childeric. "Anyway, you can't fight them all and hold me too, so what choice do you have?"

"Oh, I do have a choice," said Ambrosius. "I can just kill you now."

"A risk though, eh?" said Childeric. "And what would you gain by killing me?"

"I'd prevent you stabbing me in the back!"

"True enough, I might do that," conceded the Frank, "but not before we've hacked down these three…"

As Puglio took a step towards the pair, Ambrosius could see no other way out. And, if it came to it, what did it matter whether it was the Frank or the Roman who was the instrument of his death? Childeric was right: he had to release him to defend himself against Puglio. The scutarii had chosen their killing ground well, for none of them could be seen from Ambrosius' waiting ship. Thus, his own comrades would not even know what was happening.

"What's with that shit pile you're holding, Dux?" enquired Puglio. "For Christ's sake, save me another task and cut the young bastard's throat, will you?"

When he released his grip on the Frank, Ambrosius took a swift pace away – just in case.

With a wolf-like grin, Childeric swept out his spatha and swivelled to face the Romans.

"Oh, like that, is it?" scorned Puglio. "All friends now, are you? But then I hear you're a bit of a Frank yourself, Dux. True blood will out, eh?"

"Your blood, true or not, will very soon be pouring out, tribune," growled Ambrosius.

"Enough jawing," said Puglio and, as if perhaps by some prearranged agreement, he made straight for Ambrosius while his two comrades combined to attack Childeric.

Ignoring the young Frank now, Ambrosius concentrated all his attention upon Puglio, for the tribune came with a formidable reputation. Worse still, at that moment, they were ill-matched for Puglio wore not only a helmet, but also a breast plate and a few other assorted bits of armour – all of which Ambrosius lacked. And, of course, the tribune carried a shield - a considerable edge for a fighter who, like Puglio, relied very much upon brute strength.

Wasting no time, the imperial officer launched himself at Ambrosius, battering his spatha at head and shoulders. Using both knife and sword, Ambrosius deflected every blow except one, which scraped across his scalp like a razor. He really should find a helmet again; his months in Ardelica had truly made him only half a soldier.

Content to allow his opponent to retain the initiative for the time being, he backed away, getting closer to the harbour with every step. A glance across at his temporary ally told him that the clever Childeric was also retreating - but in the other direction. There was every chance that when he got closer to his own men, they would see his predicament. But Childeric's gambit also helped Ambrosius, for Puglio was being drawn further from his two comrades and he knew it.

"You're going to have to kill me before I get to that harbour wall," taunted Ambrosius, "because, after that, my men will swarm all over you."

"I think you'll find that your men are a little too busy just now," replied Puglio, with a gleam of triumph in his eyes. "Last time I looked, they had one or two… troubles of their own."

That was all too likely, Ambrosius had to concede, but still he backed away, for the closer he was to the ship, the better his chances of survival. Perhaps Puglio recognised that too, for he launched another brutal assault with his spatha and for good measure swung his shield hard at Ambrosius. Slamming into his left shoulder, the rim of the shield bit into his flesh. Numbed fingers let fall his knife, but he managed to carve his spatha across the wrist that bore the shield. Knowing that he had hurt the tribune badly did not alter the fact that his own left arm was hanging limp at his side. So again, it suited him to retreat a little further and draw the tribune on.

Though forced to discard his shield, Puglio was no less dangerous. His wrist might be dripping blood, but it would only prove a telling wound if Ambrosius could stay alive long enough to take advantage of it. Each man now fought with one arm and Ambrosius' left was little use even for maintaining balance.

His attention was focused solely upon his opponent's eyes for the eyes would tell him more about his adversary's intention than anything else. Puglio darted to his left in a clever attempt to stop Ambrosius from slipping away to the harbour wall. When tribune then renewed his assault upon Ambrosius' head and body, just blocking each of the heavy blows was exhausting him. Survival was his first objective, so he swayed and parried without any thought of a riposte. Even when he turned aside the tribune's blade, he was still sometimes cut and soon the tribune was not the only one losing a steady trickle of blood.

Again and again they went to it, sinews straining as their sweat-soaked bodies were pushed beyond all endurance. Like two tired wrestlers who only knew one manoeuvre, they seemed doomed to replay their bout over and over again. Yet surely one man's patience or concentration would break soon.

Out of the corner of his eye, Ambrosius saw that Childeric had cut down one of the two scutarii but was limping heavily as he tried to fend off his remaining assailant. All the while though, the young Frank was retreating towards the crossroads where he knew that scores of his comrades would finally be able to see him. Time was thus not on Ambrosius' side for, at any moment, a host of Franks could descend upon the two Romans – and when they did, he knew it would be a bloody end for them both.

Though Puglio redoubled his efforts to pound Ambrosius into submission, his eyes began to betray his own doubts and therein, for the first time, Ambrosius detected a trace of fear. Seizing the moment, Ambrosius flew at him, aiming to distract him with a wild slash so that he could slip past and make his way to the harbour wall. Before the tribune could come at him again, he was rewarded with a glimpse of the waiting ship. It was certainly still at the jetty, but what he saw filled him with horror.

Far from getting any assistance from his comrades, he wondered whether he would ever see them again for the ship was rocking and dipping beside the dock under the relentless assault of a large crowd. Next moment, Puglio attacked again. Damn the man! Did he never tire? Any normal man would have bled to death by now! Just for an instant, Ambrosius was forced to admire the tribune's dogged determination to carry out the imperial orders – for what did the emperor's orders matter now, here in this graveyard of Roman power?

"Give it up, Puglio!" he cried. "For God's sake, give it up!"

Narrowly dodging another swingeing slash at his chest, Ambrosius tried persuasion once again: "You've more than done your duty, man - what does it matter to you whether you take that fool of an emperor my head, or not?"

For the first time Puglio laughed out loud, which was as unnerving as it was surprising.

"You think I care this much about the emperor? Anyway, it was Petronius Maximus who sent me to kill you, not the emperor!"

"Aye, and paid you a fortune in gold for it, I dare say!" snarled Ambrosius, knocking aside a sudden lunge at his belly.

"Oh, he did, Dux, but I'd have done it for nothing," admitted Puglio.

"Did I offend you, tribune?" asked Ambrosius, snatching a few short breaths while he could.

"Offend me?" said Puglio. "Your very existence - your rank and position - offend me, Dux, because they should have been mine!"

Attacking again, he carved his weapon at Ambrosius, as he hurled more bitter words.

"I was Aetius' man too, you know - poised for great things under his protection! But then along came a sullen, arrogant youth!"

Puglio's spatha rang against his and the street echoed with the clash of their weapons. "A half-Roman and half–Frank mongrel who was just a butcher of men," continued

293

the tribune. "Every man sent against him, the youth despatched and then – God help us - he saved Aetius' life! And, in that one fortunate moment, that youth stole the glittering future I had earned – earned! So, you see, Dux, no amount of gold was needed at all…"

From behind them, where Childeric was still scrapping gamely, came a rumble of sound. Puglio and Ambrosius exchanged a glance, knowing what it meant. It was the sound of the roaring voices and pounding boots of Childeric's Franks; and very soon, the outcome of their struggle would no longer be in their own hands.

If Ambrosius hoped that Puglio's relentless assault had exhausted him, he was wrong because the tribune kept on coming. Trying to adjust his footing, ready to meet the next onslaught, Ambrosius slipped sideways and, quick as an eel, Puglio seized his chance. Crashing blow after blow at him, Puglio bludgeoned him to the ground and it was all Ambrosius could do to meet every lunge and cut. And, of course, he could not do so forever; with a final, mighty swing of his weapon, Puglio knocked the spatha from Ambrosius' grasp.

"Oh, how I'd like to savour this moment, Dux," he groaned, "and make it as painfully slow as possible; but sadly, as you know… I can't stay long..."

A tumult of cries informed them both that the Franks had rescued their leader, Soon they would be there, but too late for Ambrosius - not that Childeric had any intention of sparing him in any case.

Utterly spent, Ambrosius could not move. "Get on with it then, old man!" he urged, for what was a soldier's lot, but death?

With an exultant roar, Puglio lifted his sword up to punch it through his fallen opponent's chest. As the tribune's sword plunged down at him, all Ambrosius saw was a sliver of steel slicing through a beam of sunlight.

33

Having embraced death so completely, it was a shock for Ambrosius to discover that he was still alive – but how could Puglio have contrived to miss his aim? After another moment, a raging pain in his side told Ambrosius that the tribune had not missed – at least not completely. The imperial spatha had torn through his flesh to leave a wound which, though it hurt more than a wolf's bite, was not, he decided, a mortal one.

Looking up at his adversary, Ambrosius could see that Puglio was as bemused as he was, glaring down, uncomprehending, at a knife hilt protruding from under his ribs. As the tribune's trembling hand dropped from his own weapon, a bloodied figure crawled out from behind his bent torso. Though astonished by Inga's sudden appearance, Ambrosius at last made sense of it. With a swift lunge, he pulled the knife from Puglio and thrust it straight back in again, but this time closer to where the tribune's heart lay. Eyes dimming, his relentless enemy surrendered at last and fell onto him.

Reaching out for Ambrosius, Inga mouthed words that he could not hear amid the growing clamour from the jetty and the roar of Childeric's approaching Franks. With her help, he wrenched out Puglio's spatha, which threatened to pin him to the ground, and rolled the dead tribune aside. Staggering to his feet, he tried to embrace Inga but she gasped with pain and he realised just how weak she must be.

"Placido couldn't carry me to the ship," Inga murmured, "because there were too many on the jetty... so he laid me down by the wall and went to get help..."

A swift appraisal of the skirmish around the ship persuaded Ambrosius that there was no way they could get aboard – indeed Placido and Cappa were still trapped on the jetty as they tried to fight their way through. But with the Franks now coming up behind him, he could not leave her. He could not leave her, could not carry her and could hardly even fight since he was using his sword to lean on.

"Roman!" came a cry from behind him and, without looking around, he knew it was Childeric.

"Better start praying!" he told Inga.

"Your god, or mine?" she muttered.

"Roman!" bellowed Childeric once again, a few yards closer. "How mighty is your empire now, Roman?"

With a groan, Ambrosius decided it was hopeless, and told her so.

Gripping his arm more tightly, Inga stared into his eyes. "You are Dux," she whispered, "and we are bucellarii; for us, nothing is ever... hopeless."

With a bitter smile, he pulled her close, touched her lips with his and then steered her towards the dockside, where a bloody mêlée raged. The crowd was a strange mix of folk and most, he thought, appeared to be ordinary men of the town trying to escape a fate which was far from ordinary. They were so numerous that, if they ever did manage to clamber aboard, Ambrosius' ship would be sent swiftly to the bottom of Caracotinum harbour. Yet what could he do about it?

Childeric was bawling at them again. "You can't get away, Dux; you and your few bucellarii will be the very last of the Romans here!"

Dux smiled at that, for he had almost begun to forget that he was Roman – and a sudden thought struck him that perhaps these folk, wrestling for control of his ship, still had a trace of Rome left in them. It was worth a try at least...

Shutting out all doubts and fears, he cleared his throat, and shouted as loud as his tired voice would allow: "I am Dux Ambrosius Aurelianus, son of Aurelius Honorius Magnus, and I command you to cease your assault upon my ship at once!"

The effect was immediate; everyone stopped, including his own surprised bucellarii. Folk glanced around as if the much-feared Magnus himself might appear on the jetty at any moment. But a low murmuring among the throng told Ambrosius that the magical effect would not last for long.

"Placido!" he cried, pushing his way through the bemused crowd, with his good arm still wrapped around Inga.

At once, the bucellarii sprang to life: Placido bellowed commands to his dogs and then joined Cappa in flanking Ambrosius and Inga, but they were only halfway to the ship when another voice was heard again: it was Childeric, offering a generous price for the head of Ambrosius Aurelianus.

Varta was surging towards them from the ship with Germanus, but the spell cast upon the unruly mob was already broken. Weapons were raised once more and, had

Placido not been at his side, Ambrosius would have perished several times over. The indomitable warrior, aided by his two murderous dogs, hacked folk aside with his sword. No quarter was given as he forced his way through. Inching ever closer to Varta, Ambrosius was at last able to grasp his friend's hand and Germanus then seized hold of Inga.

"Get her aboard!" roared Ambrosius, noticing with approval that several men were already at the oars, preparing to drive the ship from the jetty. "And give me an axe!"

While Germanus lifted Inga onto the deck, Varta tossed Ambrosius a weapon, and at once he turned to face the murderous crowd, axe in hand. With relief, he found Placido and Cappa beside him.

"Get on the ship!" he told them.

"You too, Dux," yelled Varta, from the deck.

"Oh, I'll keep him safe," promised Placido.

Further along the jetty, several men were still trying to leap aboard and were only kept at bay by the ranging blows of Rocca's great war axe and spear thrusts by Stavelus and other comrades.

"Cast off, Varta!" ordered Ambrosius. "We'll jump aboard!"

Though it hurt to do so, he could now move his left arm a little more freely and decided that one or two more swings of his axe would suffice to deter their opponents – just long enough to escape onto the ship. Once Cappa had leapt aboard, he swung the heavy axe in a massive arc around him. A few among the crowd, keen to scramble on at the last moment, were chopped aside by the merciless blade. But the movement ripped open the wound in his side and the very weight of the axe almost pulled the exhausted warrior off his feet.

Though the ship was now several feet away from the jetty, some desperate souls were still attempting to clamber onto the deck. Deep-throated cries rang out as spears and thrown axes fell among the crowd. Childeric must have decided that he must intervene, or lose his quarry. One impaled figure fell from the jetty onto the oars which prevented the ship from moving away.

"Get on the damned ship, Dux!" cried Placido.

"Come on, Dux!" shrieked Inga, from the deck.

Amid the flurry of thrown weapons, Ambrosius realised that he might have left it too late, so taking hold of Placido's strong right arm, he said: "Come on, we'll jump on together!"

"Yeh, and probably sink it!" laughed Placido, with a dark grin.

Just as they were poised to leap, Varta yelled a warning and Ambrosius looked up to see that the Franks were driving forward through the crowd.

"Come on, Placido!" he yelled, but as they turned to jump, a spear point was thrust into his comrade's back.

With an angry blow of his axe, Ambrosius severed the assailant's entire arm, but the damage was done and more spears were already poking and prodding at them. Placido could never make the leap to the ship, which now floated more than a yard from the jetty, Though Ferox and Patricus were burying their sharp teeth into the Franks, their grim-faced enemies kept coming and soon Patricus was clubbed down by an axe and speared through several times.

With a grimace of rage, Placido pushed Ambrosius away. "Go, Dux! I was never any good on a ship anyway!"

"No, no! Take hold of my arm, man!"

But Placido used what strength he had to hurl Ambrosius towards the edge of the jetty and, as he overbalanced, he knew that if he did not jump he would fall into the water.

"Ferox!" bellowed Placido, "guard Inga!"

By the time Ambrosius sprang aboard, landing heavily on his side, the ship was two yards from the jetty. Placido's surviving dog, Ferox, covered in blood, stood motionless beside his master on the jetty. But, when Placido went down under a dozen spear thrusts, Ferox slowly turned away, loped along the dockside and took a great leap onto the ship's deck. The animal only just made it, scrambling his bloody paws across several oarsmen in the process.

Ambrosius, shaking with rage, could do nothing more for Placido for more spears were launched at the retreating vessel. Once the ship had rowed further away he just stood staring back at Childeric and the body of brave Placido at the Frank's feet. They had so nearly managed the impossible... As the bucellarii took their places to join other men at the oars, the ship fell silent.

Remigius seemed to know his business, for the vessel had to turn sharply to make it into the channel out of the harbour and he carried out the manoeuvre expertly, despite the clashing of oars perpetrated by several of his inexperienced rowers. Soon the vessel slid away from the ruined port of Caracotinum and began to pick up speed into the estuary. But after a short distance the rowers got out of time, snagged each other's oars and tempers flared.

Remigius glared at the culprits. "Listen, you useless dogs!" he snarled at them. "I'm shouting out the mark for you! So, unless you want to be sitting on the mud all night, I suggest you start rowing in time!"

When Varta told Ambrosius that Marcellus too was lost, it was the last straw and he wept.

"The very last thing he did," explained Varta, "was quell a revolt amongst the soldiers. Though his wound was grievous, it didn't stop him. When he was struck down, the shock was the jolt some men needed, Dux… to pull together at last – and, for Marco, they did."

Leaving Varta at the stern where Florina and Lucidia, along with three other women and two boys, were crammed into a small covered area, Ambrosius moved forward, grim-faced, to find Inga.

∞ ∞ ∞ ∞

They had been fortunate, for once, because wind and tide conspired to help them. So the ship did not wash up onto the salt marshes along the north bank of the Seine estuary, instead it reached the sea where its new mast, and a favourable wind in its sail, drove it north-west. It would not be an easy journey to Britannia and Ambrosius still harboured many fears about what they would discover when they got there – if it pleased God to allow their shallow, river boat to cross the sea at all…

At sunset, he stood at the prow and spoke to the ship's company. Weary soldiers slumped at their oars, while the women and children huddled together, wracked by fear.

"All of us, in our different ways," he began, "have owed allegiance to Rome. But Rome is rotten to the core and its empire grows weaker by the day. For years, I fought to defend Rome, but now it has abandoned me - as it has abandoned all of you.

"I was born to a British mother in a Roman household, so... I'm taking this ship to Britannia – my mother's homeland – but I do not go there as a Roman. Whatever I was once, I'm not that man now. Whoever any of us were before, we are not those people now. And, though we carry some memory of Rome in our hearts, I believe that we'll be seen as the last of the Romans..."

His words were not greeted by any acclamation – nor did he expect it, for only a fool would celebrate the terror of the unknown. But he had to say it... had to make it clear: Rome was dead to him; Britannia was where they were going. Perhaps Lucidia was right: that Britannia had nothing to offer; but it was the land of his mother and he wanted to see it.

Once at the arse-end of the empire in the west, Britannia was not now part of the empire at all. It was one of the few places he'd never been, nor ever wanted to go. But, given that he and his men were under a sentence of death in the empire, it was as good a place as any to run. And whatever chaos they found in Britannia, it would be a new beginning for them all in a new land.

As the light faded in the west, Inga, shadowed by the grieving Ferox, clambered forward to join him again at the prow. Knowing what to say to her was an altogether different challenge, for he was unsure how it was between them. She was the first woman for whom he had lowered

303

his guard - in truth, even amongst the men of the bucellarii, only Varta, and perhaps poor Marco, had ever got close to him.

Like most of the others aboard, he and Inga carried wounds which would take a long while to heal and would leave ugly scars – and there were many types of scar. Yet, sitting there as darkness fell, he was glad to feel her head resting upon his shoulder and content simply to listen to her steady breathing. It was enough for now. When the morrow came, they would live or die – for such was the fate of true soldiers.

∞ ∞ ∞ ∞   ∞ ∞ ∞ ∞   ∞ ∞ ∞ ∞

Historical Notes
The Fifth Century – Late Antiquity

The nature of evidence in this period, often referred to as Late Antiquity, is in a state of flux. For a long time history relied only upon written sources, but increasingly archaeology is leading the way in trying to make some sense both of the events and lifestyle of this period. The traditional idea of a sudden "fall of the Roman Empire" in the fifth century is now discredited in favour of the view that the empire was already changing, socially, politically and economically in the third and fourth centuries. The fifth century therefore marks a period of further development in the society of Western Europe in which the authority and structure of the Roman Empire no longer held sway. Since this book is set in the year 454 AD, it shows evidence of the ongoing changes in the lives of people within the boundaries of the empire – boundaries which had already started to change.

PEOPLE:
Ambrosius Aurelianus

This book centres upon Ambrosius Aurelianus - one of the few individuals mentioned by name in the history of Britain in the fifth century. Unfortunately, we know almost nothing about his origins or much about his life at all until he features in the struggle between Britons and Saxons. It is the sixth century monk, Gildas, who tells us about Ambrosius in his work: *On the Ruin of Britain*. To Gildas, writing a century later in a land much dominated by Saxons, Ambrosius was a heroic figure - in contrast with his successors.

In this story, we see Ambrosius before he goes to Britain and I have given him a plausible, but entirely fictional, backstory. Only at the end of this story does he even set off for Britain itself. It seemed to me to be an interesting idea to explore the possibility that Ambrosius lived within the empire in his early life, but it is wholly fiction.

Flavius Aetius

Flavius Aetius was a Roman general who rose to prominence in the Western Empire during the 430s and 440s when he managed, in a series of campaigns, to keep the empire more or less intact. He did so not just by astute military strategy but by clever alliances with some of the barbarian tribes which now formed the backbone of the Roman Empire in the west. The last great threat he faced down was that of Attila the Hun, whose armies swept across Europe in 451 AD and threatened Italy in 452 AD. Aetius defeated Attila and the threat from the Huns was lessened by the death of Attila in 453 AD.

Aetius served a weak Emperor, Valentinian III, who grew to manhood under his control, so Aetius was always struggling to maintain his position. Valentinian came to resent Aetius – and perhaps also feared him. Egged on by a leading court official, the eunuch Heraclius, and by a rival of Aetius, Petronius Maximus, Valentinian killed Aetius in September 454 AD when our story begins. But Valentinian did not long survive his rash action, for six months later two adherents of Aetius killed him, along with Heraclius. Petronius Maximus then seized control of the Western Empire but, within a couple of months, he too was dead –

torn apart by the people of Rome. It was an unforgiving time for politicians and emperors!

Childeric and the Franks

Childeric was an actual historical figure and ruled the Franks in the mid-late fifth century. In this story, he is ambitious and has an eye for the ladies – both features which are supported by the evidence we have about him. I must confess that the Franks were based much further north than Caracotinum in the period when the story is set – around modern day Belgium and there is no evidence that Childeric himself was ever in Caracotinum let alone attacked it. However, there were Franks serving as foederati in several areas of Gaul and it seems plausible to me that some might have been drafted in to meet the threat of coastal attacks by, for example, Saxon pirates.

The Bucellarii

The word bucellarius means 'biscuit-eater' which suggests that these men were used to campaigning on hard-baked biscuit rations. Bucellarii were basically private soldiers hired by a prominent individual to protect them, their families and their property. In the late empire of Rome the creation of bucellarii was encouraged because, since they were funded by private citizens, they cost Rome nothing. Aetius certainly employed bucellarii such as those described in the story. This is a small group but they were usually numbered in hundreds, or even thousands. Though they took an oath to the emperor, they also took one to their employer, so it's easy to imagine that a conflict of interest might arise. They were usually very well-equipped and recruited from virtually anywhere in the empire, or even beyond.

By the sixth century these elite cavalry units reigned supreme and one can see how they might have developed over several centuries into something approaching medieval knights.

The Schola Scutariorum Prima

After the Praetorian Guard was abolished, other military units were set up to be under the personal control of the emperor – i.e. some sort of imperial guard. We do not know exactly when the schola came into being but we do know that at one point there were five schola units in the late roman army of the western empire. The prima was the first, then secunda, etc. etc. and each was a cavalry unit of perhaps 500 men in theory, though by the fifth century any estimates are purely guesswork.

Tribunes, such as the fictional Puglio, were high ranking officers of the schola and many - among both officers and lower ranks – were recruited from tribes outside the empire, such as the Franks and Alamans from north of the Rhine frontier. These were elite troops who were highly paid and much esteemed. Like most soldiers in the fifth century they were equipped with spathas and oval, or round, shields, rather than the traditional, and much more familiar, Roman gladius, or short sword, and rectangular shields. When picturing in one's mind Roman soldiers of this period, it is helpful to think of them as looking more like the tribes against whom they were fighting rather than the soldiers of the early period of the Roman Republic and Empire.

PLACES:

Caracotinum

Caracotinum, on the north bank of the broad River Seine estuary, is modern day Harfleur in Normandy. It was a port for many centuries during antiquity and, though it is not listed as one of the forts of the so-called 'Saxon Shore', I think it is a possible candidate to be Grannona - a port not yet firmly identified. I am suggesting that it was as good a place as any for a concentration of any remaining Roman forces by the mid-5th century, when Roman control of the region – especially north-western Gaul – was tenuous.

The Franks had steadily been assimilated into several areas further north of the Seine in the years around 450 – along with other tribes - and it is highly likely that, if there was a residual Roman garrison in the area, they must have been hard pressed to maintain any sort of control, especially after the threat from the Huns had been neutralised in 451 AD.

Britannia

By 454 AD Britannia was no longer a part of the Roman Empire. Whilst the date 410 AD is frequently – indeed almost mechanically – cited as the date imperial control was withdrawn, it must have been a little more fluid than that. Even as late as around 446 AD, it appears that a British request was sent to seek help from Rome against several opponents. Aetius refused because Rome was already hard-pressed by then and simply did not have the resources to commit to Britain; but presumably the desperate Britons must have thought there was a chance of reclaiming their status as part of the empire.

By then, Britain was not the only part of the empire where Rome had lost control: most of Spain, modern day Brittany and much of North Africa, for example, were already ruled by others. The difference with Britannia, of course, is that its isolation was emphasised by the fact that it was an island. Thus, for many of those with Ambrosius in my story, the thought of going to Britannia seemed a very extreme solution to their problems!

Towns in Late Antiquity

The route, by which my Ambrosius journeys to Caracotinum, is a genuine one. The roads he uses, as well as the towns through which he passes: Leucerae, Centum Prata, Vesontio, etc, did exist - though evidence about their state in 454 is naturally almost completely non-existent. Some are known to have fallen under the control of others, such as the Burgundians, but most would still have been under nominal Roman control.

Towns had been shrinking for decades – perhaps centuries – by 454 AD. Some common features were: the subdivision of large buildings, the reduction in size of fortifications due to lack of manpower and the cultivation within town walls of some of their food since the traditional trade and supply routes across the empire had already become unreliable.

The landscape of the fifth century, against which this story is set, was a changing one – and change can often be painful!

About the Author

Derek was born in Hampshire in England but spent his teenage years in Auckland, New Zealand, where he still has strong family ties. For many years he taught history in a secondary school in Berkshire but took early retirement several years ago to concentrate on his writing.

Derek is interested in a wide range of historical themes and has written action-packed fiction set during the late medieval period. This book is the first of a new series of books set in the fifth century and focussing on the shadowy historical figure of Ambrosius Aurelianus. Though Ambrosius' later life is closely associated with Britain, Derek has placed him, in his early years, in the Western Roman Empire.

His debut historical novel, **Feud,** is set in the period of the Wars of the Roses and is the first of a series entitled **Rebels & Brothers** which follows the fortunes of the fictional Elder family.

The **Rebels and Brothers** series [in order]:
Feud
A Traitor's Fate
Kingdom of Rebels
The Last Shroud
The **Craft of Kings** series [in order]:
Scars From The Past
The Blood of Princes
Echoes of Treason

To find out more about my books, or to contact me, you can go to my website: www.derekbirks.com

Made in the USA
Monee, IL
16 August 2021

75829063R00184